"We're going to take up a fight with the church."

Shinichi Sotoyama
An abnormally brave high school student and the dirty advisor for the Blue Demon King.

The **DIRTY**
WAY to **DESTROY** the **GODDESS'S**
HEROES

3 | I'm Not a Bad "Evil God," You Know.

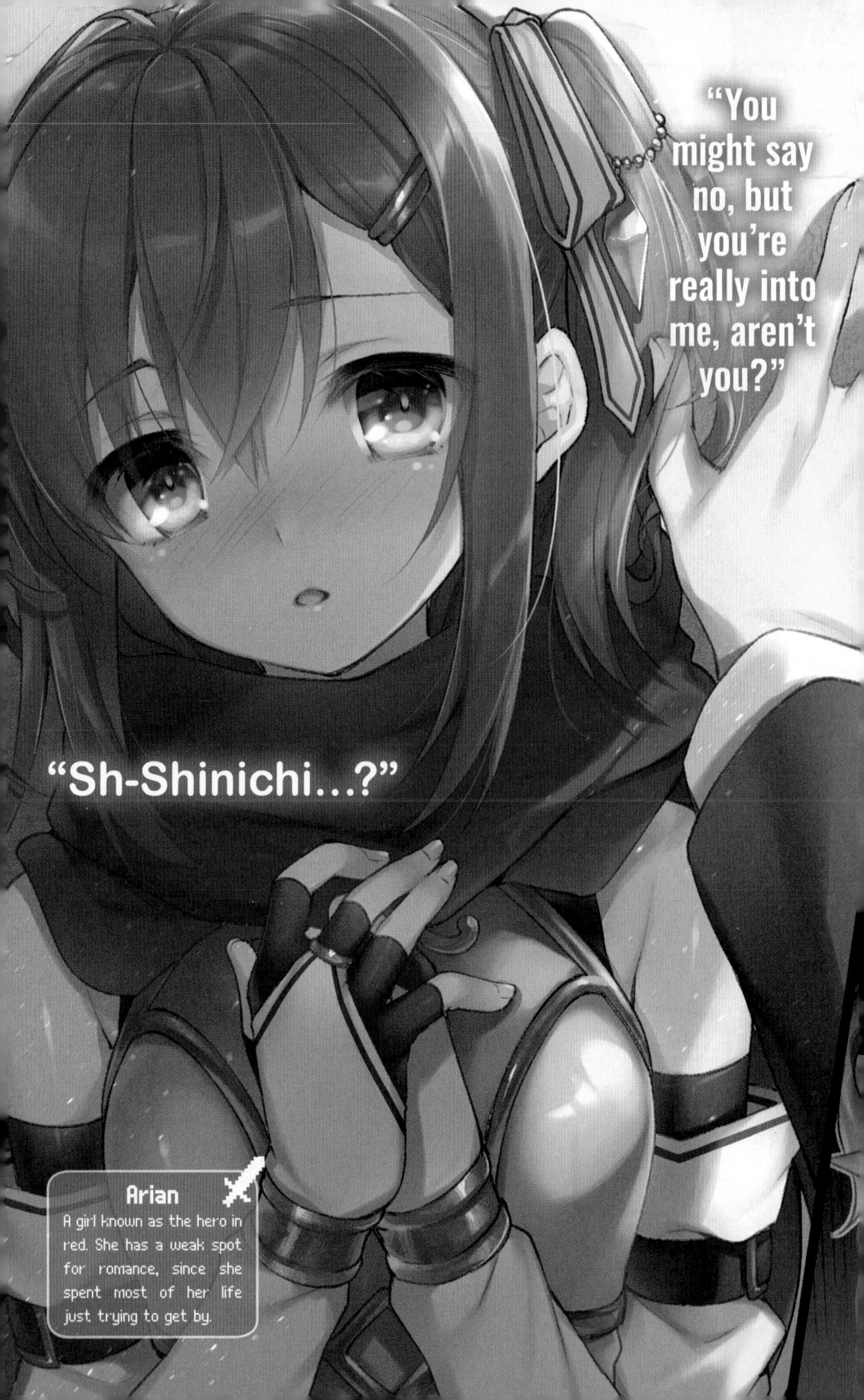
"You might say no, but you're really into me, aren't you?"
"Sh-Shinichi...?"
Arian
A girl known as the hero in red. She has a weak spot for romance, since she spent most of her life just trying to get by.

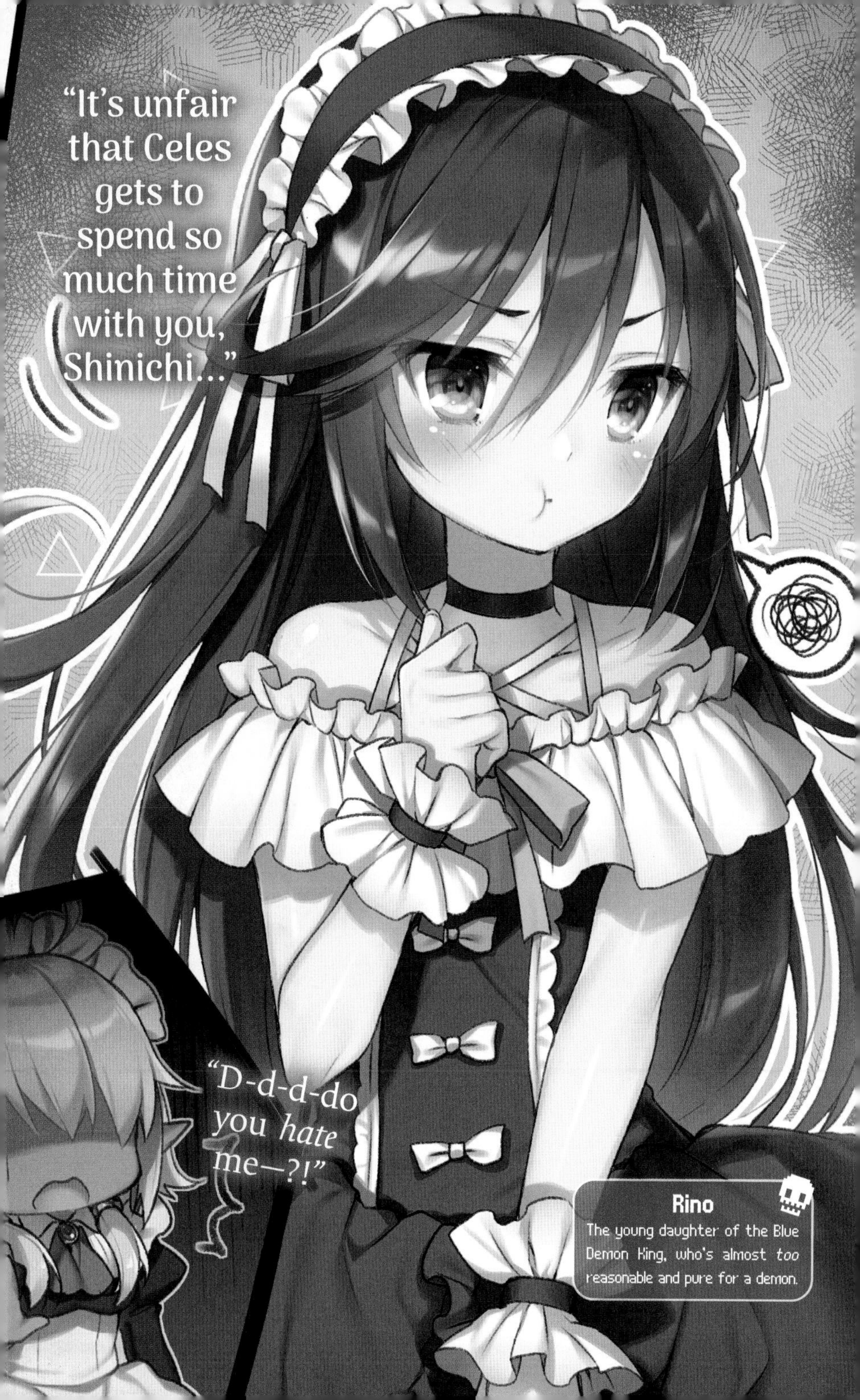
"It's unfair that Celes gets to spend so much time with you, Shinichi..."
"D-d-d-do you *hate* me—?!"
Rino
The young daughter of the Blue Demon King, who's almost *too* reasonable and pure for a demon.

"Keep up your spineless whining, you freeloader, and I'll toss your corpse to the *parbeguts*."

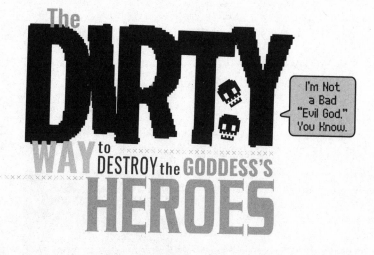

3

SAKUMA SASAKI
Illustration by ASAGI TOSAKA

YEN ON

New York

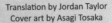

The Dirty Way to Destroy the Goddess's Heroes
Sakuma Sasaki

Translation by Jordan Taylor
Cover art by Asagi Tosaka

MEGAMI NO YUSHA WO TAOSU GESU NA HOHO Vol. 3 BOKU, WARUI JASHIN JA NAIYO
©Sakuma Sasaki 2017
First published in Japan in 2017 by KADOKAWA CORPORATION, Tokyo.
English translation rights arranged with KADOKAWA CORPORATION, Tokyo through TUTTLE-MORI AGENCY, INC., Tokyo.

English translation © 2020 by Yen Press, LLC

Yen On
150 West 30th Street, 19th Floor
New York, NY 10001

Visit us at yenpress.com
facebook.com/yenpress
twitter.com/yenpress
yenpress.tumblr.com
instagram.com/yenpress

First Yen On Edition: March 2020

Yen On is an imprint of Yen Press, LLC.
The Yen On name and logo are trademarks of Yen Press, LLC.

Library of Congress Cataloging-in-Publication Data
Names: Sasaki, Sakuma (Novelist), author. | Tosaka, Asagi, illustrator. | Taylor, Jordan (Translator), translator.
Title: The dirty way to destroy the goddess's heroes / Sakuma Sasaki ; illustration by Asagi Tosaka ; translation by Jordan Taylor.
Description: New York, NY : Yen On, 2019. | Series: The dirty way to destroy the goddess's heroes ; Volume 1
Identifiers: LCCN 2019011081 | ISBN 9781975357115 (v. 1 : pbk.) | ISBN 9781975357139 (v. 2 : pbk.) | ISBN 9781975357153 (v. 3 : pbk.)
Classification: LCC PL875.5.A76 O613 2019 | DDC 895.63/6—dc23
LC record available at https://lccn.loc.gov/2019011081

ISBNs: 978-1-9753-5715-3 (paperback)
978-1-9753-5716-0 (ebook)

10 9 8 7 6 5 4 3 2 1

LSC-C

Printed in the United States of America

The DIRTY WAY to DESTROY the GODDESS'S HEROES

I'm Not a Bad "Evil God." You Know.

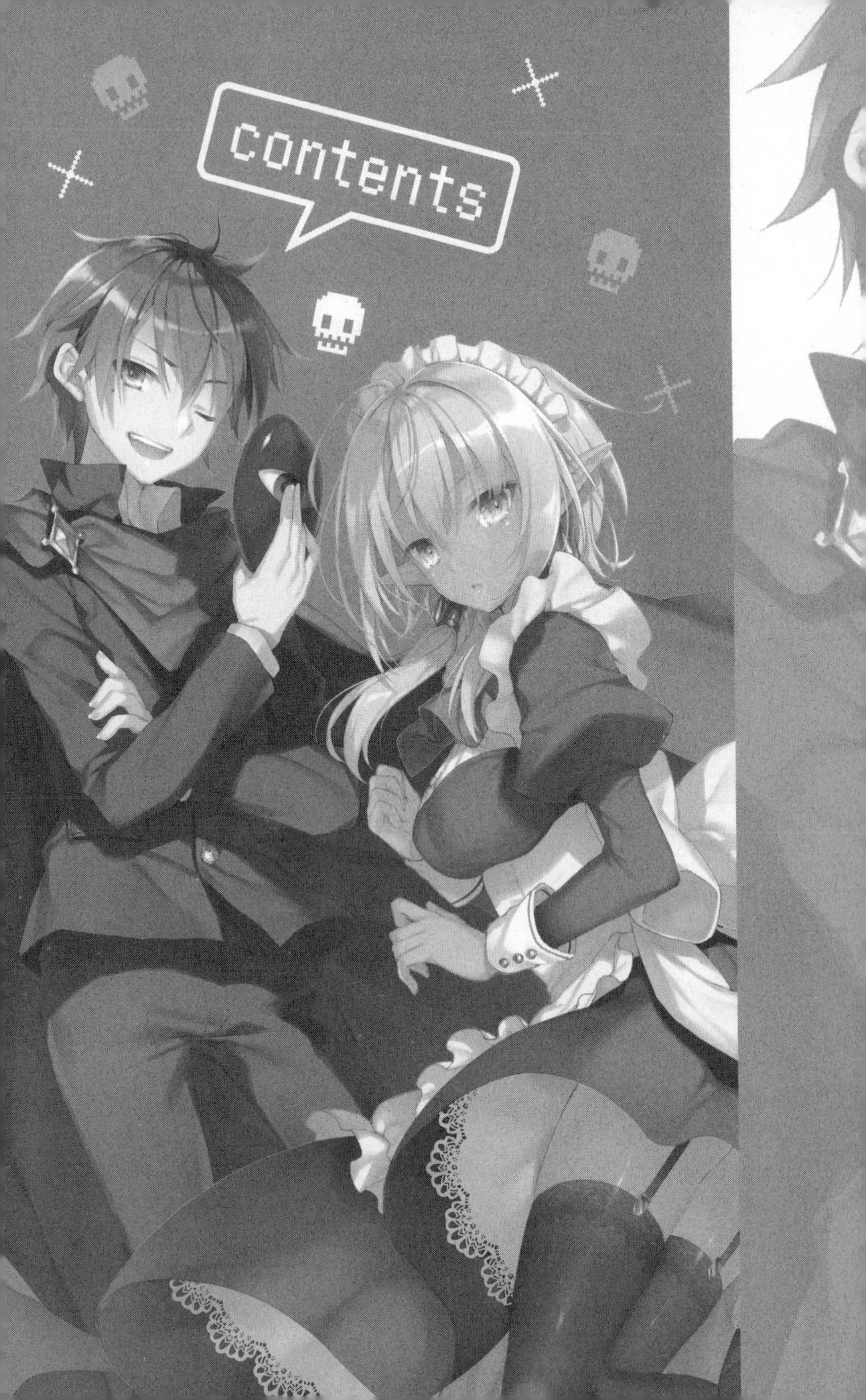
contents

Illustration by Asagi Tosaka

Holy City. The Archbasilica of the Goddess Elazonia.

Marble walls gleamed under the sunlight—blindingly beautiful, as if the walls were the transmuted form of the Goddess herself. All were moved to offer their devotion in the face of this divine sight.

But the brighter the light, the darker the shadow. That was the nature of things. The sinister truth of the church was buried deep beneath the glaring luminance of the Archbasilica.

"AAAAAaaaaaahhh—!"

Beastly howls ricocheted through the dank space—the pits of the earth, far removed from the face of the sun. In fact, it was almost deep enough to reach the bowels of hell. A ten-floor underground prison sealed off from the world by an iron cap.

The Pit of Divine Punishment was used to cast away any unlawful heroes. No one could know of its existence, especially the followers. It was a wasteland of the worst and impure, the filth and dregs of the Goddess's church.

"Gack! Gragh! Aaah!"

From it erupted childlike sobs, shrill laughter, incomprehensible roars, and the dull thuds of heads slamming against stone walls. It made it hard to believe that every single cry was made by a hero, someone who had once received the Goddess's blessing.

And yet, that was exactly who they were. Each one displayed the Goddess's sun symbol emblazoned somewhere on their body, granting them their undying status. That was precisely why these prisoners were psychologically beaten and bruised: It'd be impossible to kill them. Well, to be exact, they would be resurrected at the nearest church upon their death.

Head cleaved off? Evaporated into thin air? Not a problem. Their bodies and memories could still be resurrected—granting them the miracle of life. This was limited to the exclusive use of heroes, drawing followers to the church and eliminating any dissenters. It was how this organization had the entire continent of Uropeh wrapped around its little finger.

In the end, however, a hero was still a human being. Meaning their personality could deviate as time went on… Or maybe it would be more precise to say they could have a complete overhaul of their old ways *because* they were once a hero.

Their golden rule was to be humble and kind to others without exception. That might sound like some ridiculous dream, but it was actually the key to self-preservation. In theory, a warrior could get strong enough to fight back against flames and kindling, but that would easily become a double-edged sword if it elicited envy or fear in others—meaning it had the potential to lead to his downfall.

The secret to longevity was to be well-perceived and liked by others. That way, they wouldn't be compelled to hold a grudge against you. That meant the best self-defense hack was to befriend your would-be murderer.

A "good nature" and "friendship" were the best weapons for keeping death at bay.

But what about these undying heroes? They wouldn't need to exhibit humility or kindness if death wasn't even in the equation. As soon as they realized this, the heroes became arrogant, leading them to harm or kill civilians—and contributing to their own downfall. The elite warriors of the church kept them in check by sealing them deep in this secret pit.

"Dammit! I'm going to get out of here and exact my revenge!"

A young hero might swear at his captors when he was brought down here, but with time, he would be reduced to a shell of his former self, smiling as he chased an imaginary butterfly in his jail cell.

It was impossible to build a prison that could detain a hero forever. After all, they'd been chosen for their strength as skilled swordsmen and magic users. More importantly, if they killed themselves, they would teleport and resurrect at the nearest church, allowing them to escape at their leisure.

If they couldn't be killed or detained forever, that only left one choice: They needed to perish...psychologically.

Which sounded like an idea concocted by a certain dirty boy. But in truth, the church had been using this method since its very inception.

First, they would let flesh-eating insects crawl into every orifice in the hero's body: eyes, mouth, nose, ears, urethra, anus. Then, they would allow these heroes to be eaten alive from the inside out to their terror and excruciating pain. But even if they perished while managing to hold on to their sanity, they'd be resurrected at the nearest church: the Archbasilica right above their heads, where they would be immediately recaptured and dragged back down to the pit. Rinse and repeat.

They'd be subjected to these horrors over and over again until their minds yielded and caved in. Once their souls had become null, they would become powerless dolls, the husks of once-grand heroes. Their only trait would be their inability to die.

"Hmm-hmm, la-la-la...," sang an old woman with a wholesome little smile. Her hums echoed through the prison.

In her past, she'd been betrayed by a lover, leading her to loathe all human beings and to incinerate over a hundred people, reducing them to a pile of ash, fated never to be resurrected. There had been a time in her life when she had been indifferent to casting her diabolical spells. By now, she was nothing more than a feeble old lady, senile at best. She'd lost her ability to conjure clear images in her mind, which were necessary to cast any form of magic.

This feeling of powerlessness wasn't limited to magic users: Warriors suffered under similar circumstances. Their Herculean strength was born from their subconscious use of *Physical Enchantment* spells even before they became heroes, which meant their muscle mass wasn't all corporeal. By losing control of their mind, they'd be unable to cast this spell, and that rendered them impotent.

In many ways, the fallen heroes were trapped in hell—until the day they died of old age, when they were finally released from their undying curse.

Oh, Goddess Elazonia. Why did thou choose me to be a hero? They would have demanded answers from her if they weren't so broken on the inside.

But there were a handful of prisoners in the Pit of Divine Punishment who were holding on to their sanity by a thread—the ones who hadn't committed acts that were heinous enough to warrant complete psychological annihilation. They were being detained because the church didn't want their crimes to come to light.

One of those prisoners was ex-Bishop Hube of Boar Kingdom, driven from his position when the cathedral was destroyed.

"Bastard, bastard…!" he muttered and cursed as he thumped his head against the gray stone walls of his cell. There was nothing other than a bed, a toilet, and the Goddess's holy book atop a small table in the room.

The screams from the other prisoners hadn't rattled him, and he was still sound of mind. In fact, the chaotic chorus around him didn't reach his ears. Any normal person wouldn't be able to handle this clamor for more than three days, but all he heard was a voice playing over and over in his mind, drowning out the noise. It was the voice of a certain girl—his beloved.

"Good-bye, bishop."

She'd looked forlorn when they parted for the final time, and then she'd turned her back and walked away for good. She didn't have the heart to blame him, even after all the pain he'd put her through. Her red hair grew distant as he watched her from behind. And then her slender figure was shrouded in a black fog which twisted into the shape of a boy, the corners of his mouth curling up in a dirty smirk as he mocked Hube.

"You lost your love, your title, your honor. Now tell me, how does that feel?"

Hube was unable to move, forced to watch as the boy tore off her clothing and defiled her in front of his very eyes.

His imagination was playing tricks on him. That wasn't what had happened in real life. It was a projection of his innermost desires.

That's why Hube shrieked in rage and clawed the walls, so he wouldn't have to look at this image any longer. "Bastard heretic—!"

His nails tore off, causing blood to trickle down his hands. The pain was unbearable. He blamed it all on the black-haired boy, despising him all the more. He didn't even realize the irony behind the fact that this all-consuming hate was his saving grace, pulling him back from the edge of insanity.

"You won't get away with this... I'll shame you, ruin you, a hundred times over!"

He'd destroy them all: the demons who'd covered for the boy, this fun country or whatever he was so set on making, and even the red-headed girl who giggled by his side. He would make the boy suffer until he begged for death. Only then would he rest.

"No matter how long it takes! No matter what I have to do!"

Scenes of revenge cycled in his mind, imagining new iterations of his actions and etching his hatred for the boy deep in his soul. Trapped by these sweet fantasies, Hube didn't notice his surroundings. Inside his cell, closed off by a heavy iron door that none could enter, behind him where he stared at the wall and spouted curses...stood someone, staring silently...

Potato Village was among the many small farming towns that dotted Boar Kingdom. The village chief went bug-eyed when he saw who was driving the horse-drawn wagon that was pulling into town.

"Y-you're still alive?!" he stammered.

"Of course," replied a merchant of average height and average build, blasé as ever. Manju smiled and nodded as he climbed down from the wagon. "And I'm still standing on my own two legs, too."

"Come again?"

"Whoops, apologies. It's, ah, a joke from my home country. Pay me no mind," he assured him. Under his breath, he muttered, "Oh yeah, do they even *have* ghosts in this world?"

But the chief was eyeing him like *he* was the ghost. "Ya went to Dog Valley, and you're really okay…"

"See? I told you. There's no *dangerous* demons there."

The chief heard a cute giggle erupt behind the merchant. When he peeked around, he met the gaze of an unfamiliar maid with pale-pink hair. She looked young, maybe fifteen, but she had the alluring smile of an escort and spoke in a drawn-out purr.

"Well, there may be no dangerous demons…but there is a dangerous *human*, now isn't there?" she teased.

"I have no idea who you're talking about," countered the merchant, feigning ignorance.

"You, obviously," spat a nearby maid with blue hair who was drop-dead gorgeous. She'd come with the merchant last time.

The village chief balked at their exchange but started to talk after some hesitation. "Um, I believe we haven't met..."

"Oh yes, sorry for not introducing you sooner. This is Ribido, my employee."

"Delighted to make your acquaintance, sir," cooed Ribido with a bewitching smile, clinging to the chief's arm and squeezing her large chest against him.

"A-another lively little lady, I see, ha-ha...," chuckled the chief uncomfortably.

"You're pretty lively for your age, too," she panted, flashing him a delighted expression as her slender fingers started to inch toward his groin.

But before she could reach, the merchant karate chopped her head.

"Owie, you're so mean...," she said wordlessly with a glance.

"You freakin' idiot, I told you to keep it together today," he scolded with his eyes.

"And by today you mean...?"

"If they're single, I don't see why not. You're free to love whoever you want."

"Aha! You get it!"

It was as if they were exchanging telepathic messages. After this silent exchange, they both smiled as if nothing had happened.

"I do apologize. To tell you the truth, I'm going to be very busy soon. I won't be able to come myself, which is why I was hoping Ribido could handle some transactions with you. I brought her along today to introduce you two."

"O-oh, I see," the chief replied in a fluster, nodding feverishly.

"Yes, I look forward to working with you! ♡" she chirped as she bent down, pressing her boobs together and staring up at him.

The chief was over sixty, and his wife was long gone. But the moment this sight filled his eyes, the withered old man sprung back to life. In a fluster, he hunched over to hide it the best he could, faking a sudden pain in his hip joint.

"Ah-ha-ha, ahem. Anything else I can help you with?"

"Yes, I was hoping to purchase some more potatoes and oil, as long as it's not too much trouble…," started the merchant, pretending not to notice the chief's newfound vigor by turning the conversation to sales.

Meanwhile, the two maids began playing with the children who'd gathered around them.

"Oh yay, miss, you came back!"

"Let's kick some rocks around," the one with blue hair suggested.

"Do you have more of those sweet things?"

"No need to get so worked up. I have some right here."

"Ooh, cute little kiddies. Would you like to come and have some fun with your big sis…? Celes, I'm just joking! Please let go of my head!" begged Ribido.

"What the hell are you two doing?" The merchant snickered as he watched Ribido screech in pain as Celes administered her punishment. He passed over the money for the goods.

It wasn't as much as last time, but still far more than the market price. The chief was a bit hesitant to accept but eventually squirreled it away in his breast pocket.

"Thank you very much. Please come again any time." Joined by the other villagers, the chief lowered his head in unison.

"Of course. I'm sure we'll be back during next harvest season, if not sooner."

The merchant and his maids bowed in reply before boarding the wagon. When the village was far enough away and no longer in sight, the *Illusion* magic cloaking all three of them melted away. The merchant turned into the black-haired boy Shinichi; the blue-haired maid into the dark-skinned, silver-haired elf; and Ribido into her succubus form, complete with bat wings and a pointy tail.

"Hee-hee-hee, human men seem so tasty. I can't wait until next time!" she moaned, as she messily mopped up her saliva with the back of her hand.

"Are you *sure* we can leave it to this floozy?" asked Celes incredulously. Her brows knit together in concern.

Shinichi smiled wryly as he nodded. "There aren't many demons who can pass as human. We don't really have a choice."

Unlike humans, all demons possessed large amounts of magical power. But most of them chose to focus on *Physical Enchantment* spells. There were surprisingly few who could handle a complicated spell like *Illusion*. Plus, the spell only distorted things visually. Meaning if their original form was too different, their true identities would be given away on physical contact.

That's why the lamia or arachne wouldn't be able to morph into humans even though their species had high competencies in magic. Their peculiar bodies made them more difficult to successfully conceal. That meant the list of possible candidates was cut down to dark elves or the incubi and succubi—hence, Celes and Ribido.

"It'll be okay, Celes. I mean, even my little brother is hard at work in Tigris Kingdom, remember?" Ribido said.

"That's why I'm so concerned…"

They were talking about the cross-dressing incubus working hard—with his, erm, bottom half—to brainwash the holy warriors. With this brother, known for being an extreme pervert even by incubi standards, it was no surprise that Celes would be concerned about his older sister's "potential." But even though Shinichi was aware of the dangers, he'd put her in charge of purchasing food.

"We have to let her handle it, so we can do what we need to," he reminded her with a look of steadfast resolve.

"……Fine." Celes let a small smile play across her lips.

The succubus suppressed a giggle as she noticed the two treat each other warmly.

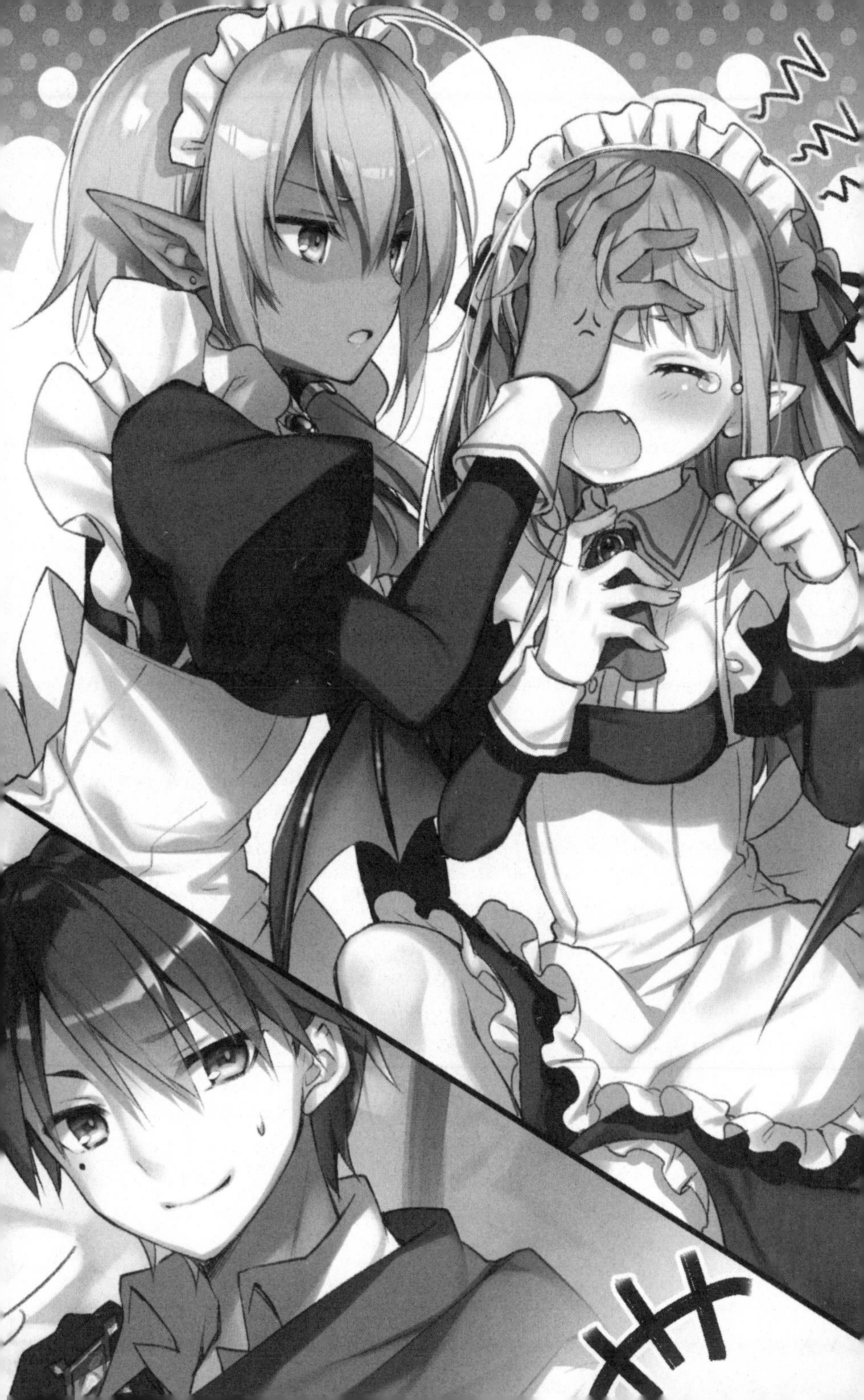

"Tee-hee, I see it's about time for Ms. Prim 'n' Proper to finally lose her virgin—"

"Quiet, you walking obscenity." *Crunch.*

"Owieee, I don't wanna hear it from a pervy deviant like you—AAAaaack!"

Expressionless as ever, Celes clamped her best clawhold on to the succubus's face, administering her punishment for pouring fuel onto the fire. Shinichi chuckled as he watched the good-natured fight and urged the horse-drawn cart forward.

The Demon King's castle stood on a strip of land that was narrow and rock-strewn—the long-abandoned Dog Valley, left to its own devices due to its barren soil. Now, however, tilled patches of soft, brown soil stretched across the terrain in the form of potato fields.

"Shinichi, welcome home, *oink*," cried Sirloin, a pig-headed orc. Wielding a plow, he ambled up to the horse-drawn cart the moment he saw them approaching. By his feet was the pet pig that the demons had taken in. He'd gotten quite plump while they were gone.

"Why the plow? We've finished planting the seed potatoes, and it's too early to harvest them," Shinichi noted.

"We were gathering food from the forests, *moo*," replied Kalbi, the bull-headed minotaur, trudging behind Sirloin. On his back was a basket filled with treasures from the mountains: bracken, butterbur, and bamboo shoots.

"My brother here found all of this, *oink*!"

"*Squee!*" announced the pig proudly as the orc stroked him.

"I've heard of people using pigs to find truffles, but I didn't realize he'd be one of them." Shinichi marveled at the pig he'd originally bought for slaughter. "He's gotten huge in the blink of an eye."

When Shinichi'd bought him, the cute little piglet was just over a foot long. But not even a month had passed, and he'd filled out into a full-size adult—three feet long and weighing in at over two hundred pounds. And he didn't seem like he was done growing, either, as he gulped down the weeds sprouting up in the fields.

"It's because he eats everything! No preference for taste, *oink.*"

"He doesn't even have any problems eating *parbegut* or *beossla* from the demon world. He's amazing, *moo!*"

"*Squee!*" rejoiced the pig as the minotaur showered him with compliments, but Shinichi's expression turned grim.

"This…is a bit *too* fast, even for a pig. He's not turning into a monster, is he?"

A monster, the mutilated form of normal animals that soaked up too much magic. In most cases, they grew larger and their muscles became stronger than normal animals, but there were some that had even been able to cast magic. Shinichi fretted that this was happening to their pet pig, but all the demons looked blankly at him in confusion.

"Has the little piggy turned into a monster?" Ribido questioned.

"Don't ask me. Monsters might be commonplace in the demon world, but I don't know if an animal from the human world can turn into one," explained Celes.

"I don't even know the difference between the two, *oink.*"

"I thought the strong ones were monsters and the weak ones were animals, *moo.*"

If Celes didn't know, no one did. After all, she was the most knowledgeable one in the demon clan, who were all indiscriminately meatheads.

The former hero and monster hunter Arian was the person who'd told Shinichi about this theory, which she'd pieced together from rumors through the grapevine. Meaning she didn't really know the underlying principles.

She said they change when they're exposed to too much magic, but what exactly is magic?

At its base, he knew it was the power necessary to cast spells. And that it could be used up and gradually restored with proper R & R.

He'd experienced that much with his own body. But he didn't know the scientific details at all: What was it made of? What were its properties? What kind of energy did it use?

And it's not just inside the bodies of humans and demons. It seems to exist in the air. Is that how I should think of it?

What was the source of this mysterious power? His best guess was that they were mana or aether particles—things that were only in myths and legends on Earth. By absorbing that in their bodies, the cells of the organisms in this world turned it into energy, which must be what they called *magic*.

A body part that takes in these particles and converts them to magic, huh... I'll just call them the magic organs *for now.*

Shinichi was living proof that humans without magical abilities could cast spells if they were exposed to magic for prolonged periods of time. Based on that, it seemed that all living creatures were born with this magical body part.

But, save for demons, the ability was dormant in most organisms. They were only able to use magic if it was activated by an external force or awakened within. That's how magic users were born.

So would it be more accurate to call them spell-casting animals?

To go back to the basics, magic was a way to alter reality to match your imagination. Humans could create complex phenomena by unleashing this energy to launch fireballs or heal wounds. But that was only possible because they're highly intelligent creatures. On the other hand, animals were only able to form simple images: to defeat their enemies and catch prey to survive. As a result, they became bigger, stronger, faster, tougher.

A creature modifying itself based on its instincts is a monster...

Shinichi met the pig's gaze as he came to his conclusion.

Around the castle, there should be a higher concentration of magic in the atmosphere than usual since there are a lot of demons who can use magic—and in particular, the almighty Demon King. Is that what's causing this?

"*Squee?*"

Shinichi stroked the pig's head as it looked at him in confusion. A certain fear ran through his mind: *If animals can become monsters from prolonged exposure to magic, then humans can become—*

"I don't have a problem if you need to think over our dishes for dinner...but shouldn't we take care of something else first?" Celes interrupted.

"...Ah yeah, you're right," said Shinichi, returning to Earth and patting Celes on the shoulder.

"Dinner?! But you said we weren't going to eat my brother, *oink!*"

"*Squeee—!*"

"Calm down. We're not gonna." He flashed a wry smile at the orc shielding his brethren with his body before he urged the horse toward the castle. When they reached their destination, Shinichi and Celes moved their most recent purchases into the cellar and headed toward a room with a magic circle drawn on the floor.

"All right, I'm counting on you."

"Understood. To where we wish to go, to go where we are needed, *Teleport*," chanted Celes.

The moment she finished her incantation, a pure white light illuminated their bodies, accompanied by a feeling of weightlessness, as if they were drifting in space. But it quickly passed as the scene in front of their eyes suddenly shifted.

The sunlight dripped through the skylight and bathed the sparkling statue of the Goddess in the center of the prayer room, dignified yet lavishly decorated. Three beautiful girls were healing the injured.

"Rino, I see you're hard at work."

"Ah, Shinichi, I didn't think you'd come to pick us up!" squealed Rino, the Demon King's daughter. After she finished healing her patient, she dashed up to Shinichi with a wide grin, leaping into his arms. "There was an accident in the caves today, and some people died, but everyone's feeling much better now."

"Good girl," Shinichi praised as he stroked her hair.

Her eyes crinkled in delight.

Nearby, the redheaded ex-hero Arian pouted with envy. "I worked hard, too. I helped pull people out of the rubble…"

"Yeah, yeah, you did good, too." Shinichi chuckled dryly as he patted her head. She burst into giggles and a happy, crooked smile.

"As dumb as always, I see," Celes observed with a hint of annoyance.

"I find her simplicity charming," objected the pale-haired ex-saint Sanctina.

After she'd betrayed the church and joined the demons, she'd been here in the Tigris Kingdom Cathedral, supporting her beloved Rino by healing the sick and injured. There was just one problem.

"Lady Sanctina, the next patient is ready," announced a holy warrior who was into little girls and had denounced the church, too.

Sanctina turned around, face plastered with the fake smile of a seasoned pro. "Is it a woman?"

"No, a man."

"Rino, the next patient is ready," she echoed, attempting to pass him off to Rino without so much as a flinch.

"Hey you! Yo, Saint! You can't cherry-pick your patients," Shinichi warned.

Cold sweat sprung to her brow. "Y-yes, but…when I go near men, my whole body goes numb, and I can't breathe…!"

"Wow, what a serious malady," he replied in monotone exasperation at Sanctina, who was pale and on the verge of collapsing. "I thought you healed men before, no problem. What happened…?"

"I'm pretty sure it's because of you," quipped Celes.

After all, she'd been traumatized by Shinichi, who had psychologically broken her to within an inch of her life. This, compounded by her hatred of men, must have spurred a change in Sanctina.

"What if you used an *Illusion* spell to make all men look like Rino?" Shinichi offered.

"…I hadn't considered that before."

"Hey, I'm obviously just kidding."

As the ex-saint beamed in delight imagining a world full of Rinos, blood started to drip from her nose. Shinichi couldn't help but recoil in disgust.

While they went on with their banter, Rino finished healing the patient, and the day's work was over.

"All right, let's go home," Shinichi proposed.

"Yessiree! Juda, please take care of things here while we're gone," Rino asked.

"Leave it to me!" replied the holy warrior, Juda, with a vigorous nod. His eyes sparkled as he was handed a task from his idol. He saw them off as they went to stand on the magic circle.

"Shinichi, why'd you come to pick us up today?" asked Arian suspiciously.

(Which was shorthand for "It's usually just Celes.")

Shinichi answered with a tense expression on his face. "Nothing major. I have something important to talk to you about."

"Huh?! Is it—?"

Just as she started to ask him, Celes finished the incantation for the *Teleport* spell, washing them over in light and whizzing them back to the Demon King's castle.

"We're going to take up a fight with the church," declared Shinichi.

This was the first thing out of his mouth after the necessary agents had gathered in the dining hall.

"We've fought off the heroes three times now, but I don't think the church will let up. They'll keep sending them in."

After all, the church had decided that they needed to destroy demonkind. As long as that was the case, a handful of losses wouldn't be enough for them to back down from the good fight.

"With His Highness's strength in mind, it wouldn't worry me if they attacked us—even if they sent in every last man. But things could get bad if they sent their troops to Tigris Kingdom."

The young king of Tigris, Sieg, had broken off all ties with the church, after enduring their abuse for many long years, and joined hands with the demons. He had yet to make a formal announcement, seeing that this change of heart might cause his subjects to dissolve into chaos. But anyone who was the slightest bit observant would notice that the holy warriors had all but disappeared from the cathedral. Not only that: Rino and Sanctina were on friendly terms, performing healings and treating patients side by side. There was obviously a huge change underway.

"Today marks the fourth day of our alliance," Shinichi announced. "I doubt word has reached the Archbasilica, but it's only a matter of time."

If the cardinals found out about what had happened, they'd surely send heroes or their troops to storm the Tigris Kingdom under the guise of suppressing heretics.

"They can't let Tigris cut off their ties without a fight. Otherwise, more countries might follow their lead and pull away from the church. I imagine they'd kill off all the ruling class, including the king, and take over, subjugating the citizens to heavy taxation—at the very least."

"Likely," Sanctina bolstered. "When the first pope destroyed the heretical capital of Mouse, the church rounded up the criminals. They're forced to work in the fields until they die of exhaustion. The church is essentially harvesting slaves."

"Absolutely diabolical...," muttered Shinichi.

Not that he could talk. Two hundred years prior, slavery remained at large on his home world of Earth. Even now, prisons in developing countries had horrendous conditions. In truth, he had no grounds to act all holier-than-thou toward the church, but it wasn't something that he could accept, either.

"They're all humans... Why would they do such terrible things to one another...?" whimpered Rino. Her eyes glistened with tears as she imagined this cruel scene.

Celes pressed a hand to her own chest, clearly holding something back, then kindly offered a drink to Rino to calm her. "Don't forget: There are some demons that act the same way. It'd be an oversimplification to blame the humans alone."

"I guess you're right…"

"I cannot allow anyone to make my daughter sad! I will annihilate every corrupt person, human or demon!" the Demon King boomed.

"That's exactly the kind of thing an evil villain would do," joked Shinichi, breaking out into a cold sweat upon seeing that the Demon King was raring to carry out a genocide in the name of parental love.

There were dictators on Earth attempting to do the same thing with their political authority, but they had their work cut out for them. With the Demon King, however, it was no joke. He actually possessed the power to massacre millions.

"Anyway! It's a pain to keep fighting off the heroes. I want to defeat the church and end this ridiculous war before trouble hits Tigris," said Shinichi.

"I have no interest in the affairs of humans, but it would besmirch my honor as the Blue Demon King to abandon those who have come to rely on my power." The Demon King nodded deeply in agreement.

"I don't like fighting, but it would be even worse if the captain and everyone else in the city got hurt," Rino remarked, supporting Shinichi with a grimace.

As for Arian, she had been silent this entire time.

"When you said you had something important to talk about, I thought…," she trailed off, embarrassed at herself for her romantic flight of fancy, turning beet-red as she collapsed on the table.

"I'm not saying that you can't daydream, but I think it'd do everyone good if you could regain some of your esteem as a hero," Celes scolded as she handed Arian a damp towel.

"Ugh, I'm so sorry…" She wiped and cooled down her burning face as Shinichi looked at her in wry amusement.

With that, he continued to explain his plan: "By 'fighting the heroes,'

I'm not talking about Your Highness reducing the Archbasilica to ash or anything. 'Cause the heroes won't die anyway."

"Absolutely aggravating," grumbled the Demon King through clenched teeth, recalling with visible vexation the time when Ruzal's party kept resurrecting over and over again.

"That's why we're gonna keep feeding them the same underhanded methods to break their spirits and manipulate them."

"You dirty scoundrel," Celes spat back without missing a beat.

Insults had become a normal part of their conversations. Shinichi just waved it aside and turned to look at the former saint.

"Our targets are the four people who run the church: the cardinals. I want you to tell me everything you know about them."

"Anything for Rino." Sanctina sighed without batting an eye at the prospect of stabbing her adoptive father and his colleagues in the back.

The Demon King grimaced. "Shinichi, will we gain anything from listening to this girl? This could just be a trick to lead us astray."

"I don't think she's the type to lie to us at this point."

"It's true, Daddy! How could you doubt Sanctie!" cried Rino crossly as she jumped to Sanctina's defense.

"Oh, your saintly kindness never fails to surprise me...," marveled Sanctina.

As she leaned against Rino's small frame, a vein popped up on the Demon King's forehead. "You tramp! I can't believe my daughter uses a cute pet name for you!"

"*That's* what you're angry about?! Not for making Rino cry or anything?!" Shinichi protested.

"Of course, I haven't forgiven her for that, either! A hundred deaths would not be penance enough!"

"Welp, that came back to bite me in the ass."

"But a nickname! I simply won't allow it! She's only called me Daddy her entire life!"

"What else would she call you?" Shinichi retorted. He was genuinely flabbergasted by the Demon King and his unreasonable helicopter parenting style.

"The name Sanctina is just so long," Rino argued. "Was it bad for me to shorten it?"

"Of course not. It's the first nickname I've ever been given. It makes me very happy," Sanctina assured her.

"Ooh, I want one, too. I don't have any…," Arian lamented.

"I suppose the nickname 'Red' isn't very endearing, even though the demons think very highly of it," Celes remarked.

The girls prattled among themselves, chattering on in an animated way…meaning there was no one to back up the Demon King.

"Aaagh—!" he growled.

"Seems Rino's already forgiven Sanctina, so don't let a stupid nickname upset you. How about it, pops? Or should I say, father-in-law?" Shinichi jested.

"…Shinichi, have you finished writing your death poem?"

"My sincerest apologies. I took my jokes too far," Shinichi spouted, hastily kneeling on the ground and bowing in apology upon seeing the murderous look flash across the King's face.

He sighed instead of giving a response and jabbed his finger at Sanctina again. "In conclusion! This girl displeases me!"

"Daddy…" Rino balked at her father's childish tantrum.

Upon seeing her gloomy expression, Sanctina suddenly stood up. "Your Highness, I realize I have committed grave crimes. I cannot expect you to pardon me. But is there any way I can prove my loyalty toward Rino?"

She was in front of the great Demon King—a matchless figure and, on top of that, a *man*. But her face didn't betray any emotion though she must have experienced full-body chills. And yet, she was composed when she knelt in front of his towering body.

He looked down at the ex-saint coldly. "Well then, would you die for Rino?"

"Happily," she chirped.

Shinichi didn't even have time to open his mouth before she placed her right hand at the base of her own throat with a gentle smile—

"*Wind Cutter.*" Her head flew off her body.

"Aah?!" screeched Rino.

The blood spurted out of the severed neck and painted the dining hall a brilliant crimson. Sanctina's head was still smiling faintly as it rolled away.

Shinichi and Arian were frozen in place, unable to respond to the sudden act, but the Demon King stood quietly from his seat, picked up Sanctina's head, and placed it in line with her body on the ground. Before her brain cells completely died from lack of oxygen, he held up his hands and spoke an incantation.

"*Full Healing.*"

Light blanketed her body and severed neck, joining the two together as if time had been turned back. Sanctina continued to smile when she was pulled back from the deep abyss of death, her face pale from blood loss.

"Would a million more deaths be enough?"

If that wasn't enough, she'd die a million and one times.

To Sanctina, this act amounted to nothing. If this was all it took to prove her love for Rino, so be it. She smiled boldly back at the Demon King, steadfast in her resolve.

The corners of his mouth twitched in amusement, and he waved his large hand.

"That will not be necessary. I acknowledge your loyalty to my daughter."

After all, the demons valued strength above all else. And not just physical strength. It was the same for spiritual and emotional power, too. The Demon King was impressed by Sanctina's insanity and happily changed his mind.

"I'm very grateful," she replied, bowing her head deeply.

In truth, she was happier than she'd ever been, more than when she'd received the Goddess's blessing. Now she was being accepted for her true, authentic self.

What a truly moving scene— Er, well, they were the only ones who thought that.

"...Yeeeah, the people in the Goddess's church are actually insane," Shinichi griped, cringing.

"...I doubt many are as bad as Sanctina," Arian objected, but her argument was pretty weak.

Up until then, Rino's face had been white as a sheet, stiff with surprise. But she'd broken free from her initial shock to run up to Sanctina in a frenzied panic.

"S-Sanctie, wh-why would you do something like that?!"

"My life is a small price to pay to prove my loyalty to you."

"And you're a hero, so you'd be resurrected anyway," Shinichi bluntly cut in.

Rino glared at him and raised her voice. "It doesn't matter if she's a hero! Pain is bad, and treating life with indifference is even worse!"

"...I'm very sorry," Sanctina replied.

Of course. That was common sense. But that might be why it resonated so strongly with Sanctina.

All her life, she'd spent time in the church where injuries, disease, and even death were no problem. For the first time in her life, she was being seriously admonished for dismissing life and inflicting pain—to herself or otherwise. Rino was the first person to point that out.

"I was right all along! Rino *is* my goddess," Sanctina extolled, looking absolutely blissed out.

"Erm, did she...level up?" Shinichi groaned.

"Never mind that. Could you please do something about this blood?" Celes hissed to Sanctina.

After she cast a *Purification* spell to tidy up and ate dinner to replenish her excessive blood loss, they eventually got back to the topic at hand.

"Right. I think we left off at the point when you said you'd like to know more about the cardinals and their weaknesses?" Sanctina said through gulps of wild-boar steak. Color was gradually returning to her face.

"Yup. But I think it'll be a good opportunity to learn more about the church itself," Shinichi proposed, asking the questions he'd been waiting so long to ask. "When did the religion start? What's its doctrine? What's their general history? I want to know everything."

It might not be necessary for their plan to overthrow the cardinals, but there could come a day when it'd be useful.

I mean, something as small as a termite can bring down an entire palace. It could help me if the Goddess ever decides to show her face. It might be good to get a better understanding of the hand behind the system that resurrects heroes again and again.

If he could just get a better peek into the secret behind these resurrections, he could end this pointless battle. But he wasn't expecting to glean that much information.

Sanctina silently thought for a moment before she began talking calmly. "Well then, I guess I'll tell you the story from the beginning, based on our holy book. Long, long ago, when the world was one—"

Long ago, gods of righteousness and virtue created this world of Obum, making one great continent.

The people lived in resplendent prosperity. Even in the dead of night, their cities were bathed in light. Residents filled their stomachs with bountiful food and drink. They sang and danced day after day. In essence, it was paradise.

But something appeared that would destroy it: the diabolical Evil God and its demonic kin.

The Evil God led its hordes and the Evil Dragon, waging a war against the humans. It was hell on Obum—humans shredded and crushed by the Evil God's magic, the Evil Dragon's breath, the demons' fangs and talons.

When humanity was teetering on the precipice of destruction—with a survival rate of one in ten—the Good Gods descended from the heavens to save humanity. Goddess Elazonia led them in a raging battle lasting ten days and ten nights. Its ferocity tore the single great continent into three. Dust and soil erupted into the sky and plunged the world into a harsh winter.

The Good Gods found a bitter victory and sealed the Evil God, Evil Dragon, and the demons deep below the earth, but the victory came at a steep price. Most of their kin had been slain, and Elazonia, having exhausted her power, returned to the heavens and fell into a long slumber.

The Good Gods were all but gone, the sunlight was choked out by debris, and the remaining few humans withered from hunger and cold.

Yet, they continued to scrape a life from the bleak land for many years—

"—and so, that's the creation story according to the holy book," Sanctina wrapped up.

"Interesting, sure, but there are a ton of plot holes," Shinichi objected.

He knew it was absurd to expect a myth to make perfect sense, but he just couldn't keep his mouth shut. "First, the story about the creation of the world is weak, slipshod at best. I get that the Good Gods created it, but is that all you know?"

"Yes. The holy book only says that Goddess Elazonia and the other Good Gods created Obum, leaving it in the humans' care before disappearing to the heavens."

"I was told the same story at church. What's wrong with it?" asked Arian.

The pair were confused that Shinichi questioned it.

"Don't you think it lacks details—no? Am I the only one?"

Shinichi tried to reason with them but realized something partway through. He had a point of reference—other creation myths—which was why he could observe it was weak. There would be no reason for people of this world to question it, especially if they'd been hearing the creation myth from the Goddess's church all their lives.

"Okay, listen to this as an example: In some religions on Earth, it's said one god created the world in six days and then rested on the seventh, and he made the first human from soil. Then there are myths about how Chaos was born from nothing, then Gaia was born from Chaos and later gave birth to a bunch of different gods."

"Wow, those are supercool," Rino gasped.

"Oh, the island country that I'm from is said to have been born from two gods, a brother and sister," he added.

"An island born from incest. What a perverted legend," Celes scoffed.

"Save that for Greek mythology: Brothers, sisters, parents, children, even animals and sculptures do it. Plus, the main god was the epitome of a chronic cheater."

The myths were written long ago, before moral restrictions. Of course they'd be packed full of sexual, grotesque nonsense.

"Anyway, I just thought that story's a bit sloppy, that's all."

Why does the world exist? The age-old question. It was a question that all people carried with them. It made them uneasy to not know the truth. That was where religions and myths came in, filling the role of a teacher, explaining that it was "created by the gods" or whatever to give them peace of mind. It was also the reason that many iterations of creation stories were passed down as myths.

But the Goddess's holy book seemed to cut it out, missing this chunk entirely.

As if to say, *There's no need to explain how the world was created after all these years*, or something…

There was something about it that bothered Shinichi, but he couldn't quite put his finger on it. He returned to the main topic.

"Okay, so if the Good Gods created this world, where'd the Evil God and Evil Dragon come from? Did the Good Gods create them? Why did the Good Gods let them be until they almost destroyed humanity?"

This was a common argument on Earth: An omnipotent, omnipresent god wouldn't just let a devil to do his own thing.

"On Earth, some people claim that God came and saved humanity from the devil that tried to manipulate them, for which the people were grateful. And God let the devil be so he could keep taking credit for doing good, yada yada," continued Shinichi.

"Are you trying to tell me that it's not just the humans who are twisted? That the gods are, too?" Celes asked, looking put off by the stories.

"Don't you think the humans and gods here are pretty dirty, too?" retorted Shinichi with a wry smile.

Beside him, Sanctina tapped a finger to her lips as she thought.

"Where did the Evil God and Evil Dragon come from…? Now that you mention it, it is strange, but I'd never put much thought into it before. I was taught that the beginning of the holy book is the Goddess's own words, recorded by the first pope, so it is wrong to question them."

"…I see," said Shinichi with a slight frown, catching glimpse of the extent of their brainwashing tactics. "But it can't be just me. I bet scholars would have something to say about it, too."

"I'm not sure of other cities, but anyone who doubted her teachings in the Holy City would be thrown in jail," Sanctina explained.

"Wow, unbelievable! But hang on… If we spread rumors that they doubted the holy book, we could take them down like—"

"No, if they had a *Liar Detector* spell put on them and gave testimony, the truth would come out. I don't think it would work," interrupted Sanctina.

"No false testimonies?! Ever?! Zero percent?! Glad justice has got something going for it."

"That doesn't mean a judge hasn't lied about the truth, even after he knows everything using *Liar Detector*."

"Just kidding! They're really friggin' corrupt!"

It was a perfect example of the splendor of magic rendered totally worthless if the caster was a rotten scoundrel.

"Well, if you aren't stupid enough to pick a fight with the cardinals, you won't have to deal with anything so corrupt," Sanctina assured him.

"Yeah, but we *have* to be that stupid…," said Shinichi, his head in his hands at her uncomforting words. "Anyway, the story about the demons being led by the Evil God and killing off the humans… Did that really happen?"

It was likely that the church had twisted the creation story to fit their agenda. They had free artistic rein, seeing as it was about an event that supposedly happened long ago. Shinichi was asking to hear the demons' side of the story, but the Demon King just shook his head.

"I have never heard such a tale. I hadn't even heard of the Goddess until we came here."

"They cast our grand Black Dragon in the role of their Evil Dragon. I must say, it's quite offensive," Celes added.

"It was so far back that I don't know anything about it, but I don't want to believe that my great-great-ancestors did such horrible things to the humans..." Rino shuddered.

They didn't have any proof to rebuke it, but both Celes and Rino seemed to think it wasn't true.

"I see... By the way, does the demon world have a creation myth, too?" Shinichi asked.

"Yessiree, we do," Rino confirmed with a nod before standing from her seat and dashing out of the dining hall. She returned carrying a book. "It's written in this book."

It looked like a picture book titled *The God Who Became the Sun*.

"One of the nice dvergr ladies made it for me," Rino exclaimed.

"Those guys can make anything, huh?"

"Because every dvergr—young or old, man or woman—is a craftsman. Sir Ivan is a master of the forge, but others exceed in their own arts, including pottery or painting," Celes explained.

"On the other hand, they refuse to assist with projects that disinterest them," the King lamented.

"Sounds about right. Artists through and through." Shinichi gazed at the book constructed with such skill that it was hard to imagine it was handmade. "Can I read it?"

"Yessiree," replied Rino, reaching out to pass it to him.

"Stop right there. I think this would be a perfect opportunity to hear Rino read aloud," Sanctina suggested, extending her hand to stop him from taking the book.

"You'd like *me* to read?"

"Yes, if you read it in your clear voice, it will flow through the world as gospel, reaching deep into our souls."

"Hmm, a fine proposal indeed," the Demon King agreed.

"Yo, reel it in. Same goes for you and your helicopter parenting," Shinichi chided.

But Rino blushed at all the compliments, bashfully opening the book to read. "Long, long ago, a great calamity came to Obum—to the place where the demons lived."

"Calamity, huh...?" murmured Shinichi.

"God appeared before the panicked demons, telling them, 'I have created a new world below the surface of the earth where the calamity cannot reach. Everyone come with me to safety.'"

Guided by God, the demons trudged down below the surface of the earth to begin their new lives there. There was one major problem: There was no sun underground.

"No one could see in the inky darkness. No grass or flowers sprung up from the ground. That is when God became the sun."

God turned itself into the sun, illuminating the land underground with blue light.

"And so, the demon world was created, and the demons lived happily ever after. The end."

"What a beautiful performance!" wept Sanctina.

"Bravo! I'd expect no less from my daughter!" boomed the King, clapping his hands with the concussive force of a bomb, but Shinichi ignored them, lost in thought.

There's a slight overlap with the origin story taught by the church.

Other than the obvious difference between this calamity and the hordes of evil creatures, it was pretty obvious that *something* big and serious had happened a long time ago. He still couldn't put his finger on *what* it was, but it had resulted in the majority of humans perishing and the demons moving underground.

I can't really take them at face value. I mean, who knows how much of the

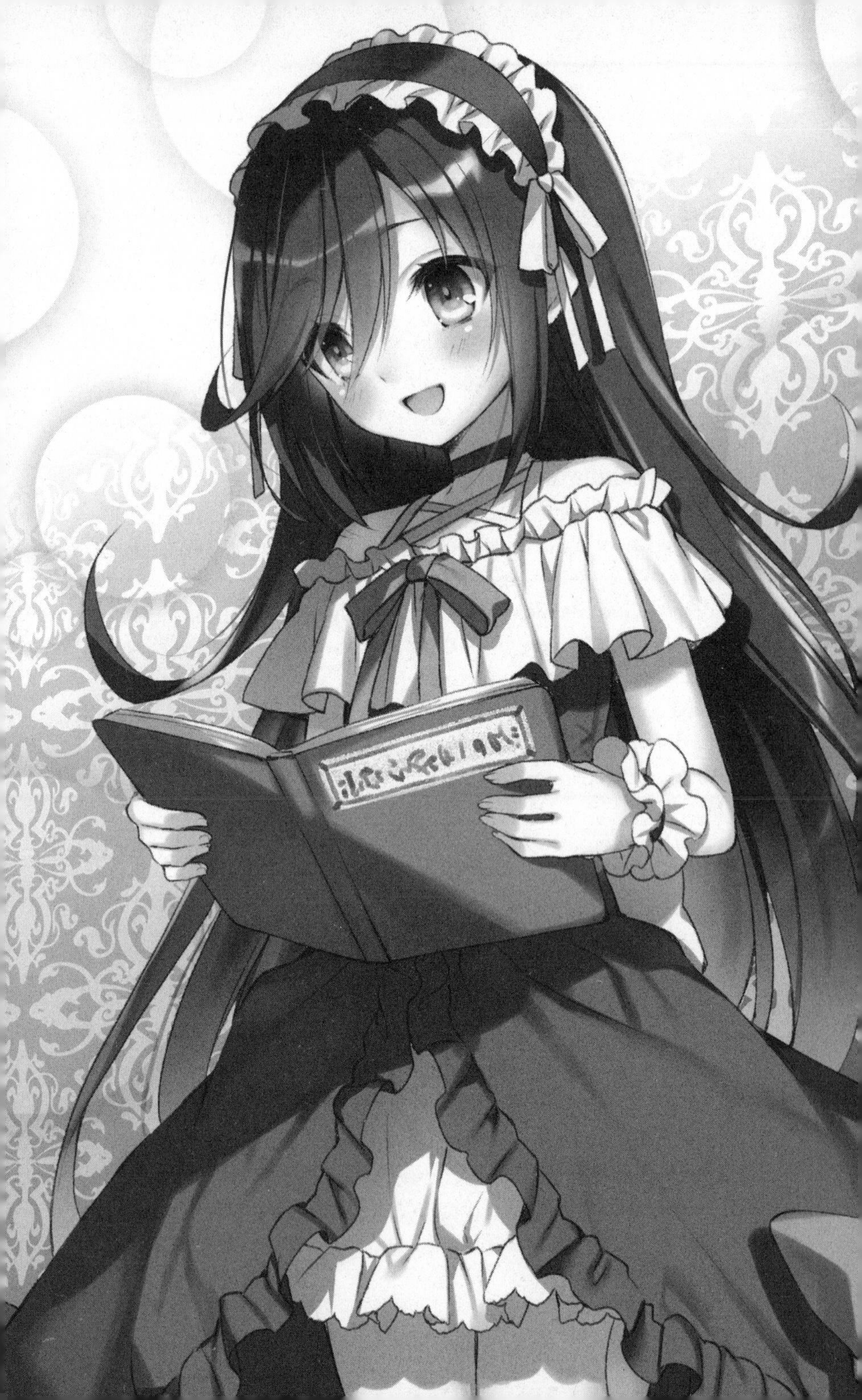

stories have warped over the years, especially since they were passed down for generations... But I wonder if there's some truth where they overlap. Like an archaeologist uncovering long-lost ruins, Shinichi let his mind run though the possibilities. *Reminds me of Noah's Ark for some reason.*

The story of the great flood appeared in *The Epic of Gilgamesh*, the oldest piece of literature on Earth. According to the tale, it rained for forty straight days to eliminate the sinners. It was all part of God's plan, even though God had been the one to create humankind.

Maybe the Goddess herself brought this calamity onto Obum.

But he might just be projecting his suspicions on her because he viewed her as the enemy.

Either way, it seems the Evil God who was sealed below the earth and the god who became the sun might be the same being.

Just as he came to this conclusion, he shot a glance at the Demon King, who pounded his cerulean chest with a proud thump.

"I claimed the title of the Blue Demon King—in part for the color of my skin, but also as a tribute to the god who saved demonkind."

"I see. Since the color of the sun is blue," Shinichi concluded.

In human terms, it'd be like having the name "King of the Golden Sun."

"How strange," Arian said to herself, nodding in admiration as she noted their cultural differences once again.

"Speaking of, is this calamity the reason why demonkind doesn't come to the surface?" Shinichi asked.

"Yes, we've been taught that it's a dangerous place. We must not leave the demon world since the calamity fell," explained Celes.

"And that's why those who do go to the surface are those looking for danger, like my wife," the King added.

"I bet she was pretty bummed out," Shinichi commented.

After all, they'd been told that the surface was more dangerous than the demon world—the land of roaming monsters, where strength was king. And when they gritted their teeth, determined as all hell to go up to the hellish scene aboveground, they were met with...a peaceful sight: animals wandering through lush greenery under a golden sun streaming through the clouds.

Oh, and humans—weak as hell and mostly incapable of using magic, save for a special few.

"Some of the jaded demons returned to tell their tales of the 'human world,' a place where there wasn't a single dangerous thing. But the majority of the demons couldn't see it for themselves since they'd need to *Teleport* a great distance. And with a few travelers never returning, they'd rather believe that the land aboveground was fraught with danger," Celes explained.

"My guess is that they didn't come back 'cause the heroes did them in or they fell in love with the food," Shinichi offered.

There might even be some who'd fallen in love with humans and settled down on Obum.

"It's incredible if you think about how we got here. First, Your Highness's wife brought back stories of good food."

"Yessiree, and I was able to meet you, Shinichi, thanks to Mommy. I'll have to tell her thank you when she comes home!"

Rino's joy was contagious, and Shinichi found himself smiling, too.

"Which is the truth: The hordes of evil creatures or a calamity from the sky? Or are they both wrong...? This would be a whole lot quicker if we had someone who'd been there. Are there any high elves that live for thousands and thousands of years?" he asked.

"What exactly do you think an elf is?" Celes fumed, glowering at him to the max.

Just who do you think you're calling an old hag? seemed to be what she was implying.

Shinichi remembered what she'd told him earlier. "Oh yeah; elven life spans aren't too different from humans, right?"

They'd talked about it not long after they'd defeated Bishop Hube, around the time Arian had joined them for good.

"Yes, we live to about a hundred and twenty years," Celes hissed.

"I'll never get used to hearing that...," he muttered.

Based on popular fantasy worlds and stories in Japan, he'd had the impression that elves generally lived long lives. That's why he was a bit resistant at first, but there wasn't anything strange about it.

In reality, the demons were saying the word *aulice*. Shinichi was under a *Translation* spell, which had been cast on him when he'd been summoned. This is how it broke that word down: *aulice* → "a race of beautiful people with long ears" → *elf*. That was finally a word that he could understand. But there wasn't actually any relationship between the "elves" here and the race featured in high-fantasy stories on Earth.

"Well, forget elves then. Are there any demonkind who were around when the calamity fell?" Shinichi tried again.

"Don't be dumb. How long ago do you think that was?" The King gave him a hard no. "We can live to be two hundred years. In fact, some can live to see three hundred, but none have lived the thousands of years from the time of myth."

"You're right; it's a waste of time... Wait, hang on," Shinichi said when one possibility popped into his mind: "The dragon would know everything, wouldn't it?"

The legendary Black Dragon. This was the incredibly powerful creature that slumbered in the demon world—the Evil Dragon that the Goddess allegedly sealed beneath the earth.

"Indeed. The Black Dragon would know everything," Celes asserted.

"But nobody knows where it is," Rino chimed in.

It was a legend even among the demons. There wasn't even any proof that it existed.

"That's true. We don't even know if the Black Dragon exists. We know with certainty that a Red Dragon does," declared Shinichi as he looked pointedly at their proof, Arian.

"Ah..."

Arian was startled to find herself at the center of their attention. Her hand shot up to touch the red scales that cascaded down the base of her throat. She was a half dragon, the child of a dragon father and a human mother. This was more than enough proof that dragons existed.

"Arian, I know it must be difficult to talk about, but do you know where your father is?" asked Shinichi, trying to be as considerate of her feelings as possible.

"...Sorry, I don't know anything about my father at all." She hung her head apologetically. "My earliest memory is traveling alone with my mom. I haven't met him even once. When I asked my mom, the only thing she'd tell me was that he was a dragon and so I'm a half dragon..."

Since her mother had passed away from an illness, the secrets of how she'd met Arian's father and the circumstances that had led to Arian's birth would remain shrouded in mystery.

"I see," he said.

"But you know, whenever I asked my mom about Dad, she'd seem a little embarrassed and hesitant, but she never looked like she disliked him. So..." Arian trailed off.

...*I want to believe they were in love*, she seemed to want to say.

Shinichi stroked her hair as he smiled reassuringly. "A dragon and a human created a child. Two different races, two different forms. There's no way you'd convince me that child *isn't* proof of their love."

"...Uh-huh!" Arian wept tears of happiness as she jumped into his arms. His gentle words washed away a lifetime of fear.

"Hmph, Arian! No fair!" Rino whined.

"...... (*gazing intently*)."

"Uuum, yeah, let's see: Does the church have any stories of the dragons' whereabouts?" Shinichi strategically changed the subject as he released Arian upon seeing Rino pouting and Celes glowering at him coldly.

"Other than the story of the Evil Dragon sealed beneath the earth, not really. I've heard of dragons hiding in mountains and rumors of heroes going to defeat them," replied Sanctina.

"But you don't know of anyone who has seen them, right? Much less defeated them."

"I do not," she confirmed.

Shinichi's shoulders slumped in defeat. "Oh well, let's give up on the dragons then. We don't even know if the Red Dragon would know anything about that time anyway, and we have to come up with a plan to deal with the church."

"I could go look for them instead if you have no time," suggested the Demon King, his eyes sparkling with excitement.

"No chance," Shinichi shut him down immediately.

If Arian's dad is anything like the Black Dragon, then the Demon King would be no match for him...

But, of course, demons were *exactly* the kind of meatheaded war-mongers that'd be itching to fight with a matchless opponent. With that in mind, Shinichi decided it would be too risky to talk about the dragons any longer, so he turned the topic back to the church's legends.

"So humanity was pushed to the brink of destruction by a gaggle of demons or the calamity. Then what?"

"For a long time, humankind lived in the world without gods, suffering along the way. But they scraped by. Then 287 years ago, the Goddess suddenly woke again—"

Smack-dab in the exact center of the continent of Uropeh, there was a small village where a man named Eument lived. He worked as a woodcutter and carpenter, an honest and good young man, but it's been said he was a commoner without any magical abilities.

Then one fateful night, he woke from his slumber to find a ravishing, radiant woman standing by his bed. Eument was frozen in surprise, but the woman spoke to him with a gentle smile.

"I am Elazonia, the Goddess of Light. I have awakened and descended from the heavens to save my lost children. You are their savior, destined to spread divine light to the people," she commanded.

With that, Eument was bathed in brilliant light as if the sun itself stood in his room, showing him that his late parents' polytheistic beliefs were lies, false idols. He swore his everlasting devotion to the Goddess Elazonia, who was filled with joy and bestowed upon him great magical power and the holy symbol of the sun.

That was the moment that the first follower of the Goddess was created: the first preacher, the first undying hero, and the magnificent first pope.

Eument used his magic to heal the sick and injured, even to raise the dead, and to fell fearful monsters and evil men. Awed by his acts of faith, the people began to toss aside their old beliefs in local spirits and nature to praise the Goddess Elazonia instead. The number of followers multiplied right away, and the particularly skilled followers received the Goddess's symbol from Eument to begin their work as heroes, further spreading her word.

Then, in year twenty-two of the Elazonian calendar, Eument led many followers in a triumphant return to his hometown where they established the Holy City, the center of the church. With his own hands, Eument carved a statue of the Goddess from stone and placed it in his home, which later became the site of the Archbasilica, where the Goddess had descended to Obum.

"—and that's the story from the time when Elazonia descended from the heavens until the Holy City was created," Sanctina concluded.

"......" Shinichi was silent, lost in thought, as Sanctina took a deep breath and sipped some water.

So it isn't wrong to think the Goddess Elazonia "existed"...

It was more realistic to think there was a paranormal entity pulling the strings than to believe an average young man suddenly developed the ability to use magic and started spreading the word of a made-up religion.

Which means that the Goddess Elazonia isn't some system or machine, but rather a single entity.

And if that is true, what is her goal? While Shinichi was thinking, Rino spoke up in a voice tinged with sadness.

"Everyone abandoned the original spirits and the other gods? That's so sad..."

"Tsk, the people in the church are all the scummiest scumbags! I can't believe they'd make my sweet girl cry!" Sanctina screeched, exploding in anger.

"...Should I say something?" asked Arian.

"Let her be. You'll just wear yourself out." Celes sighed.

The pair were understandably exasperated at Sanctina, ready to chuck the blame at someone else when her own past was intrinsically tied with them.

Upon hearing Rino's words, Shinichi had another question. "Speaking of, do these spirits and gods actually exist? I mean, could we meet and speak with them?"

"In Tigris, there are people who believe in the mountain god, and I've heard of forest gods in other places, but I've never met any or heard of anyone else having those kinds of encounters," Arian started.

"If other gods did exist, I imagine the church would attack them, claiming they were false gods, but I don't remember ever hearing of such a thing," Sanctina added.

"There are stories of spirits living in stones and trees in the demon world as well, but I've never seen one," Rino concurred.

"Well, the ghosts of the deceased often appear on battlefields," said Celes.

"Yeah, but I punch them down," the King admitted, "since they annoy me."

"So (physical) exorcisms are effective, huh? Man, fans of horror movies would be so disappointed," joked Shinichi.

On one hand, he'd learned the stunning truth. On the other hand, there was no useful intel on whether or not spirits or gods existed based on personal accounts alone.

It sounds like Earth. Do they also worship the spirits and gods that don't materially exist? If so, why is the Goddess Elazonia the only one that "exists"?

The only person who'd ever seen the Goddess was the first pope, Eument. But there certainly was something that gave him his massive magical power and something that continued to make the undying heroes.

"I have one question. Heroes didn't exist before the first pope, right?" Shinichi asked.

"Correct. If what is written in the holy book is accurate, Eument was the first hero," Sanctina confirmed.

"So we can be fairly certain that the Goddess started doing things about three hundred years ago," he guessed.

If they believed that it was true she'd slept after using her powers up in a battle with the Evil God, then they could theoretically handle her in a fight. Even if she was undying like the heroes, they could potentially take her out of the picture for a long, long time. Then the system that resurrected the heroes would collapse, and they'd be able to put a stop to this nonsense and the church's reign of terror.

The only problem is whether or not the Demon King can win against the Goddess.

If they considered the fact that the Goddess could resurrect people from nothing—something that even the Demon King couldn't do—it'd be a gamble with poor odds.

"I guess we have no choice but to do something about the cardinals..."

"Shall I continue telling you what I know?" asked Sanctina.

"Yeah, please," Shinichi urged, pulling himself out of his spiraling thoughts and listening again to her stories.

Unfortunately, the remainder of the stories were about how the various popes throughout history spread the word of the Goddess. They didn't contain any hidden intel on Elazonia. Rino started to doze off while they were talking about the current cardinals, so they ended their strategy meeting and went off to their respective rooms to sleep.

Chapter 2
The Diamond Bribe

The morning after the meeting, Shinichi was ready to head to the Holy City, but there was one more problem to take care of before he left.

"All right, we're off," he announced.

"We leave the castle in your care," Celes deferred to Arian and Rino. But they were met with angry pouts and puffed cheeks.

"Hey! Why do *I* have to stay behind?" Arian complained.

"I wanna go, too!" whined Rino.

They'd been blindsided by the news this morning. The pair tugged on his arms, pleading with him and throwing tantrums.

"Oh, come on. We already went through this. Rino, you can't come along 'cause you need to continue treating the injured in Tigris," Shinichi explained again.

Not only had the bishop and his subordinates in Tigris jumped ship to Boar Kingdom, Sanctina's thirty holy warriors—with the obvious exception of their traitor, Juda—were in jail and in the middle of being forcibly "brainwashed" by an incubus.

That meant there was a huge shortage of healers. With Sanctina's androphobia, she couldn't handle an influx of patients by herself, which was why it was essential for Rino to support her by her side.

"According to the mage Dritem, they're planning on finding and recruiting the magic users that were booted from the city thanks to the church. I think things will get better soon. But you gotta keep at it until then, Rino," Shinichi reasoned.

"Gah, I know, but…," Rino grumbled as she hung her head, unable to argue with him.

It was their fault that the people of Tigris Kingdom got pulled into this mess, so they had to help them out whether they liked it or not. However—

"It's unfair that Celes gets to spend so much time with you, Shinichi…," she complained, directing her pout at Celes in an uncharacteristic move—the polar opposite of her usual kindhearted, gentle demeanor.

This was the first time ever that Celes had been on the receiving end of any sort of negative emotions from Rino, whom Celes had served since she was a baby.

"D-d-d-do you *hate* me—?!" stammered Celes, flinging off her expressionless mask to reveal a pale face trembling with full-bodied spasms.

"Geez, you're dramatic."

"I—I don't!" Rino objected. "I love you so much, Celes! It's just when I hear that you get to be alone with Shinichi, I get this tickly-prickly feeling in my chest…"

She couldn't quite put a finger on this new feeling… *Jealousy*.

But Shinichi was able to guess, albeit bashfully, as he knelt down to look Rino in the eyes.

"If anything happens, Celes will *Teleport* us back right away. Once I take care of this, I promise we'll play together. Can you wait until then?"

"…Do you mean it?"

"Yep. What should we do?"

"I wanna draw with you! Celes said you're supergood."

"All right. If you're okay with heavily stylized manga drawings, I can teach you."

"Yay!"

Her previous mood dissipated as Shinichi patted her head, and she jumped up and down with joy.

This time, Arian eyed Rino with envy. "I get why she has to stay, but why can't I go?"

"Because people would recognize you," Shinichi explained.

In the past, she'd visited the Holy City on a mission to defeat the giant black wolf and was known all around as Red, the famous hero. One look at her, and they'd be toast.

"But couldn't I just wear a disguise?" she argued, looking pointedly at Celes's long ears.

Her dragon scales could be easily concealed with a scarf, whereas they needed to use *Illusion* to hide Celes's elven ears. Plus, the stakes were higher if she accidentally revealed her true form.

Celes was very aware of this problem, toying with her ears as she proposed a plan. "Shall I cut them off? If we claim I'm a human with dark skin—"

"No!" Shinichi cried out. "You can't get rid of them! Taking away an elf's long ears is like taking away glasses from a cute girl who always wears them!" He grew increasingly flustered as he tried to stop her.

"I'm grossed out that you're so adamant about this," Celes sneered, her eyes wide with surprise.

To put things in perspective, it was as criminal as taking away the fill-in-the-blank of a femme boy.

"I would heal them once we have completed the mission. Besides, didn't you scorch your face before?"

"I don't care what happened to this old mug, but the face of a beautiful woman is one of the few wonders of the world! It's my personal duty to protect it at all costs!"

"…You dirty rat. I can't believe you'd treat people differently based on their gender and appearance," Celes retorted, but averted her eyes, embarrassed by his comments.

Arian pursed her lips even more as she watched their exchange. She unsheathed her sword, pointing it to her own throat.

"Yeah? Well, I'd cut off my scales for you…!"

"Wait, wait, wait! STOP! YOU'D DIE!" cried Shinichi.

It has been said the scales at the base of a dragon's neck were akin to their Achilles' heel. They wouldn't allow just anyone to touch them. And it was far too dangerous to slice through her throat.

He yanked her hand back. "Calm down. Even without the whole disguise mess, I still want you to stay here. You know, because of that one…" Shinichi trailed off as he cocked his head at Sanctina, watching over them from a distance.

"Is something wrong?" she inquired with a saintly smile.

But that wasn't enough to hide her ulterior motives, which were practically leaking out of every orifice as she wordlessly chanted, "Hee-hee-hee, now I'll have Rino all to myself."

"…I'll worry if you're not with Rino, you know, for, uh, reasons," he stammered.

"…Yup, yeah. Completely agree."

The pair looked at Sanctina in disappointment before Shinichi placed a hand on Arian's shoulder.

"Also, we can't be certain that a hero won't attack Tigris," he continued.

In all likelihood, the Holy See hadn't yet received word that the Saint had been defeated, or that the Tigris Kingdom had turned its back on the church. But there was a possibility that some random hero or bishop would overhear these rumors and decide to take matters into their own hands.

"I don't want to underestimate the captain, but I doubt he has the strength necessary to protect the people from an undying hero. That's why I need you to stay."

"Okay, I understand," Arian declared chivalrously to his serious request.

It all made sense. Rino shared her father's magical capacity, but she was still a novice when it came to battles. On the other hand, Sanctina was strong, but only at the capacity of a magic user, rendering her worthless when it came to hand-to-hand combat. And since they'd be stationed in a city, she wouldn't be able to cast spells that tore up large masses of land.

But Arian's body was strengthened by her status as a half dragon. On top of that, her offensive strategies, defensive moves, and speed were top-notch thanks to her experience in battle. She'd give anyone a run for their money. With the exception of beasts like the Demon King or someone underhanded like Shinichi, there was no one who'd be able to get the best of her.

Arian's chest swelled with well-deserved pride. "I promise to protect Rino and the people of Tigris."

"I'm counting on you, my hero," Shinichi replied.

"Should I take that as a compliment?" She chuckled wryly with a complicated expression, and Shinichi flashed a grin back.

"I bet I'd make people back in my home world angry for saying some sexist shit like this, but I think men can go off and be stupid, 'cause we know there's a woman holding down the fort—you know, a place called *home*."

"Home?! That's like saying, hee-hee-hee…" Arian giggled.

He made it sound like she was his wife! Any and all shreds of her former heroic attitude dissolved as she melted into a sloppy smile.

"…*These sweet nothings will come back to bite you someday*," Celes telepathized.

Shinichi did his best to ignore her words of caution as he clapped her on the back.

"All right, we're off then."

"I await good news. Even better if you bring me back a powerful opponent," boomed the Demon King.

"Yeah, no. That would be bad," Shinichi corrected tight-lipped as Celes cast her spell.

"*Fly*."

He clung to her back as she was freed from the chains of gravity, floating gently from the ground and soaring high into the sky.

"Wow! I mean, I'm low-key terrified, but this feels great!" He whooped with laughter as his body flew through the air.

"You'll fall if you get too carried away," Celes warned, exasperated by his childish delight. "Did we need to use *Fly*? Are we in that much of a hurry?"

"Oh, we don't have to. Especially if it's putting a strain on you."

"As long as we rest occasionally, I should be fine. I just wanted to know why."

"Oh, right. Celes, you've always been a curious one."

There were a few times when her thirst for knowledge came in handy, but more often than not, she'd use it against him to call him a pervert—which was honestly a figment of her imagination. Anyway, he hadn't decided if it was a good thing or a bad thing yet.

"If we hurry, we should be able to make our move before they get the info."

"Which is?"

"That Sanctina has betrayed the church."

In Tigris Kingdom, it was common knowledge by now that the Saint had realized she was in love with Rino and jumped ship. But news of this incident hadn't reached the Holy See...as far as they knew.

"Cardinal Cronklum or whatever—you know, her superior—must know something's up since she's stopped telepathically communicating with him, but he has no way to know the details," continued Shinichi.

That was because there was no one to report back to him: Sanctina herself betrayed the church, and her thirty holy warriors were either captured or sleeping with the enemy.

"Plus, she's the only person strong enough to send a telepathic message over a long enough distance to reach the Holy City. Oh, and I checked with the captain, just in case, to see if any of the more devout followers had tried to run off and inform the cardinals, but they haven't seen any messengers on horseback speeding away from the city. Meaning the cardinals will have to wait until the news reaches them through the grapevine."

There's an old saying about how you can't put a stop to talking mouths. It wouldn't do them any good to impose martial law in Tigris, and the news wasn't really a secret to begin with. It would travel across cities and towns on the backs of merchants, minstrels, and other wandering travelers, and eventually land in the ears of those in the Holy City.

"Without amateur radios and *Telepathy*—at least for most people—it seems the rate of news spreading equals their walking pace," he concluded.

"Meaning it hasn't yet reached the enemy?"

"Apparently, it takes about twenty days to walk from Tigris to the Holy City. It's already been five days since the incident in question, meaning we have fifteen more days. It would also take us about twenty days on foot to reach the Holy City from here, but if we use *Fly*, we can go faster since we're circumnavigating mountains and forests. How long do you think it'll take us to get there?"

"About five days, I believe."

"Which means we have ten days to work with."

Ten days where the people in the Holy City would be in the dark about the defeat of their high-class magic user, Saint Sanctina. Ten days where they wouldn't expect spies to infiltrate their borders.

"It's the perfect time to take advantage of them. Right when they're off guard," Shinichi commented.

"Will it really go that well?"

"Well, I am worried about one thing: If Cronklum takes the loss of contact with Sanctina very seriously, he might consult the other cardinals...but I don't think that's likely."

Based on Sanctina's story, the cardinals were heavily involved in a battle for the next papal appointment. It wouldn't be very strategic for Cronklum to bring his own failures to light.

"It's possible that he'll attempt to squash the rumors in order to hide the truth. That'll buy us even more time, heh-heh-heh," he snickered sinisterly.

"But wouldn't he know this isn't the time to quarrel with his own allies?" asked Celes. She cocked her head in confusion, finding human thought processes incomprehensible.

Shinichi replied with a wicked smile. "Ah, won't it be so fun to give them a rude awakening when they think they have all the time in the world to bicker with each other?"

"You're dirty," Celes snapped, taking her usual jab as she increased their speed and soared through the sky.

Shinichi and Celes didn't encounter any bad weather conditions or turbulence on their flight. Thanks to that, they reached the church's main base, the Holy City, in five days as planned.

"All right, let's go."

Under the familiar disguise as the middle-aged merchant Manju and his blue-haired maid, the two figures took their first steps into the Holy City, taking notice that it lacked guards and city walls—a total change of pace from the fortified surroundings of the Boar and Tigris kingdoms. Hordes of people moved in and out freely, whoever they happened to be.

"Which means they're confident," Shinichi observed.

He guessed there wasn't anyone stupid enough to attack the Holy City, especially with the teachings of the church spreading across the entire continent. And even if someone chose to storm the city, they'd be against undying heroes and a mountain of holy warriors collectively capable of fending off tens of thousands of soldiers.

Once again, Shinichi acknowledged the strength and size of the church as he observed the peaceful atmosphere of the Holy City. He steeled himself again for the task ahead.

"We've gone and made enemies of some pretty nasty people, haven't we?" he commented.

"Then why are you smiling?"

"Whoa, no kidding?!" He gingerly touched his face in disbelief, completely bewildered by this revelation.

She sighed, frustrated. "Is His Highness rubbing off on you?"

"N-no, impossible."

It might be masculine instinct firing him up in the face of a strong enemy. That went for humans and demons alike.

Regardless, Shinichi was slightly embarrassed and cleared his throat before changing the subject. "*Ahem.* Anyway, I was thinking we should gather info—"

"Understood, let us find a tavern."

"Yo, you're definitely just in it for the food."

"What an absurd accusation." She rebuked his claims immediately, but her eyes were glued to a sign: THE ORIGINAL STUFFED FRIED PEPPERS! ONE OF POPE EUMENT'S FAVORITE THINGS!

"It's not a bad idea, but I don't think we'll get much good information in one," Shinichi reasoned.

Sanctina had already covered all the information available to the average follower. He wanted to know something to help him understand the cardinals on a deeper level.

"I don't think a tavern owner will know that much—even though they're general purveyors of gossip."

"We could ask around?" offered Celes.

"No, that'd attract too much attention, and I assume we'd get apprehended real quick."

Everyone in the city was a follower of the Goddess, meaning they were smack-dab in the middle of enemy territory. If they went sniffing around for rumors about the cardinals, it'd be like begging to get the holy warriors called on them.

"If I were one of the cardinals, I'd keep tabs on the taverns for any news, befriend some of the owners; you know the drill. I bet Cronklum's doing the same, at the very least."

After all, he'd made powerful magic users have children, promptly brainwashing them to eventually create a monster: the Saint. He was definitely the kind of guy who'd keep his ear to the ground.

"I suppose it takes a twisted person to know one," Celes snarled in an annoyed-but-impressed way, and Shinichi flashed back a crooked smile.

"It's times like these that make me realize how nice it'd be if there was more organized crime, or like a bandits' guild where you could buy information…"

He spoke about other towns, figuring that the church would have squashed out any criminals lurking around in their Holy City.

"Is the church the greatest crime syndicate of them all?" asked Celes.

"Ha-ha-ha. Oh Celes, you're finally starting to get a grip on human society." Shinichi chuckled as he glanced around the wide street. "Who would have information on the bougie guys? Where could we talk without standing out—?"

He scanned the rows of shops—just fancy enough to be appropriate for a Holy City—and his eyes came to rest on a black building that had a particularly high-class feel.

"Let's try that one."

Over the entrance was a sign that said ZAIM'S JEWELERS. Shinichi and Celes went to an inn for moment to prepare then came back to open the door to the jewelers.

"Welcome," the young woman working the counter greeted them as Shinichi stepped in and glanced around the shop.

It's all carved wood combs and bracelets with glass beads… There aren't any rare jewels or anything.

It was obvious once he thought about it. It wasn't like modern-day Japan with its glass cases, security systems, and theft insurance. That meant they wouldn't place the valuable items up front, especially ones that could lead to huge monetary losses if they were stolen. The higher-end items were ordered by customers, made-to-order and one-of-a-kind.

As Shinichi made these guesses, he received a telepathic message from Celes.

"Further in the shop, there are three men. They appear to be workers. And one guard with a sword. There are three more people on the second floor, who seem like the shop owner and his attendants."

"They must make enough money to employ a guard," he observed telepathically. "Not bad."

Of course, there were very few idiots who would try their hand at stealing something inside the Holy City. But their goods must be valuable enough to warrant this kind of caution.

Even the woman at the counter seemed wary of Shinichi as he slowly took in the shop. He grinned in order to reassure her.

"Hello, I am a merchant by the name of Manju. I would like to meet the store owner. Are they in?"

"Do you have a letter of introduction?" she asked firmly, even as she smiled.

There was no way she'd let in just any old man, especially one that she'd never seen before.

Shinichi smiled back and gestured to Celes, who stepped forward softly and placed a fist-sized object wrapped in cloth on the counter.

"This is my letter of introduction," he announced.

"Sure...," replied the worker, disinterested.

He gestured for the worker to uncover the object. When it broke free from the cloth, a blinding sparkle refracted through the transparent rock and filled her eyes.

"I-is this a diamond?!"

It was a large gem—uncut, around two-thousand karats, and worth a fortune.

"Wh-what...?!" The shop worker trembled more out of fear than reverence. She'd never seen a diamond so massive.

Shinichi smiled gently at her as he repeated himself. "This is my letter of introduction. Would it be possible for me to meet the shop owner?"

"One moment, please!" she cried out, clutching the massive diamond with shaking hands and dashing into the back of the shop as if making a grand escape.

She returned after a little while, slightly more composed as she gestured toward the back. "This way, please."

"Thank you," Shinichi replied as he followed her into the back of the shop, up the stairs to a reception room on the second floor, then to a frowning man in his forties waiting on a couch.

"It's a pleasure to make your acquaintance, Mr. Manju. My name is Zaim; I'm the owner of this store."

"It's nice to meet you as well, Mr. Zaim. Thank you for meeting with me," replied Shinichi as the proprietor gestured for him to take a seat on a couch facing him.

Between them was a high-quality ebony table on which the giant diamond sat gleaming.

"I presume you wish to sell this gem to my establishment?"

"Of course," replied Shinichi.

"Might I evaluate it?"

"Please, as you wish."

Zaim lifted the diamond and closed his eyes.

Through his career, quite a few people had attempted to sell him rocks disguised as gems using *Illusion,* which is why he was attempting to use touch, a sense unaffected by visuals, in order to determine its authenticity.

"The surface, its weight; it all seems like the real thing, but… May I use this?" He took out a huge iron knife, and Shinichi nodded with a smile.

"Of course, do as you feel necessary."

"Thank you." Zaim brandished the knife and swung down with full force on the diamond. Even the best imitation gems would crack in half—or, at the very least, be damaged. However, with a loud clink, the diamond deflected the weapon, breaking its blade in the process.

"It does seem to be genuine. I'm sorry for doubting you, Mr. Manju," Zaim admitted as he bowed his head deeply.

"Not at all. I'm glad to know you are a cautious and reliable merchant." Shinichi smiled and waved off his apology.

Zaim lifted his head and smiled back in relief, but his expression quickly soured again.

"I'm incredibly grateful that you would offer my shop this exquisite item. But—and this is just a rough estimate—I can't imagine this diamond being worth less than fifty thousand gold coins. I, unfortunately, don't have enough cash on hand to purchase it..."

Even if he scrounged together all the money in the safe, he'd still be short. Then there'd be the issue of finding a buyer because it was just too expensive.

"I can offer one thousand gold pieces up front. If I'm able to find a buyer, I will request an advance payment from them, and then the rest—"

"That won't be necessary," interrupted Shinichi, holding up a single finger. "I will accept one gold coin as payment."

"Come again?"

"And in exchange, I would like some information from you."

"...Of what sort?" Zaim asked, suspicious. His dumbfounded expression immediately turned dour.

Running his mouth—especially about something appraised at fifty thousand gold coins—could cost him his business. Zaim steeled himself. It could be information on how he obtained his gems or his customer base.

Shinichi eyed him with a hungry look. "I want you to tell me everything you know about the cardinals."

"...I see." Zaim nodded.

With the pope nearing the end of his life, the cardinals were running the show as the real leaders of the church. Any intel on them would be well worth fifty thousand gold coins, even for a jewel merchant.

Here in the Holy City, the higher ups in the church—the bishops and cardinals—were some of their biggest clientele. The first pope, Eument, might have been a humble woodworker, and the church might reject materialism, but that didn't stop bishops and cardinals from roping precious metals and gems around, and around, their necks. This was doubly true for the bishops who were sent to other countries as envoys and the cardinals who led sermons in front of tens of thousands. They justified it by telling themselves they needed to look the part.

On many occasions, Zaim had taken orders for jeweled crowns and scepters. From the infamously materialistic Cardinal Snobe, the owner received requests on a monthly basis for gifts of all kinds for his mistresses.

He did indeed have information and connections worth the fifty thousand gold pieces, but—

"I must decline your offer," he stated.

He had the intel. But that was precisely why he didn't hesitate to turn this down. Zaim slid the massive diamond back to Shinichi.

If he dared to anger the cardinals, it'd be off with his head. If he lost them as customers, he'd lose more in future sales than the promised fifty thousand gold pieces.

But for whatever reason, Shinichi smiled gleefully in the face of the jeweler's rational decision. "Loyalty, first and foremost. All merchants should follow your lead."

"I appreciate the praise, but unfortunately, fate is not on our side today," announced Zaim—with just one regretful parting glance at the massive diamond.

Their negation was closed—or at least that was what he thought—until Shinichi drew a rolled-up piece of parchment from his breast pocket instead of rising out of his chair to leave. "Well then, how about this in addition to the diamond?"

"...Let's take a look, then," the shop owner said nervously, unfurling it slowly and wondering what could possibly be written there. "I-is this stamped with the Saint's blood?!"

Accompanying Sanctina's flowy signature was a crimson imprint of her hand.

"Please feel free to take that to the residence of Cardinal Cronklum to confirm its authenticity," Shinichi confidently urged.

After all, he'd been the one who'd arranged this whole thing with Sanctina—in exchange for a figurine of Rino. It was undeniably the real deal.

But it'd be a big problem if Zaim took this to the cardinal, seeing as he'd be arrested on the spot and interrogated about the whereabouts of the Saint, especially because she'd been ghosting Cronklum. That was exactly why Shinichi kept his best straight face, laying the lies on thick.

"Alas, I have absolutely no relationship with the Saint or Cardinal Cronklum. I'm no more than the traveling merchant Manju... Do you know what I'm trying to say?" Shinichi blabbed.

"Y-yes, of course," Zaim sputtered, jumpy as he wiped the beads of sweat from his brow. He knew what this man was implying.

This "traveling merchant Manju" persona was all a fabrication. He was actually a spy for Cardinal Cronklum, sniffing around for secret information on the other cardinals to get a leg up in the next papal appointment.

—That's what he'd assume anyway.

It wasn't likely that he'd realize that Shinichi was an agent of the Demon King attempting to trap the cardinals.

Well, if he'd think this through with a bit more logic, he'd see that none of this makes sense in the slightest.

It wasn't hard to imagine that Cronklum would have spies. After all, the man in question raised Sanctina for the sole purpose of exploiting her as a Saint. None of this was above him.

The question was whether or not a cardinal's watchdog would go to some jeweler to find information on the others candidates.

They'd never ask an outsider for support. That'd only lead to more backstabbing and leaked secrets.

On top of it all, a spy would never allow his true identity to peek through. In order to keep the wavering shop owner from noticing the inconsistencies, Shinichi followed up with another critical hit.

"Please don't worry. I don't intend to harm you or resort to violence in order to keep you from talking," he cooed reassuringly.

"—Ngh?!"

But Manju had shown him the seal of blood. Did that mean that when he was done with business, he'd kill him and bury him in the dark?

As the owner considered this theory with substantive fear, Shinichi could peer into his soul. But even as he trembled, he looked Shinichi straight in the eyes as he gave his final answer.

"Will you swear to the Goddess Elazonia that your word is your bond?"

"Don't you think it's easy to break verbal vows and promises?" Shinichi asked in reply.

"......"

"I apologize. I have a way to protect both the secrets and your safety," Shinichi admitted as he glanced back at the maid standing behind him.

Without a word, Celes held up her hand, flickering with magic power.

"Are you aware of the *Geas* spell? I want you to swear that you'll never speak of the events of today again," Shinichi explained.

"I see, so that's how it will be," the shop owner said with a nod, hounded by the invisible force behind the maid's magical presence.

Under the spell, they would endure worse pain than death if they tried to break this promise. There would be no need to forcefully silence each other, and there would be no chance of them betraying each other.

On top of that, the fact that she's strong enough to use Geas *lends credence to the lie that I'm Cronklum's spy. Nice.*

The shop owner was mulling this choice over—without a shred of doubt about Shinichi's true identity.

"You're free to refuse my request. If you do, all I ask if that we're bound under the *Geas* spell. I'll give you the diamond in exchange. If you do accept, please know that nothing we talk about today will leave this room," Shinichi offered as he pushed the huge diamond back toward the shop owner.

"...I need to think for a moment," replied the shop owner as he gazed at the diamond in front of him and carefully considered his options.

Either way, he got the rock. The problem was whether he wanted to be Cronklum's ally. Did he want to lend a hand to the man closest to becoming the next pope? Even if it meant making enemies of the rest of them?

Had this happened ten days later—when rumors about the Saint reached town and destroyed her adoptive father's status—the shop owner would have instantly refused to assist. At this moment in time, however, Cronklum was still the man at the top.

"Okay, I'll tell you everything I know," the shop owner folded after a long silence, and he picked up the huge diamond.

Shinichi smiled in response and held out his right hand. "First, may I have one gold coin as payment?"

"Har-har, yes, that's right," the shop owner chuckled, getting up and handing Shinichi one coin before stepping out into the hall for a moment. "Could you please prepare some tea and snacks? We're going to be talking for a while."

"And lunch as well," the maid chirped.

"Celes, this isn't a cafeteria," Shinichi teased the greedy maid, but the shop owner just smiled and called back to his secretary again.

"You're the epitome of dirty," Celes jeered in the room at the inn after their top-secret discussion at the jeweler's was over.

Shinichi forced his lips to crack a smile at her usual insults as he collapsed into the bed. "But I didn't do anything that bad this time! We just talked, and he got a diamond worth fifty thousand gold coins. Sounds like a good deal for him if I do say so myself."

It'd been a complete lie to imply that he'd be making ties with the soon-to-be pope, but even so, the shop owner came out better off than before.

As Shinichi proclaimed his innocence, Celes shot him a glance and heaved out a sigh. "But the diamond was fake."

"How rude! That was a bona fide, legit diamond! It just wasn't natural," Shinichi said as he smirked sinisterly and rolled the single gold coin from the shop owner over his fingers. "There's no one in this world who'd be able to tell that it's coal with some *Element Conversion*."

As he had explained to the dvergr before, coal and diamonds were both made from carbon. By taking the haphazard arrangement of the atoms in coal and aligning them neatly, you could make the latter.

"If I make too many, they won't be as scarce and their value will tank, but this much shouldn't be a problem," continued Shinichi.

"Okay..."

There was no way that Celes would know about the principles of scarcity in economics, but she did understand that pursuing that conversation further was pointless. She returned to the topic at hand. "Well then, which of the cardinals will we be targeting first?"

"Cronklum's out," replied Shinichi quickly as he roused himself out of bed. "He's sometimes called the Elderly Cardinal, the oldest and closest to becoming the next pope. From the perspective of the demons, he should be the first to go. Plus, Sanctina told us that he'd be the easiest to handle, but we don't have to do anything to take care of him."

Because he'd be done for even without one of Shinichi's schemes. With enough time, the city would be inundated with rumors about Sanctina and how she'd failed to defeat the Demon King. The most damning news of all would be that she'd become a traitor.

As her adoptive father, Cronklum would suffer some serious damage to his public image. He'd be forced out of the race for pope. In a worst-case scenario, he could be stripped of his cardinal position. They'd gain nothing from breaking this old geezer or destroying his reputation.

"And I don't feel like a seventy-something-year-old man would go on a crusade himself against the Demon King," finished Shinichi.

"I agree."

"Next is Snobe, aka the Materialistic Cardinal... I'm gonna pass," Shinichi croaked, his face twisted in a grimace.

"Why?"

Of the four cardinals—and quite possibly out of all history—Snobe was the most vulgar of all. He had a voracious appetite for food and drink. But the same couldn't be said for work. In essence, he was as fat and lazy as a cow.

He'd dine on the finest steak in this world for dinner every night and drink barrels of the finest wine, crushed by the feet of virgins. He could bathe in the amount he drank.

Plus, he was a sex machine. At any given time, he allegedly had more lovers than fingers on both hands combined. Some rumors said he had enough illegitimate children to make two soccer teams for a legit game.

Of course, he naturally had a whole bunch of enemies, and according to the man-hating Sanctina, he was "a piece of shit, lower than even a c—ckroach."

"Seems like he reeks of vice. I would've thought he'd be the perfect target for you. Wouldn't it be easiest to sway him?" she asked, but Shinichi's impression was the exact opposite.

"Based on Sanctina's stories alone, I would have agreed, but judging from what the jeweler said..."

The Materialistic Cardinal had a terrible reputation, but the owner of the jewelry store regarded him highly. That's because the cardinal was simple and, most importantly, a very well-paying client.

"He wants to eat fine food and sleep with fine women, and he has the means to fulfill his desires."

He was in a position where he had financial control of the church's purse strings. That didn't mean he embezzled, though. If he did, the other cardinals would find out and he'd be chased out of his position.

What he did use his position for was to gather information from the churches in other cities and use that information to his advantage. For example, if he knew that wheat harvests in the east were unfavorable, he'd purchase all the excess grains from abundant harvests in the west for pennies on the dollar and sell high in the east. Any average merchant would do the same thing, but Snobe could receive information from loyal bishops through *Telepathy* and act on information faster than anyone else, thus generating revenue faster than anyone else.

"The jeweler vouched for him, saying, 'He's not very devoted, but he's the real deal when it comes to sales.' What's bad is he'll do anything to fulfill his desires," he continued.

"What do you mean by that?"

"Let's say I made a delicious cake. What would you do?"

"I would force you to make ten more, even if it kills you."

"Geez, reel it in, you glutton!"

"I'm joking. If I killed you, I wouldn't be able to eat another one."

"'Make me cake for the rest of my life'? Is that what you're trying to say?"

It might sound like a marriage proposal, but all Shinichi heard was the terms and conditions to a contract for indentured servitude.

"Anyway, the only reason you have an insatiable appetite for cake is because you don't come by good food often. If you had it every day, I bet you'd get sick of it pretty fast."

"In simpler terms, a womanizer can keep his cool, but a virgin won't be able to help himself."

"You're not wrong, but was there really no better example?" He sighed.

How could she remain so composed as she spat out obscenities? Especially when she always blushed to her ears when he directed them at her?

"Point is, the cardinal has become used to succumbing to his desires. I do sort of want to try and see if we'd be able to manipulate him with a succubus, but with his skills as a businessman, I just don't think it would go over very well."

"I imagine I would enjoy seeing the pathetic sight of that floozy lose to a human male."

"...Do you hate Ribido that much?"

"I wouldn't say that. I'm just annoyed by the way she yaks off my ear every time she finds a new man. It makes me want to knock her into an eternal slumber," she growled, her words dripping with murderous rage.

"Oh, I see..." Shinichi wasn't able to say any more.

I'd be willing to bet Ribido had a hand in giving Celes all her second-hand knowledge about sex, and paired with her wild imagination...

They'd be better labeled as frenemies.

"A friend, huh? Rino might— Nope, nope, she definitely doesn't need a friend like that. We'll have to look for a reserved, timid kid," he corrected himself.

"Why are you suddenly acting like His Highness?"

"Am not!"

In truth, he hadn't let Rino tag along on this mission because he was scared something bad would happen to her like last time. He was growing overprotective of her, of which he was very well aware, and it was exactly why he tried to change the topic as soon as possible, flustered that Celes had been onto something.

"Okay, next is Effectus, who people teasingly call the Agreeable Cardinal. He's, well..."

Effectus had been given this moniker because he rarely gave his own opinion, constantly agreeing to other opinions instead. But he was also the cardinal with the strongest reputation among the holy warriors. He seemed to be a man of true integrity—the exact opposite of the Materialistic Cardinal. He wanted neither gold nor women, working earnestly to uphold the Goddess's teachings with all his heart.

He was aiming to be the next pope, but it wasn't to fulfill his own desires. It was a goal born of pure faith, urging him to spread the Goddess's word. Someone describing him in a positive light might call him an honest and just man—or, on the flip side, an inflexible zealot.

"I don't think he's the type to give in to threats from the demons, and I don't think he can be easily persuaded."

"From our viewpoint, he's the most difficult opponent," added Celes.

"Yeah, his personality means he doesn't accept bribes and that gives him little power over the people, but it's actually the thing that's saving him."

The members of the Goddess's church were human, after all. It was quite normal for them to want to drink fine wine and sleep with beautiful women, but this Agreeable Cardinal didn't seem to have any of those desires. Every day, he consumed inexpensive loaves of dark bread. He was nearing his sixties, but there were no shadows of a wife or lover. It was very possible that he'd never been with a woman at all.

He took notes from the first pope and lived modestly, gaining great admiration from the lower class. Even the androphobic Sanctina spoke highly of him. On the other hand, high-ranking bishops and wealthy merchants didn't view him quite so favorably.

"If the Agreeable Cardinal becomes pope, he'll force his lifestyle onto us... The more they have to lose, the more worried they are about losing it all."

That's what the jeweler had told him, flashing a smile as he told him that Effectus's extreme ways didn't make him the "Agreeable" Cardinal at all. There was visible unease in the jeweler's eyes as well.

"I get the feeling he's messed up in the head; you know, someone who'd say something like, 'There will be no poverty if we all live equally among the poor,'" Shinichi joked.

"He couldn't be that stupid, could he?"

"Ya never know. There are people who've decided to make their country better by killing all the intellectuals in it."

"...You're joking, right?"

"Unfortunately not. It's a good example of the saying, 'The road to hell is paved with good intentions'... Wait, is this not the right time for that?" Shinichi interrupted himself, falling into thought.

He glanced at Celes who was uncharacteristically cringing, then forced a weak smile and got back on topic. "Anyway, the Agreeable Cardinal is too proper, so he'd be a pain. I'll pass on him. Best-case scenario: He becomes a tyrant and focuses on disciplining heretics and non-believers over the demons, destroying the church from the inside out."

"How might you go about making that happen?"

"If we copied his appearance and made him go around attacking and killing people until his reputation hits rock-bottom, the masses would throw stones at him, hate him, and he'd lose hope in humanity, maybe? ...No, he'd just testify with a *Liar Detector* spell and come clean; that wouldn't work."

"I regret asking," Celes sighed as Shinichi spoke casually about the dirty aces up his sleeve.

At the very least, she knew these plans were all talk since they'd only make Rino sad if they executed them.

"So then, our target is...," she clarified.

"The last one," Shinichi finished, "the Holy Mother Cardinal, Vermeita."

Vermeita was the youngest of the cardinals, in her midforties, and the only woman. She was magically powerful and a master of martial arts using a staff, so she had a record of defeating hordes of monsters and saving a bunch of people: a true heroine who'd reached the top at a precocious age. In her early years, she was called the Saint, and Sanctina admired her as a mentor and role model.

"She's young, but she's still lived twice as long as me, so I don't think we'll easily find her weakness, but I think she's the one that I'd like to have as an ally," he continued.

"Another woman... You're just a perverted dog, chasing after an older woman."

"That's not what I meant! Like most men, I prefer my girls young!" retorted Shinichi in all seriousness, refuting the accusation that he liked cougars.

In response, Celes—

"...Then I've passed my prime," she sulked, suddenly upset as she sat in the corner of the room, hugging her knees to her chest.

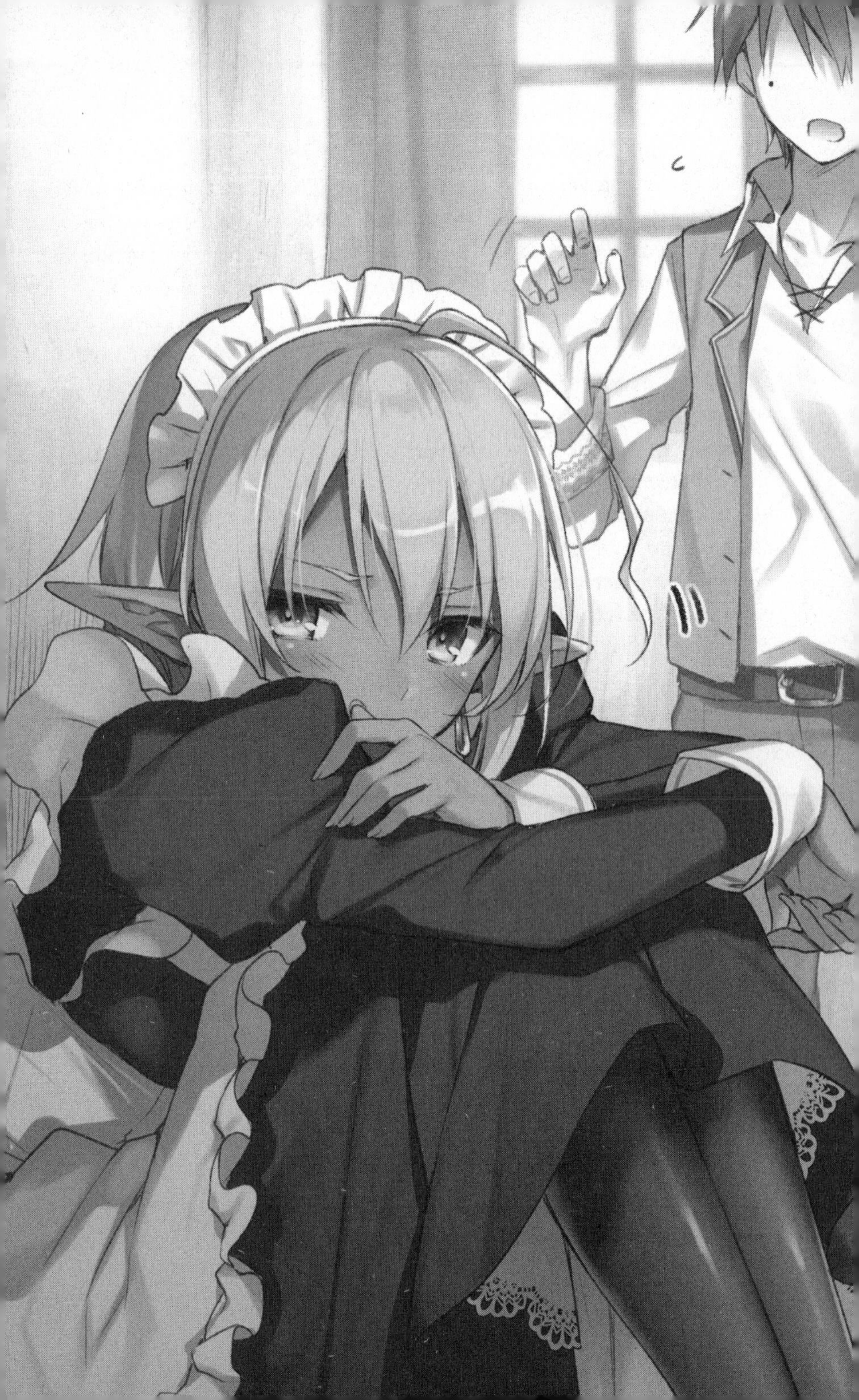

"Did I just land an unexpected critical hit?! No, Celes, you're plenty young! You don't need to worry..."

"You don't even know how old I am. Please refrain from assaulting me with your empty nothings," she quipped.

"Fine, I'll bite. How old are you?"

"It's incredibly rude to ask a woman her age, you know. I'll cut off your tongue for that." Celes didn't forget to take her jabs even while pouting.

"You're impossible!" he cried, feeling incredibly helpless. "Anyway, we're going after Vermeita starting tomorrow, so I'll need your help."

"...Are you asking me to invite her to tea? Since we're so close in age?"

"Does it really bother you that much?"

In all honestly, he did find her childish whining a bit charming. Shinichi decided to make some sweet snacks for her to cheer her up and left the room to use the inn's kitchen.

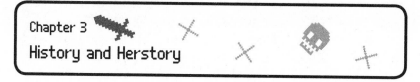
The prayer room was in the very center of the Archbasilica, adorned with the first statue of the Goddess, which had been laboriously carved by the hands of the first pope. It was where the four cardinals—including the Holy Mother Cardinal, Vermeita—gathered to hold their usual meeting.

"It seems the heroes that we've dispatched to the east are up against a difficult fight."

"Indeed. It appears the elves have caused quite the inconvenience."

"What a pain. If this continues, we'll never be able to fulfill Pope Eument's mission."

"That said, it wouldn't be the wisest move to stir up trouble with the elves, seeing that they're strong magic users."

The four discussed the locations of the heroes and how they would handle the various countries as if they were engaging in small talk. That was until the Materialistic Cardinal, Snobe, suddenly interrupted the conversation and made his move.

"By the way, are things going well with Miss Sanctina?"

The question was innocent enough on the surface. But it had dark intentions, slimily coiling around Cronklum like a snake tightening its grip on its prey. The Elderly Cardinal, however, smiled and nodded, betraying no emotion.

"Yes, our plans have been set back somewhat by the people in Tigris Kingdom—all obstinate—but they're proceeding smoothly."

Things were not "proceeding smoothly" at all. Cronklum was wracked with anxiety since he'd been unable to contact Sanctina for quite some time, but he wouldn't have made it this far if he was the sort of person to let that show.

"I see. Very good." The Materialistic Cardinal backed down from the inquiry surprisingly quickly.

However, for just a brief moment, Vermeita saw an amused smile flit across his face, causing her to wonder: *Hmm, does he know something?*

The Materialistic Cardinal lacked popularity in the Holy City, but of all the cardinals, he had the greatest influence in other countries, giving him a wide net to bring in information. There was a chance he knew something Cronklum didn't.

In order to properly gauge the situation, Vermeita proposed, "If there's been a setback, should we send some more people to support her? I'm sure you'll all have your opinions about this idea, but we'll have nothing to show if the Goddess loses her prestige."

"Indeed. To defeat the evil demons, we must forget our quarrels and work together," said Effectus, but Cronklum immediately shook his head.

"No, there's no need for that. It is for the girl's own good that she resolve these issues by her own hand."

"...Heh." The Materialistic Cardinal accidentally let out a tiny snort of laughter.

So he does know something. Maybe it's not just a delay. Could Miss Sanctina...have failed?

Even Vermeita would never be able to imagine in a million years that their Saint had fallen for the Demon King's daughter and willingly betrayed the church.

It seems I should check up on the situation in Tigris.

She'd held back from doing anything out of line to avoid ending up on Cronklum's bad side—but if this was true, things were about to change big time.

I will not let the next pope be someone like Cronklum, who'd gleefully brainwash children to keep up appearances. Much less someone who treats women as trophies, like Snobe.

That's why Vermeita was aiming to become the next pope even though she was at a disadvantage for being the youngest candidate of the bunch.

I must make the Holy City an ideal place, one of great value—

As she burned with newfound resolve, time passed, and the meeting came to a close. Vermeita left the prayer room and met with her attending priestess who was waiting outside the door.

"Your schedule for the rest of the day is open. What would you like to do?" The priestess smiled.

"Let's stop at home for a moment," Vermeita proposed as they walked out the main entrance of the Archbasilica.

The Elderly Cardinal was in charge of the church's affairs in the stead of the ill pope; the Materialistic Cardinal controlled the purse strings; the Agreeable Cardinal spearheaded legal matters; but Vermeita was only in charge of ceremonies and rituals. That was because as a woman of considerable beauty, she could act as the proxy for the Goddess in ceremonies, even though she was well into her forties. This meant she was very busy before and during the festival to celebrate the Goddess's descent to Obum. But her schedule was relatively free for the rest of the year.

"I hope everyone's doing well," she thought aloud as she stepped into the carriage on standby next to the Archbasilica. They set off toward the south.

After they passed through the cityscape into the open fields, they came into sight of two simple yet large buildings on an estate: the residence of Vermeita and the reason for her nickname, the Holy Mother Cardinal. Just as soon as the carriage entered the grounds of the red-roofed building on the left, the door burst open, and a gaggle of girls pushed through, tumbling out.

"Mother, welcome home!" cried the children, grinning gleefully from ear to ear.

"Thank you. Were you all good today?" With a smile, Vermeita gently hugged each one.

All the children in the estate were orphans; the Holy Mother had taken them in. Of course, with spells to resurrect the dead, it was rare for a child to become orphaned because their parents passed away. This was the opposite: *Because* there were these spells, it became a real problem when parents had too many children without thinking the consequences through. In many cases, they'd find themselves with too many mouths to feed, compelling them to abandon or even sell their own children to lessen the burden.

There were also cases of parents brutally abusing their children with the knowledge that all injuries could be healed. Unfortunately, it wasn't uncommon to see children running away from home to live on the streets.

"Oh yes. Mother, the most wonderful thing happened today!"

"What's that?"

"A nice man gave us cookies!" one of the girls exclaimed, opening up her pretty little handkerchief to show Vermeita. "They're very sweet and yummy!"

"Mother, you try one!"

"Why, thank you." Vermeita gave in, succumbing to their expectant gazes, and took a bite of the cookie. "Oh, they really are nice."

"Right? I've never had such sweet cookies before."

"And they're not just brown! There's red and blue and green! They're so pretty!"

"Yes, that's nice," she acknowledged with a gentle smile. She ushered them back into the building before calling the eldest girl, who'd been in charge of minding the house in her absence. "Who was this man who gave them the cookies?"

"A merchant. I've never seen him before. He said he came to give you a donation..." With some hesitation, the girl very apprehensively held out a heavy pouch.

Vermeita opened it to see that it was brimming with gold coins. "That's an astonishing sum."

"Y-yes, I was so surprised. I've never seen a donation this big before..."

Over the years, there'd been more than a few donors acting out of pure goodwill and others to curry favor with the cardinal. Telling one to *not* be suspicious of an unknown merchant and his outrageously large donation? Impossible.

Could it be someone working for Snobe?

Off the top of her head, she could only think of the Materialistic Cardinal. He'd be the only one with connections to someone this extravagant and generous with their money.

It could very well be an apology: About a year ago, he'd visited the orphanage and let slip that he wanted the prettiest girl to be one of his mistresses. She'd sent him on his way with a good beating from her cane.

"Has the man left already?"

"No, he went to the blue building." The girl pointed to the blue-roofed mansion a little way away.

Vermeita suddenly hiked up her skirts, dashing off toward it.

"Mother?!" Her attendant and the girls let out surprised yelps, but she ignored them, moving forward, leaping over the hedge between the two buildings in one fluid motion. She arrived in the garden of the blue building—

"Ready, set, shoot!"

The middle-aged merchant and the maid attending him, along with the exhilarated boys of the orphanage, were battling with some flat, metal spinning tops.

"Blow 'em away, Behemoth!" whooped one boy.

"Heh-heh-heh, you might have thought a bigger, heavier top would be stronger, but you've made a serious mistake!" The merchant sinisterly snickered.

"What?!"

Just as he'd predicted, the merchant's smaller top struck the larger one in rapid fire succession, each time making the larger top lose its grounding.

"Of course, the heavier one has more power. But the Behemoth is too heavy for its own good! Its axis is to the side, and it's easier to knock its rotation off."

"It's true! It's getting all wobbly!" wailed another boy.

"And larger tops have another weak point: Their bases are wide open. Take 'em down, Cerberus!"

"Aaah?!"

As if to obey the merchant's battle cry, the small top sent the Behemoth flying, causing the boy to collapse to the ground in defeat. The other children watching all raised their hands, clamoring to be the next to play.

"I'll take down Giesh's enemy. And exact my revenge! My turn!"

"Carlo, you went already. I'm next."

"Heh-heh, I bet I can take all of you down at once."

"Pick on someone your own size." The maid sighed as she watched the merchant goad the boys with an evil smile.

At this completely unexpected sight, Vermeita had been frozen at a standstill.

"...What are you doing?" she finally found it in herself to ask.

"Ah, Mother, you're back!" called out one of the boys, finally noticing Vermeita.

One after another, the boys pulled themselves from the game and ran over to greet her.

"Welcome home. We're playing BeySpinners!" explained one of them.

"BeySpinners?" asked Vermeita.

"Mr. Manju showed us how! It's super-fun!"

As if beckoned by their cheers, the merchant named Manju stepped to the front of the crowd. "It's wonderful to meet you, Cardinal Vermeita."

"And you. Thank you for playing with the children."

Their exchange was outwardly pleasant enough, but she'd noticed how the merchant's body was cocooned with magic.

An Illusion *spell, huh. And I'm gathering that woman over there cast it.* Though the merchant seemed to possess some capacity for magic, it wasn't any more than the average priest. His maid, on the other hand, was radiating wave after wave of magical power. She couldn't hide it even if she'd tried.

At the very least, she's as powerful as a bishop, possibly even more powerful than I am...

That unnerved Vermeita somewhat. But she didn't show it. Instead, she continued to give him a gentle smile, befitting the name of the Holy Mother Cardinal.

"I must say I feel uncomfortable receiving such kindness from someone I've just met."

"Ah yes. You're right. I guess I was too eager and overstepped my bounds. Please forgive me." The merchant bowed. When he noticed the group of boys looking at him strangely, he grinned devilishly. "Grown-up business is boring as hell. Run along and keep playing BeySpinners with that lady over there. I'll give the last man standing the prize of battling against my Cerberus."

"Oh man, I'm definitely not losing this time!"

The boys chattered energetically as they scurried off to play with the maid. The merchant watched them go with a smile then suddenly looked at Vermeita with a dead-serious expression.

"To put it bluntly, I doubted you. I wondered if you were gathering orphans to do the same thing as Cronklum." He explained that he came in her absence to check, but that his fears were groundless. "They're all good kids. They obviously love you very much. You wouldn't be able to raise them like that if you didn't love them back."

"Thank you."

"I came here prepared to take them in if their condition was bad enough—and with the money to do so—but thankfully that wasn't necessary."

"Oh, you flatter me." On first glance, she seemed humble, almost bashful, but she was heightening her defenses on the inside.

I don't think he's lying, but I don't think he's telling the truth, either. On top of that, he knows about how Cardinal Cronklum raised the Saint...

He didn't just have money backing him: He had information. Just like the Materialistic Cardinal. As she continued to think, the merchant looked up at the clear and balmy sky before speaking as casually as possible.

"I'm not going to lord the fact that I made a donation, but I was wondering if I could ask you a few questions. Would that be all right?"

"Go ahead."

"What do you get out of gathering and raising these children?"

In all truth, Vermeita was taken aback by his bluntness, but she flashed him a gentle smile almost immediately. "Would you not accept the answer that their smiles bring me great joy?"

"Well, I know there are some angelic childr—excuse me, kind people in this world. But I'm a crooked and dishonorable person myself, and I tend to doubt other people's good intentions." His wicked smile showed her a sliver of the merchant's true form, disguised under the mask of a philanthropist.

Refreshingly straightforward. But his bluff could use work. Is he actually a young man?

Even as she tried to sniff out her opponent's actual identity, she grinned genially and repeated herself. "It would be dishonest to say that my reputation isn't better off because of it, but I'm not lying about my desire to see the children smile." Vermeita glanced at the boys battling their tops.

"Let me go again! One more time!"

"Fine. But if you lose, you have to do whatever I say, all right?"

"D-deal! And if you lose, you have to be my servant!"

"Hmph, you're all talk! Hold up, is your leg shaking?"

Vermeita watched the boys as the started arguing, getting worked up over the game, and remarked, "…Precious."

"Hmm?"

"Don't you think the sight of children having fun is more precious than money?" Vermeita broke into her signature smile from ear to ear—as honest as the Holy Mother herself.

The merchant was struck silent for a moment, but then the corners of his mouth twitched up. "You're right. I'm sorry I doubted you."

"No, I'm glad you understand now."

"I have one final question, if it's not too much trouble. Why are the boys and the girls in the orphanage separated?"

The orphanage was divided into the building with the red roof for girls and the building with the blue roof for boys, complete with a tall hedge to separate the two.

"But no one was upset at me for entering the girls' dormitory, and it doesn't seem that the boys and girls are forbidden from visiting each other, so I was wondering why they were separated at all."

Vermeita recited an answer that she'd given countless times before: "Many of the orphans were abandoned by parents who had too many children to take care of. That's why we give them lessons on sexual education, so they don't repeat their parents' mistakes."

She didn't need to explicitly say that's why their dormitories were separated. It was a sound argument. However…

"I see. It's one of those 'separate the children once they're old enough to realize their differences' type of thing. I wish the people who confuse gender difference and discrimination would get an earful of this."

"What?"

"Just talkin' to mysel—"

"AAAAaaaaaahh—!"

Just as he scrambled to piece together some explanation, a scream pierced the air, drowning out his half-assed excuse. As the merchant tried to grasp the situation, the maid barreled over, clinging to him with a pale face.

"H-hey! Celes, what's wrong?"

"No! No! Keep it away!" She squirmed like an infant, almost smothering him in her large chest.

Vermeita was just as perplexed and looked over in the direction that the maid had come running from. She found a group of boys standing stock-still, their faces bewildered.

"Were you being mean to this nice lady?" Vermeita asked.

"N-no, we weren't doing anything!"

"Will was just showing something off when she suddenly screamed and…"

The group of children nudged one boy to the front—mild-mannered Will. He took a step forward. In his hands, he held a box made from slender sticks, holding something inside. Because Vermeita knew absolutely everything about the children, she immediately realized what it was.

"Ah, it's Will's bug—"

"No! No! Don't let it near me!"

"Calm down, Celes. It's not what you think it is. It's just a female rhinoceros beetle!" The merchant looked in the box—the insect cage—and tried to console her, but she was on the verge of tears with no intention of letting him go.

"I-it doesn't matter if it's a rhino something-or-other beetle! They're all the same… Please don't let it near me!"

"I knew you hated those nasty roaches, but I didn't realize all other bugs were no-go, too." He gazed at her with weary yet gentle eyes as he held on to her. He bowed his head to Vermeita and the boys. "I apologize for this fuss. We shall take our leave for today."

"No need to apologize. My children were the ones who caused it. I'm sorry."

"Um, I'm sorry, Miss…," stuttered Will.

Vermeita, Will, and all the boys hung their heads in apology.

The merchant flashed his pearly teeth at the children. "No worries! We'll play some soccer next time."

"I—I was just a little surprised. You need not worry about it. I hope we can play again," consoled the maid, trying her best to smile. The two then headed on their way.

"Next time," huh...? Vermeita thought as she and the children saw them off.

She still couldn't guess their motives, but she knew she'd be seeing them again and would need to prepare for when that time came.

Vermeita sent a telepathic message to her priestess-in-waiting.

"I am truly very sorry for being so disgraceful."

The moment they'd returned to the inn and Celes had dissolved the *Illusion* spell, she bowed so deep, her head was about to hit her knees. But the merchant, aka Shinichi, didn't blame her or anything. He just sat on the bed with a wry smile.

"Don't worry about it. Everyone's got something they don't like."

"...I'm sorry, are you running a fever? Wouldn't you normally demand for me to 'strip down and grovel on the ground'?"

"Yep, that's my Celes." Shinichi felt reassured to hear Celes had returned to her foul-mouthed ways. "Why do you hate bugs anyway? I'm surprised I don't see you make a scene on a regular basis. There's all sorts of creepy-crawlies around."

"That would be because I keep an *Insecticide* spell in place. It exterminates all bugs near me by shaving down their life span."

"A broad-spectrum Ra—d?! Just use an insect-repellant spray instead! Is that even healthy to inhale?!"

"I dispel it when I'm with others. That's why I was particularly surprised to see a bug while my defenses were down..."

"I see. Wait, how about now?"

"I'm currently releasing it at 200 percent."

"What about *my* health?!"

It was a pretty big waste of magical power, but the fact that Celes was constantly using it could be one of the reasons she'd become a top magic user, second only to the Demon King.

"Well? Why do you hate them to the point you'd use specialized magic?"

"That's..." Celes's face suddenly clouded over, and she turned away.

"You don't have to tell me if you don't wanna." Shinichi tried to end the conversation, sensing that this memory was too difficult to recount.

But Celes shook her head and looked up at him. "No, this is a good opportunity to talk it out. But I would like to hear something from you in return."

"Like about the day I decided to check the locations of all the fire extinguishers at school, just out of the blue? And how I thought I could use them as weapons in case the school was taken over by terrorists?" Shinichi joked, teasing her with an example that was incomprehensible to someone in this world.

But Celes didn't laugh—much less make fun of him. Her expression betrayed no emotion, as if she had forcibly squashed it down.

"Who did you lose?" she whispered.

At times, Shinichi would show anger or envy toward the heroes' ability to resurrect from the dead. She'd picked up that it was emotional scar tissue, left behind after he'd lost someone precious to him.

"...I see. That's how deep this conversation is going," Shinichi murmured after a moment of silence, letting out a self-deprecating sigh. "It's not something you want to talk about lightly."

"Well, you don't have to tell me if you don't want to?" Celes echoed his earlier phrase, making him smile wryly as he shook his head.

"No, I'll tell you. I want you to know... But it's not a happy story. I wouldn't want Arian or Rino to hear it, but I think you'll be okay."

"Excuse me? What exactly do you think I am?"

"A dark-skinned, big-boobed, sharp-tongued, sexy-ass maid."

"Understood. Increasing *Insecticide* strength to 500 percent."

"Hey, I'm actually getting chills here!"

After they finished their usual comedic banter, her face dissolved into a warm smile for a moment before she released the spell and sat on the bed next to Shinichi.

"I can go first," she offered.

Celes began to tell the tale, as wearisome as an attempt to fish out clothes from the back of a dresser. "I have never known my parents. My earliest memory is being forced to work as a slave for the Gray Demon King, a were-elephant."

She'd been born in a country controlled by violence—one that was the manifestation of the demon world as imagined by humankind.

"Anyone who attempted to go against the Gray Demon King or run away was slaughtered mercilessly—even infants. There were only two ways that the weak could survive: if they curried the favor of someone greater or if they worked obediently as slaves."

"...Yeah, I guess violent brutes really exist," murmured Shinichi.

He'd spent so long with the demons, especially with Rino as their leader, that he'd forgotten they lived in a dog-eat-dog society. The strong triumphed, and the weak were killed. It was actually normal for demons to use their power to control people, like this Gray Demon King. Shinichi's master—the Blue Demon King—might be a big softy with mad respect for the strong, but beneath that shell, he was cruel and vicious. He'd have no problems completely obliterating the human race on the ground of their weakness. His conscience was cleaner thanks to an angel by the name of Rino, but he wasn't all that different from the Gray Demon King.

"While I was a slave there, I worked to gather *beossla* with the other children."

"*Beossla*?"

"An edible, man-eating plant. They were allegedly the Gray Demon King's favorite," Celes explained.

"But I'll bet it's disgusting. Like all plants from the demon world."

The *beossla* had a number of tentacles protruding from its round green body—the monster version of the carnivorous sundew plants on Earth. If Shinichi dared to nibble on it, he'd find it inedible, sputtering something along the lines of *I'd rather nosh on some weeds on the road.*

But of course, demonkind had unsophisticated palates. The Gray Demon King was no exception, delightedly scarfing down *beossla*. Its biggest problem wasn't even its flavor: It was the fact that it was a man-eating plant that could move of its own accord.

"At the time, I was so weak, I could only cast about four magic arrows a day."

"Stronger than the average human adult. Terrifying." Shinichi shuddered.

"We were constantly under the supervision of soldiers, which made it impossible to run away. We spent every day desperately hunting for *beossla*. There were a lot of slaves in the mix who were unlucky enough to be swallowed whole, but the Gray Demon King apparently laughed it off and thought it tasted 'best when fattened up with little brats.'"

"......"

"The strongest wins and takes all; the weakest loses and forfeits all. Those are the rules of the demon world, regardless of if you're a demon, a monster, or a man-eating plant." She was trying to say that she didn't resent them, but she couldn't help but avert her gaze, mourning the death of the other children. "Based on these circumstances, I'm guessing you can imagine that my room was vile as well."

It was a small, damp, stone cell, holding upward of ten children packed in together. They were never allowed to bathe, much less have a proper bathroom. Instead of a toilet, they'd used a bucket, and the gag-worthy smell of urine and feces reeked across the room. Their scraggly blankets were full of holes and ticks. Those filthy conditions were bound to attract nasty pests.

"*They* would scurry across the room," Celes continued, referring to the bugs. "At the time, I just didn't have enough energy left to care. But there was this dark-elf boy sleeping next to me, and one day he started whining to me that his ear was in pain…"

"Nope! I know where this is going! Spare me the details!"

"I peered in his ear and saw that *they* had l-l-laid eggs at some point and…they ha-hatched and tiny, black ones scuttered out…!"

"AAaaaaaaagh—!" Full-body chills shivered up and down his spine, and Shinichi shrieked in spite of himself.

Celes's tanned skin paled as she recalled that gruesome spectacle. "Ever since, I can't help by be petrified at the sight of *them* and any other type of bug…"

"Yup. Anyone would be traumatized by that incident."

Celes covered her long ears with shaking hands, which Shinichi found particularly adorable, but he couldn't really bring himself to smile in this situation.

"After all that, I was so sickened by *them* that I could no longer bear to be in that tiny stone cell. I tried to make a run for it."

But she was immediately apprehended by an ogre on lookout who beat her until she couldn't stand any longer.

As she lay on the ground and blood dripped out of her nose, the ogre swung a massive club in an attempt to cut her young life short.

But a gale blasted between them at the last moment.

"Someone snatched the club with one hand and punctured the ogre's chest with their fingertip."

"Sounds like the kind of guy who could make the sky fall with the power of his love."

This figure was the Savior of the Century's End—or at the very least, a savior in the eyes of Celes and the other children.

"This person cast a *Healing* spell on me before sprinting off to the Gray Demon King's castle without another word."

On the way, this so-called savior clobbered the gang of small fry desperately trying to prevent their advances, as if flicking off some dust, and in no time, reached the tyrant.

"With a single spell, the feared and hated Gray Demon King was reduced to ash."

"Wow, totally rigged! A cheating bastard. The only beast who can bend the rules is the Demon King... Oh?"

"Do you get it now?" She smiled gently at him, as something in Shinichi's mind finally clicked. "It was His Highness's future wife, my magic teacher and trainer: The Blue Princess of War, Regina Petrara Verlum."

She was the alluring azure woman who'd squashed the Gray Demon King out of existence and gazed down at the trembling demons with boredom. This image of her was burned into Celes's young mind. It was as if the blue sun of the demon world itself descended down in a divine and dazzling display.

"After Lady Regina defeated the Gray Demon King, she seemed to lose interest, determined to leave the area."

She didn't intend to partake in some generous, feel-good act of freeing the slaves from their pitiful conditions. She'd come to this land to fight the brute upon hearing rumors of his strength. She only had eyes for combat. That was why she was called the Blue Princess of War.

"Even if this Gray Demon King was a benevolent ruler, she wouldn't have hesitated to strike him down and slaughter him."

"Well, she sounds just about rabid."

"To top it off, she'd resurrect the good if their corpse was in adequate condition."

"You're telling me she'd eliminate the bad and resurrect the good? I guess that's fine—"

"According to her, 'I do it 'cause we can brawl over and over if I bring them back to life, eh?'"

"Yep, positively insane!"

But Regina was only stoic with the strong; she was gentle with the weak. After all, she'd healed Celes in her time of need.

"I chased after Lady Regina and begged her to make me her apprentice."

And surprise, surprise, the Blue Princess of War allowed her to tag along. "Oh, Lady Regina is a master of martial and magical arts. She tried her very best to polish her battle techniques. But on the flip side, she had absolutely no interest in cooking or cleaning. She was just searching for someone to help with day-to-day chores when I approached her."

Regina was the type to train to the brink of exhaustion—physically and magically—if left to her own devices. If it reached her ears that there was a strong warrior in the east, she'd dash off and beat him into submission. If she heard there was a powerful magic user in the west, she'd whiz over there and blow her away.

As Celes frantically followed her teacher every which way, she'd gone through a magical growth spurt.

"It could be because Lady Regina was getting sick of her impossible quest to find a suitable opponent. I think she was hoping to train me until I surpassed or defeated her."

"Like some sort of final boss. Geez..."

But before Celes reached that level, the Blue Princess of War learned of another with the "Blue" title. She was on the verge of a fateful encounter—with the Blue Demon King, Ludabite.

"I still remember how Lady Regina was grinning ear to ear as His Highness awaited her arrival with a smile. That marked the beginning of the now-famous incident, 'The Last Day of the Timoar Mountains.'"

"Oh, when those mountains were turned into empty fields..."

This "Last Day" part of the name wasn't a figure of speech. On that day, the Timoar Mountains were wiped away from the surface of the demon world, caught up in the scuffle between the two behemoths. For the first time, the Demon King and Princess of War had found an opponent capable of fighting on equal ground and withstanding their full strength.

"I was watching from above, using a *Fly* spell, but I came close to dying a few times from the sheer force of their combat. It could have knocked me straight down."

From dawn to dusk, the decisive battle had stretched over the course of more than half a day. The curtain had finally closed after the pair clashed against each other, squeezing out the last of their strength to cast their most powerful spell.

A flash had burst through the sky, momentarily blotting out the inky darkness of twilight. The Timoar Mountains were swept away, leaving nothing behind other than a cloud of dust. After a moment, the debris settled to reveal the Princess of War laying in the bottom of a crater and the Demon King coated in blood, kneeling but somehow still conscious.

"I rushed to Lady Regina's side and healed her, then used my remaining magic to heal His Highness."

"Did you consider finishing him off right there in his weakened state?"

"Excuse you! If I had, it would have sullied the honor of not only the victor but also that of Lady Regina."

"Right, yup. Celes, you're definitely a demon."

The victor was strong—therefore, righteous. That was why she didn't try to skew the results by meddling in their affairs. Shinichi couldn't argue with that: He actually liked the simplicity of their muscle-headed ideals.

"Then the two fell in love, got married, and had Rino," he concluded.

"Yes. For a time, Lady Regina stayed in the castle. Was well-behaved. She helped me train, and I cared for Lady Rino." Celes broke into a soft smile, imagining baby Rino in her nappy.

Celes had never known her parents, but Regina had acted as her mentor and mother figure. And Rino was both like a little sister and her master at the same time.

"Compared with them, you really roughhouse your 'father'…"

"How rude. I respect and love His Highness, just as much as the other two. But I wish he would grow up a little and stop his helicopter parenting."

"I can't agree more." Shinichi nodded.

Celes let out a big huff as she remembered one particular incident.

"When Lady Rino was three years old, she was bit by a tiny mosquito on her arm. His Highness was so enraged that he spent two months clearing the surrounding sixty capra (about 120 miles) of all mosquitos."

"If he exterminated an area the size of Hokkaido, I'm sure that completely obliterated the ecosystem..."

"Obviously, I helped him with this mission."

"You're just as bad!"

Well, in Celes's case, she had the added reason of hating bugs.

"Time passed, and two years ago, Lady Regina abruptly declared that she's 'gotta train again, gotta test out the human world.'"

"And then she came back from the human world with bread, which brought us here."

"Yes. After that, she left again. This time to search the demon world for the Black Dragon."

She didn't seem worried in the slightest for her master's life. But she cast her gaze down, pining to reunite with this precious person.

Shinichi thought quietly as he looked at her profile. *Her earliest memories. Hmm. Let's say that's about five years old. Then she was a slave for about a year. Then she traveled with her teacher for, like, a year. Her current masters got married, and then Regina got pregnant and gave birth—that's another year. And Rino's fourteen years old now. In total, that makes her at least twenty—*

"What are you calculating?" *Crunch.*

"E-erm, can you mind read with magic?"

"I'm not using magic. It's what they call a woman's intuition."

"Even scarier!" Shinichi shook with fear as Celes's hand clenched his face. His skull started to make some seriously ominous creaking noises. Geez! He couldn't hide anything from that maid.

"It's your turn. Spit it out."

"I'm about to spit out my brain juice!" he protested, wiggling out of her death grip. Shinichi took a ragged breath as he forced a wry smile. "Don't worry. You don't have to continue with your slapstick routine. I'm not going to be too upset at recounting my tale."

"…I'm not particularly worried about you."

Shinichi thought about teasing Celes as she turned her face away, but he'd risk his skull getting crunched again. He obediently started his story.

"Mine isn't as bad as yours, Celes. Eight years ago, a girl in my neighborhood drowned in the ocean and died."

There were approximately a thousand fatal accidents at sea every year in Japan. That was one in every hundred thousand people. It just so happened to be his childhood friend.

"Like I've said, we don't have these superconvenient spells to resurrect the dead on Earth. If you die, that's it. It's over."

Even though people learned best from failure, there was one failure they couldn't come back from: death.

"I don't think she understood that. She was such a dumbass." A smile crept across his face.

She was the kind of person who was all smiles, all the time.

"I've always been cold and distant even when I was a kid. All the adults in the neighborhood said I was an unpleasant little brat."

"I think you're quite unpleasant now," Celes offered.

"Don't. Anyway, she was different: honest and endearing, a bright and lively idiot."

"Which is why…"

"She reminds me of someone I used to know."

…Which is why he'd whispered that when he decided to save Arian. But Celes didn't say that aloud.

Shinichi guessed what she was thinking and shook his head, chuckling. "I said she reminds me of her, but Arian's *way* prettier and *way* smarter. Plus, Arian might seem happy-go-lucky on the surface, but she's got a pretty dark past."

"Right. Just when you think she's gotten too soft, she'll pout and throw a tantrum."

"Compared to Arian, this girl never had anything going on in her mind. She was a dumbass. The real deal. She legit seemed happy every day."

She'd play outside from morning to night, rolling around in the mud. And just after she'd wept as her mother scolded her, she'd bounce back with a big smile. It wasn't that weird for an elementary schooler to switch emotions so quickly, but she was still a real big idiot. At least, that's what he'd think to himself.

"She was so stupid! She'd try everything: She'd fall from the monkey bars and hit her head; she'd attempt an overhead kick and hit her head; she'd dive headfirst into the kiddie pool and hit her head."

"...Um, I get the impression she hit her head constantly."

"Yup. I'm sure that's why she was so stupid."

Even as a kid, he'd tried to warn her, fretting about how she needed to think her actions through or she'd have to face the consequences in the future.

"But she'd reply: 'It's fine! In the future, I'll have you to take me in, Shinichi!' That was the first time I seriously felt like killing someone."

"...Is that so?" She kept her answer short, seeing him smile through a difficult topic.

Celes could tell how much this girl meant to him, even if he bashed her repeatedly, dumbass or not. This girl must have warmed him like the sun, he who was cold and distant.

"Did you like her?"

"They say the idiots are the cutest. If I had to choose between liking and hating her, I'd have to say I liked her. But not romantically. Well, I'm not sure."

It wasn't a lie. It was how he'd felt.

He had no intentions of insulting young love. But he just couldn't understand it—because he was tied to logic and reason more than emotions. After all, he was a rational person at heart.

"What *is* love anyway? If it's an increased heartbeat, well, then I'm definitely in love with your boobs, Celes."

"That's just lust, you pervert."

"Um? I'm pretty sure it's *more* perverted to dislike boobs!"

"I'm creeped out that you're so insistent."

If Sanctina were here, she'd probably side with Shinichi, but she was definitely a pervert for sure.

"Anyway, she was fun, but I couldn't be around her for too long, 'cause that would just exhaust the hell out of me. We never got that close."

And that's why he didn't go that day when she invited him to the beach with her family.

"She loved the pool, but she couldn't swim at all. Her teacher was this spirited moron and got it in her mind that she 'shouldn't be afraid, just go for it!' She got riled up, you know, super-excited to go off into the waters. Then she went in the ocean when her parents weren't looking and drowned. She was really foolish. I guess that was inevitable."

He'd heard a rumor that she had drowned trying to save a kid, but he didn't know if it was true. He was certain that she hadn't considered for a millisecond that she might die—or that those left behind would be in so much pain.

"Kids always think they're invincible, that they'll be okay no matter what. You reap what you sow, I guess. It was no one's fault but her own."

Shinichi understood that in his mind, but he couldn't forgive the adults who'd always pushed her to do more and not reprimanded her for being careless. But he was most resentful of some*thing* intangible, not some*one*.

"She died for being dumb. But if she'd noticed that someone forgot their indoor slippers, she'd lend hers; or if a kid dropped their flan at school lunch, she'd give them hers, even as drool dribbled from her mouth—they were her favorite. Once, there was a kid crying because he wet himself in class, so she wet herself to cheer him up. She was a good kid."

"I'm not sure about that last one," Celes replied, exasperated. Shinichi smiled wryly back at her.

"An idiot. But she was well liked, and everyone was bawling their eyes out at her funeral."

Well, everyone except Shinichi, who was seething quietly.

"She did her best and didn't back down from a challenge. But she made this one little mistake, and that was it. How could this world be so unreasonable? An arrogant, unpleasant brat like me could keep on living just fine, but an actual good kid dies. I couldn't forgive the world for being that cruel."

That's why Shinichi decided to fight against death. But he didn't choose magic or voodoo or anything shady like that. He chose the more realistic option: science.

"I'd read books from the library every day. I'd read every page of science sites on the Internet. I was so obsessed, I even surprised myself."

Thanks to that, he knew a lot about science. But it also made him face the reality that resurrecting the dead was impossible. He gave up. And now he was here.

"Well, that talk went longer than expected. All it was was that a girl I knew died."

"Which is why…," started Celes, fumbling for words when she realized the answer to her doubts, nagging at her secretly.

From the moment the Demon King had summoned Shinichi up until now, Shinichi had never once uttered that he wanted to return to Earth.

In most normal cases, anyone would want to go back to their home, to their parents and friends. Of course, the answer in Shinichi's case wasn't so simple. He'd stuck around to satisfy his own morbid curiosity and to test out his dirty tricks in real life. Along the way, he started to worry about the well-being of Rino, along with the others, which compounded his reasons to stay.

But at the center of it all was this girl. She'd meant something to him. When he'd lost her, he'd had no other ties to Earth, especially when he'd realized that he'd never be able to resurrect her. That was what he'd been hiding in the small cracks of his heart.

"I may be stepping over my bounds, but why can't this *science* resurrect the dead?" asked Celes.

"Well, it's the same as this world. If the body was in good condition, it might be possible."

By freezing a corpse, the dead could potentially be resurrected in the future, when science had advanced enough to allow it.

But if the body in question had been cremated—losing the brain, its memories and information, its DNA—it was impossible.

"Unless we were able to computerize it, I guess. Like in sci-fi movies, you know, uploading a person's memories into a server once the brain is gone..."

"Do what now?" Celes called out to him, but after he'd blurted out some foreign phrases, he'd gone silent.

Her voice didn't reach him. He'd been stunned by another revelation, triggered by his own words.

No way. What if that's the kind of system that the Goddess is using to protect the undying heroes?

It wasn't something that could be done in his version of Earth in the twenty-first century, but it wasn't that absurd to think it could be done in a few hundred years. In theory, it was possible to achieve immortality.

Let's say you took and stored some of your cells alongside the information in your brain. If this information was transmitted automatically, it would be akin to taking a backup of your computer.

Meaning even if you died, they could make a clone out of your cells and download the information into the clone's brain—making a re-creation of "you," save for the memory of your death. If there was a technology that could transmit real-time information about your body, it'd be an even more perfect version of "you."

But then we run into the "Swampman" identity issue...

He was thinking about the philosophical thought experiment. Say lightning kills a man in a swamp at the same time that another bolt of lightning crashes into another swamp. In a miracle of miracles, it rearranges the molecules to re-create the deceased—down to the last atom. This is the "Swampman." Can you call it the same person?

This problem has existed since ancient Greece. The ship of Theseus, another thought experiment, asks: *If we swap out all the pieces of the ship, is it the same ship?*

Philosophers have struggled to come up with an answer. Each person's suggestion to the Swampman problem seemed to come down to whether they thought of humans as "collections of matter" or "collections of consciousness."

Would the heroes be able to handle the truth? If they're "Swampmen," that is.

Even Shinichi didn't know, but he did know one thing.

If that's how it's done, resurrection from nothing would be possible.

Even the Blue Demon King had said it was impossible to resurrect a corpse that'd been completely destroyed. But it'd be a different story if there was a *copy* of their memories and body.

If being a "hero" is the authentication necessary to access the Goddess's server and save backups...

Shinichi looked at the back of his own hand, which obviously wasn't emblazoned by the sun symbol, the proof of being a hero.

There are no issues in theory. If resurrection is already possible with magic, it shouldn't be impossible...

When the Demon King said he couldn't do it, it wasn't because he didn't have enough power. He just couldn't conjure a system that could make it work.

Magic was a way to alter reality to match your imagination. And there was no way the Demon King would be able to imagine a system to upload memories, clone bodies, and download information without Shinichi's knowledge of science and sci-fi. Meaning it didn't matter how much power he had. If he couldn't picture it, he couldn't replicate it in reality.

That's all well and good. But how is the Goddess able—?

"Sir Shinichi."

"Ah?!"

Shinichi jumped back in surprise when he found Celes's face inches away from his. He could feel her hot breath on his skin.

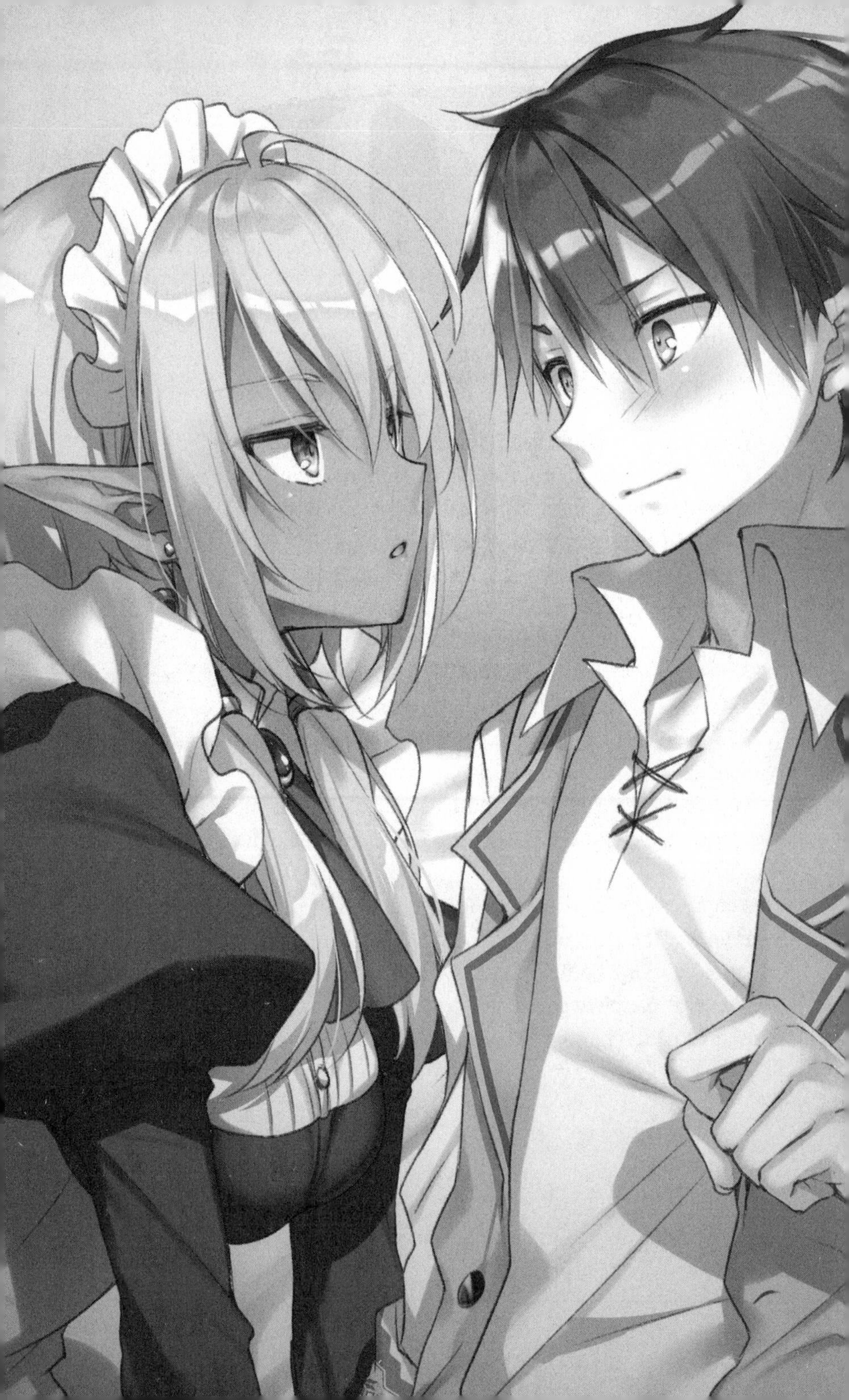

"I'm well aware that you can get carried away with your erotic fantasies, but please refrain from being swept away in the middle of a conversation."

"I wasn't having erotic fantasies! All I was doing was wondering how a centaur breastfeeds her children: Human boobs or horse titties?"

"Aha! I was right." Though she let out an annoyed sigh, she was observant enough to catch that he was trying to change the subject. "I know I won't understand what you're thinking, so I'm not going to ask. Plus, you've already told me what I wanted to know."

"...Sorry, I'll explain once I have some proof." He hung his head apologetically.

"I look forward to it." Celes stood from the bed. "I think we're done with our chitchat for now. I'd like to hear our strategy, but first, I shall go get us something to eat."

She made her way out the door, but right before closing it, she turned back. "One last thing."

"What?"

"I'm ever-so-slightly jealous of that girl—for holding a piece of your heart."

"...Huh?"

She let the door slam shut behind her before he could ask her to clarify, making him listen to her footsteps as she tromped farther away. He collapsed on the bed, completely dumbfounded.

"She's such a tease..."

Shinichi could feel his cheeks getting hot, but he needed to find a plan to defeat the cardinal, the enemy in front of them. He used everything he had to refocus his attention and fine-tune their strategy moving forward.

Four days after their initial visit to the Holy Mother Cardinal's orphanage, Shinichi and Celes returned to the red-roofed building for girls, cloaked under the guise of a merchant and his maid.

"I apologize for visiting so late. Is Cardinal Vermeita in?" asked Shinichi.

"Oh, Mr. Manju. A pleasure to see you again," the priestess warmly greeted them upon opening the door.

She ushered them in with an amicable smile, but Shinichi didn't miss the slight hostility and fear that flashed in her eyes. He stepped in and acted like he hadn't noticed.

"I can't tell you how happy I am that you stopped by. Lady Vermeita has worried herself sick that she hadn't expressed her thanks properly."

"Ha-ha, well, no need," he dismissed.

As they exchanged pleasantries and feigned ignorance of their ulterior motives, she guided them to the far end of the estate, a room for the cardinal's personal use.

"Lady Vermeita, Mr. Manju has arrived," the priestess chirped when they arrived at the door.

"Please come in." The Holy Mother Cardinal beckoned them from inside the room.

As directed, Shinichi went to take a step inside when Celes yanked his arm and made him stop in his tracks. *"It's a trap."*

"Yeah, I know." Shinichi chuckled in response to her short warning via *Telepathy*. He could guess that they'd been expecting his return and had planned something based on the priestess's nervousness, even without checking for the presence of magic. *"Anyway, it's a bit late for a warning. If it were me, I'd have set a trap capable of blowing away the entire building. At the very least."*

"That's absurd! The children are sleeping on the floors above us."

"Which would make it the biggest ace in the hole ever. That's a mental blind spot, right? You'd assume no one would ever do it. Well, I don't think she's that despicable."

Shinichi stepped inside the room. Celes didn't hesitate to follow him in, and the door clicked quietly shut behind them. With that, a set of complex magic circles emerged out of the ceiling, floor, and all four walls, ensnaring them.

"Brave of you to walk so fearlessly into a trap." The Holy Mother Cardinal rose slowly from the desk, one of the few pieces of furniture in her minimalistic room.

The glow from the magic circles illuminated the tender, loving smile of a mother, as if she were looking at her mischievous little children.

"Cardinal Vermeita. Thank you for seeing us on such short notice. By the way, what do these do?" Shinichi jabbed the magic circles, completely unbothered by the situation.

Vermeita was unable to hold back her laughter, hooting at his brazenness. "Ha-ha, well, it's so we don't wake the children. Let's see. There's a little bit of *Silence* and *Protection*. Then we have some *Acid Rain*, *Lightning Wall*, *Poison Cloud*, and *Land Bite*, along with a few others."

"Heh-heh, enough to blow a body to smithereens," Shinichi chuckled as he examined the symbols and pictures in the circles.

All you needed to cast a spell was magic power and a visualization of its effects. There isn't any need to yell something like "Fireball!" But the more vivid the mental image, the stronger the spell. Most magic users relied on words—otherwise known as incantations—to enhance them.

There were, of course, disadvantages to using an incantation. First, it took time to chant them. Second, because humans only have one mouth, they could only unleash one at a time.

On the other hand, magic circles didn't have any of these disadvantages. By laying down one's imagination as letters, symbols, and diagrams, a circle procured magic and allowed one to fire off a spell quickly. It could even cast multiple spells at once. These magic circles were helpful in complicated spells, including *Teleport* and *Summon*, by acting as additional magical support.

The only two real disadvantages were the long setup time and their lack of portability due to being such large drawings. But they were ideal in cases where one was lying in wait.

"It's so like an undying hero to set a suicide trap to kill your enemy," Shinichi commented.

"I was scared the first time, too, but I got used to it after a while."

"...That's what she said."

"I'll crack open your skull if you keep joking around," Celes growled as she latched her hand onto his head, intent on punishing him for his dirty mind.

He let out a shriek of pain, but he was still cracking up on the inside. *I wonder what you'd think if you knew you were a Swampman, Holy Mother.*

Would she even get it? Would it leave her confused? Would she lose her mind? Or would she have the will to get over it? He couldn't guess what was going on inside her head just by looking at her plastered smile.

"Well then, Mr. Manju. Have you come tonight to show off how close you two are?"

"No, no. If we had, I'm sure you wouldn't have given us such a warm welcome."

After all, she'd set a trap that'd easily kill a normal person and leave nothing behind, rendering them incapable of resurrection. Vermeita must have discovered their true identities and goal.

"Well, I thought you'd humor me with a sales talk. You know, make a deal or something," Shinichi began.

"All right. Would you mind showing me your true identities?" asked Vermeita.

"Oh, how rude of me." Shinichi had forgotten that he was still in his middle-aged merchant form.

He looked back at the maid. Celes had already guessed there was no longer any reason to hide, so she dispelled *Illusion*.

"Nice to meet you, for real this time. My name is Shinichi Sotoyama. You can just call me Shinichi."

"I am Celestia. I go by Celes."

As she got an eyeful of the young boy with black hair and the dark-skinned woman with pointy ears, Vermeita wasn't unsettled, but she was bug-eyed at the sight of the first demon she'd ever seen. "A dark elf... You really are an agent of the Demon King."

"How did you figure it out anyway?" He didn't hesitate to ask a bold question.

Vermeita nodded pleasantly. "I may not be as well connected as Cardinal Snobe, but I have my ways. I happened to come across the name of the merchant Manju in Boar Kingdom."

Even after the orphans left the orphanage for good, Vermeita continued to fret about their well-being, often visiting their homes to check in or sending letters and telepathic messages to those far away. Out of them, there was one man who'd become a priest in Boar Kingdom. She'd happened to hear him talk about a strange merchant, Manju. After Shinichi's visit to the orphanage four days ago, Vermeita had started collecting information on Manju when she remembered the priest. She asked him to look into it further and eventually determined it was the same person.

"A certain figure had proposed that the king of Boar Kingdom make a deal with the demons. This individual also visited one of the most prominent jewelers in the Holy City and immediately afterward handed one of the cardinals an incredible sum of money. His companion was an inhumanly powerful magic user... Well, even with just that information, it's enough to connect the dots and make one suspect he's connected to the demons."

"This is what happens when you're lazy and use the same name," Celes scolded.

"Whoops, how careless of me..."

Vermeita smiled patiently at them, just as when she was speaking with the children. But her eyes glinted, sharp. She was prepared to activate the magic circles if they made the smallest move. "And what is it you wished to speak with me about?"

"You've already guessed, haven't you?"

Otherwise, she would have activated the magic circles when they walked into the room, instead of prattling on with a pointless conversation. Vermeita smiled at his guess but remained silent. Shinichi offered to answer in her stead.

"I want you to join us."

It was an extreme request, especially to one of the highest members of the church. It was essentially asking her to betray her own organization.

But she must have predicted this was the case for she was neither startled nor angry. She nodded as if her suspicions had been confirmed.

"Before that, may I ask why you selected me?"

"Cronklum is gonna be defeated soon anyway. There's nothing to gain from working with him. Snobe is too hedonistic and greedy. It makes him dangerous. Effectus is too stubborn. He'd never listen to what we have to say. On the other hand, you strike me as a good person. You're popular with the people. Plus, you're open-minded enough to listen to the likes of me."

"I'll take your words as a compliment."

He'd basically admitted she would be the easiest cardinal to manipulate, but she didn't seem to care.

"By the way, do you know why Cronklum is gonna be defeated soon?" he asked.

"Only a bit. As I was looking into this 'Manju' character, I stumbled upon information that a popular singer was interfering with Miss Sanctina's mission."

"Hmm. It seems you're missing the most recent development."

"Care to enlighten me?"

"That singer is the daughter of the Demon King. Sanctina has fallen head over heels in love with her and has gone so far as to betray the church."

"What?!" Vermeita shrieked, unable to suppress her shock.

She'd figured from their interactions that the outward purity of the Saint was hiding something sinister. But never in a million years would she have guessed that Sanctina would realize she was interested in the same gender and betray the church.

"If you work with us, we'll give you other pieces of information. They'd benefit you, for sure. Obviously, we're also prepared to give you gold and material goods."

"You're a generous one. Even with that donation of yours," she commented.

"Oh, that'd be the Demon King's money, not mine."

"...Sir Shinichi?" Celes sent him a piercing glare.

He whistled, pretending not to notice.

As she witnessed their friendly exchange, Vermeita broke out into a smile, but her face clamped down immediately into something more serious.

"A tempting proposal, I must say. But if this alliance ever came to light, I'd lose everything. That means the children would have nowhere to go." She explained that was why she couldn't take such a risk.

"If that happened, all the children could go to the castle of the Demon King. We're going to be swamped with the potato harvest soon, and I want to try sowing wheat, so we could use the extra help.

And then there's the Demon King's daughter—her name's Rino. It'd make me really happy if she could have more friends to play with."

"That sounds nice. But I have to wonder if the children wouldn't end up slaughtered and stewed."

"If you'd just meet Rino, you'd immediately understand why that would never happen. She's a total angel. I mean, even Saint Sanctina fell for her."

"'A total angel'?" Vermeita repeated the unfamiliar words slowly.

"Oh, that just means she's a supercute, supergood kid."

All Vermeita could do was shake her head since she didn't know the person in question.

"I'll also let you know that the Demon King doesn't eat humans. He doesn't have weird ideas like trying to conquer the world. He likes to fight with the powerful and dote on his daughter. He's basically a big-ass muscle head."

"That's not a very nice way to speak of your master." Vermeita chuckled wryly, but she didn't seem to doubt him.

She didn't even need to use *Liar Detector*. Based on the way Shinichi talked in excitement and exasperation, Celes silently affirming him by nodding along, Vermeita knew they were telling the truth.

"Let's stop talking about what I'd do if I were discovered. I even admit that it's possible we misunderstand the demons. But the church could never coexist with these 'evil creatures.' What would you intend for me to do about that?"

"All you need to do is keep sending your heroes. We'll keep up appearances as enemies. If there's an attack once a week, well, let's just say the Demon King would be happy to have someone to tussle with."

It would dishearten the people to know the demons hadn't been beaten back yet, but if the two parties continued with this little tableau of combat, the people would be none the wiser.

"On top of that, if necessary, we'll eliminate the followers of the Materialistic Cardinal and the Agreeable Cardinal so they are pushed further and further away from becoming the next pope," Shinichi tacked on.

"I had an inkling," started Vermeita, "that the one who chased off Ruzal and his party of heroes from Boar Kingdom..."

"...was me. I broke them and forced them to surrender. Easy peasy," finished Shinichi.

The corners of his mouth curled up, suggesting he could do worse—much worse. He didn't know if Vermeita bought it, but she looked away as she quietly contemplated his proposal.

"And once you're pope and you have real power in the church, you could help us out by starting the reconciliation process with demon-kind. But if that's impossible, we can keep up the enemy act. We could even see a drop in the wars between humans, 'cause you'd have us as your common enemy. That would make things a lot easier for the rulers, I think."

"...You are a scary one," murmured Vermeita with a sigh, impressed that he'd planned this far ahead despite his age. "You're offering me an escape route if things go south. You'd make me pope... There's certainly a lot to gain."

"Right? If your goal is to become pope and not annihilate the demons, it'd do you a lot of good to work with us. We'll make your dreams come true."

Vermeita felt a sudden shiver run up her spine as she wondered how much Shinichi actually knew about her. But she kept her emotions under wraps as she began to shake her head slowly.

"This has been a fairly interesting discussion, but I must decline your offer. After weighing the dangers and returns, I still feel I have too much to lose."

"Hmm, that's unfortunate." But his expression didn't seem upset at all.

I'd say it wasn't blind faith or personal preference. She calculated the return on investment and concluded she should decline.

Meaning the scales could turn if he was able to offer a reward that outweighed the risks. He'd imagined things might end up this way. He was prepared to raise his wager.

"Can you say the same thing after looking at *this*?" Shinichi pulled a large envelope from his jacket with dramatic flair.

"What's this?"

"Open it and you'll see," he prompted as Vermeita tentatively took it from his hands.

Celes turned her back without a word, showing Vermeita that she wouldn't launch a surprise attack as Vermeita looked at the contents.

"......" The cardinal stared at the envelope in silence for a moment.

Alarm bells were ringing in her mind. She knew that there would be no going back once she looked inside. At the same time, her heart was pounding so loudly it filled her ears, as if to chorus, *What you desire is right here in your hands.*

"...I'll take a look." Curiosity trumped fear.

Inside the envelope was a sheaf of paper. The moment she saw it, her entire body stiffened. Drawn there was the beautiful, pure world that she'd always yearned for.

"Th-this...?!" Her hands shook violently, and her heart throbbed wildly, but her eyes were glued to the pages.

Shinichi smiled, satisfied. "Heh-heh-heh. Feast your eyes on this! A secret love affair between two boys...a comic about Boys Love, otherwise known as a BL manga!"

"'Bee ell manga'?!" Vermeita repeated.

The concept of manga didn't exist in this world—other than in this grand reveal. Of course, it was beyond her comprehension and almost went completely over her head.

But she understood that the pictures and words on paper depicted a passionate exchange between two boys. It was the beautiful world, a dirty world—one that she'd pined after for so long.

Four days prior, right after Shinichi and Celes did a deep dive into their tragic pasts, the pair started to talk strategy.

Shinichi made a bold declaration: "Vermeita's into BL."

"Bee ell?"

"BL, short for Boys Love. She gets off on stories about gay guys."

"Uh-huh..." Celes didn't really understand what he was saying. "I witnessed the incubus ramming into those criminals, but it seemed painful—and uncomfortable to look at."

"Ah, well, see, the real deal isn't the same as two-dimensional BL. And it's gotta be between two hot dudes..."

The most hardcore BL lovers could get off on uggos or beefcakes, but normies preferred drawings of slender, beautiful young men.

"Okay, fine. How do you know she is into this BL?"

"I could tell just by the hungry look in her eyes. She looked at the boys of the orphanage like she was a predator."

She'd tried so hard to hide it, but Shinichi had seen the dark desire flicker past her gentle gaze for just a moment.

"When I first heard that Vermeita opened an orphanage, I actually suspected that she'd wanted to make a place to get it on with young boys."

It made it even more suspicious that the Holy Mother Cardinal was well into her forties and unmarried. No shadows of lovers or romance lurked behind her. In truth, there were a few people who'd thought the same thing, leading the masses to trudge up to the orphanage out of sheer curiosity and to sniff out any incriminating details.

But no matter how much he investigated, he was unable to find any indication that she'd ever laid hands on the children.

"I'm embarrassed to have doubted her," the jeweler had admitted, even though he'd been the one to give Shinichi that information. *"But she's an ambitious woman. She's climbed her way up to cardinal. Why would she open an orphanage out of goodwill? Or even as a bid to gain popularity? Especially if it could become a liability later."*

It wasn't just an additional financial burden. If someone were to kidnap the children, they could manipulate her. And if she wasn't using them to manufacture some pawns like Cronklum had, it did seem like the risk outweighed the reward.

"That's because you're twisted and refuse to believe in the goodness of others," she quipped.

"I won't deny that. But there was also a chance that the Holy Mother Cardinal was dirty, too."

That's why he'd risked revealing his true self by going to the orphanage and engaging with her directly.

"It's no lie that she loves the children, but at the same time, she's a pervert. She gets off on seeing relationships between boys."

The little boys had chattered on casually as they played with the spinning tops: *"Let me go again! One more time!"*; *"You have to do whatever I say, all right?"*; *"You have to be my servant!"*

Most people wouldn't pay much attention to the conversations between children, but Vermeita was too excited to hide it.

"That's also why she separates the orphanage between boys and girls. It's a way to protect the girls and reduce suspicion, but she made a paradise for herself of exclusively boys. I bet she was banking on if things went really well, she'd get to witness an actual relationship blossom between them... Heh-heh-heh, I know she's the enemy, but I have to give her mad props."

"Why are you praising her?" Celes looked down at him with a cold glare.

Don't tell me you're into this, too, she seemed to say.

"Whoa! Whoa! Hold up, I'm not into this kind of thing. I only know this 'cause, like, one of my geeky friends has this sister who's really into BL. He's the one who told me all this."

"...I see."

"You don't believe me? Seriously, I—"

"I completely believe you. You're nothing more than a perverted womanizer," snapped Celes, looking all huffy as she turned away.

Not that she'd ever tell him that she was grumpy because he'd talked about other women from his past.

In all honesty, her fears were unfounded, because the girl was into BL hardcore, and she'd rather pair Shinichi with her brother than with herself.

"Anyway, I think Vermeita would happily join forces with the demons if it meant her BL dreams could come true."

"Do you think that would actually work?"

Celes was skeptical, especially since she didn't really understand the appeal of BL, but Shinichi was confident that he knew the inner workings of this crowd.

"That girl that I mentioned? Super-hardcore. She'd always attend conventions in the summer and winter, and it was standard for her to waste hundreds of thousands of yen on fan-made comics of her favorite pairings. She'd chase down her favorite manga, travel to different prefectures all around Japan to attend region-exclusive events and musicals. Geez, I didn't know if she lived for BL or if she needed it to live."

"I literally have no idea what you're talking about. But I get the sense that she's also a sexual deviant."

Celes had no way of knowing this but she was spot on, since that girl was the type of person who would screech: *If only that religion had never spread to Japan! We'd be a country brimming with BL by now!*

"That girl went all out. But Vermeita's different. She's only ever been able to fantasize in her mind. She's never enjoyed fan art or talked to a friend with common interests. I bet her desires have been simmering for a long time, and they're close to boiling over. She'd bite if we dangled some bait in front of her."

"I suppose it's better than breaking her spirit with some dirty method of yours."

She was still doubtful as she nodded and accepted his plans.

With the exception of her love for BL, Vermeita was a righteous person who'd saved those children. It wouldn't sit right with them to corner her with some incriminating rumors or torture her to mental oblivion. Their consciences would be clear if they could just entice her with a prize.

"Which means we need to go back to the King's castle to prepare said bait."

"Understood." Celes nodded before taking out some chalk, drawing a magic circle for *Teleport* on the floor.

As she did, Shinichi scampered to find the owner of the inn, placing five gold coins in his paw to pay for ten nights upfront and the promise of no one disturbing them. This was to ensure no one erased the magic circle before their return. After all preparations were made, the two went back to the Demon King's castle for the first time in a while.

"Welcome home, Shinichi!" cried Rino.

"Ah, hey! Unfair! Rino!" Arian whined.

Rino and Arian both sprang up to hug Shinichi, who was trying his best to not topple over as they crashed into him. The two had been antsy, waiting for their return after Celes sent a telepathic message that they were coming.

Shinichi chuckled. "Ha-ha, based on your reactions, I'm guessing nothing out of the ordinary has happened."

"Nope, Tigris Kingdom wasn't attacked or anything!" Arian gave him an eager nod.

Shinichi began to stare at her very seriously. "…Hey, have you been resurrected since becoming a hero?"

"Nope! Why do you ask?"

Shinichi laughed and brushed it off. Even if she was a "Swampman," he wouldn't care. Their memories together would still be real. He was more worried that she'd be upset if she found out, and he didn't want to see that, which was why he was relieved to hear his fears were baseless.

Shinichi called out to Sanctina, standing nearby. She'd been busy glowering at him, seething in envy as he held Rino in his arms.

"I have a question: How are same-sex relationships handled?"

"Oh, it's a wonderful thing. Particularly between two women. That's how love ought to be," she declared with a straight face.

"I wasn't asking for your personal opinion. I want to know how they're handled in the church," he added in complete exasperation.

"'Handled,' huh... They're not recommended since there would be no children in that union. The church won't release a public statement since there are a few people who are against doing that, but they aren't punished or anything."

"Surprisingly tolerant. I was sure they'd be super-strict, crying out 'kill all the gays!' You know, that sort of thing."

Throughout the history of Earth, there had been quite a few countries and religions that deemed homosexuality an inexcusable crime.

"But the primary deity *is* a woman, and the church doesn't really seem to take a strong stance on sex in general, so I guess it makes sense, once you think about it."

After all, the Materialistic Cardinal held one of the highest positions in the church, and he was public about his multiple lovers. Shinichi got the impression that the church didn't say much about their followers' sex lives as long as they weren't doing anything illegal.

"Meaning we won't run into any problems using *this* to negotiate."

If the possession of homosexual materials could lead to arrest, the risk would be too high, and the Holy Mother Cardinal would turn them down. Shinichi was relieved to hear that wasn't the case.

"And Rino, I'm sorry to ask you for a favor right off the bat, but I was wondering if you could introduce me to the dvergr who drew your picture book."

"I don't mind. Do you want a book drawn for you, too?"

"Yeah, uh-huh."

There was no way he was going to slip up and tell this innocent child that he wanted something with explicit boy-on-boy scenes.

"I can draw a little bit, but it's heavily stylized, inspired by the god of manga. What I need is something more detailed and artistic. Maybe even realistic."

The aesthetic tastes of this world were way different than Shinichi's, seeing that he was used to manga as a Japanese person. It was safest to go with a more realistic style when he took that difference into consideration.

"It'll take too long to draw if it's *hyper*realistic, though, and I need it to be finished quickly—"

"It's always so hard to understand what you're saying, Shinichi...," Rino murmured, warping her face into a dejected look.

"How about we go to meet the artist before we get too wrapped up in concerns?" suggested Celes with a pat on Shinichi's shoulder.

The group filed down to the basement of the castle to a room with a magic circle drawn on the floor.

"I shall be back shortly." Celes stepped on the magic circle, chanting the incantation for *Teleport*, and disappeared.

"Are there dvergr artists in the demon world?"

"Yessiree. Other than Grandpa Ivan, the others are down there. I guess the sky is too bright on the surface for them," Rino offered.

As they continued to chat, Celes reappeared with a short, rotund dwarf woman with blue-black skin.

"This is Lady Mimolette, an illustrator for children's books," Celes introduced.

"...Pleasure." Mimolette's face showed signs of fatigue as she bowed her head.

"You seem a little tired. Are you all right?" asked Arian, concerned.

"...Oh no, I'm just worrying about my craft," she grumbled. Her voice did seem to lack energy.

"Are you really okay?" He was growing worried.

"When she's inspired, she's unstoppable. I suppose it depends on what you need." Celes urged him to continue, though he remained hesitant.

"I'm sorry for calling you on such short notice. I was hoping you could draw a manga for me."

"Manga?" Mimolette echoed the unfamiliar word.

"It'll be easier to show you, I think. I have a digital copy of a weekly boy's manga magazine—" He slid his smartphone from his pocket, firing up the digital reader app. "You add words to the pictures, spice it up with some sound effects, divide them into panels. Rinse and repeat until it flows from drawing to drawing to tell a tale."

"Hmm, this is interesting." It was the first time she'd seen something of this sort. She was attracted to its novelty and technique, and a sparkle returned to her eyes. "With picture books, one page is one scene. That means long and complex stories are difficult to tell, but this resolves that issue. The successive panels make the pictures come to life. It may be hard to draw more pictures, but it might not be too bad, since it's restricted to black and white. The lines are simpler, too."

"One glance is enough for you to analyze all that, huh? So it's true: The dvergr really are geniuses…" Shinichi was petrified, but he held their talent in high esteem.

"Well then, I could easily use this manga style, but what is it you want me to draw?"

"Well, that…" He glanced to the side.

"Lady Rino, I believe it's time for your bath."

"Huh? But I want to listen to what Shinichi wants…," Rino protested as Celes gently nudged her toward the exit, obeying his pointed gaze.

"Lady Rino, I'll wash your back," chirped Sanctina as she chased after them, a trail of blood gushing out of her nose.

"Umm, should I go, too?" Arian offered, gathering from the situation that everyone should vacate the premises.

"No. You can stay if you want." He turned to the dvergr and very timidly started to explain his request. "It's a little bit of an embarrassing request. A boy-on-boy, hot-and-steamy love sto—"

"My kin!" she exclaimed with a twinkle in her eyes as she grabbed his hands before he could finish talking. "A fellow purveyor of romance between men! Oh, why didn't you tell me sooner? Ah yes, relationships between men and woman are bound by lust! It's much,

much better to witness a passionate friendship between men bloom into romance! Oh, their love is pure and true! Wouldn't you agree?"

"S-sure...," stammered Shinichi.

"Ask my pop, and he'll say it's 'unsanitary' and 'not for children'... And I'm like, 'It's not like I *wanna* show kids, you big, fat moron!' Like, shit! Can't you tell the difference?! And it's got nothin' to do with you! We're all free to draw whatever we like, ain't that right?! It's none of your friggin' business!"

"......"

Shinichi was at a loss. It was apparent that the dwarf had been bottling up all her frustration, and it was suddenly rushing out in a torrent of words.

"...I guess I know why you had artist's block. We're not gonna judge you—in fact, we'll cooperate—so could you please draw me a BL manga?"

"'Bee ell'?" asked Mimolette.

"It's short for Boys Love. In my world, that's what they call manga featuring love stories between two beautiful men. Also sometimes called *yaoi*."

"I see. BL, huh. *Yaoi*... Oh, joy. Hee-hee-hee," giggled the dvergr eerily, mirroring BL fangirls back on Earth. "Yes, let me draw this BL manga for you. But can you give me some ideas for the plot? It'll go faster if I have live models for the characters and speech."

"Models? Well, there's that man-loving incubus—" started Shinichi.

"DE-NIED!" boomed the dvergr with a severe expression. "Yeah, he's good looking and all, 'cause he's an incubus. He's got that going for him. But he only has eyes for sex, sex, sex! He'll force himself on any man! That makes him a rapist! If it was one of those stories that started off as a friends-with-benefits type situation and blossomed into love...I could go with that, but he's got no goals other than sex—and nothing else! That's not any different from hetero porn, now is it?!"

"Hmm, valid points."

"Besides! The best part is their initial resistance, right?! Like, 'I can't, but he's just so...' That's the part that gets me. But the dude doesn't even hesitate. Like, if he just bangs 'em and leaves, that makes him a gigolo! Shit, there's no love there—!" She howled from the very pit of her soul.

"Yes, of course," he agreed. "I'd be pretty angry if someone did the same thing with *yuri*, or girl-on-girl manga."

"Shinichi..." Arian was a bit disgusted, taking a tentative step back from Shinichi upon catching a glimpse of his true nature—a man from the bloodline of the pervert capital of the world, Japan.

At the same time, the dvergr seemed to be calming down from her tizzy, tiring herself out from all her shouting. "*Huff, huff*...sorry, anyway, not him, please."

"I'm sorry. I can't really think of any other models..."

"...You're pretty close with His Highness, aren't you?"

"Hey! No! Stop right there!" Every last bit of blood drained from Shinichi's face as the dwarf eyed him with a disgustingly suggestive look. Just imaging the final piece made Shinichi feel sick to his stomach. More importantly, he wouldn't live very long if the Demon King found a book pairing him and Shinichi just lying around the castle.

"But I can't get my creative juices flowing if I don't have models."

"Hmm, I don't have any manga or anime that would inspire BL situations. Or male idols that you could reference... Hey, Arian. Do you know any fairy tales that we could twist into a boy-on-boy story?"

"I wouldn't tell you even if I did...," Arian said curtly, shaking her head.

She'd really prefer not to insert a bunch of dudes into her mother's stories or the minstrels' tales, especially the ones that made her heart race with the idea of romance.

"If that's the case...there's nothing else we can do." Shinichi racked his brain for a moment before slipping his arm around Arian's shoulder with resolve. "Draw me and Arian."

"Oh? I didn't realize you're a boy in girl's clothing! Perfect!" Mimolette trilled.

"No! I'm a girl!" Arian shouted, pushing out her flat chest as proof, as the dvergr stopped pumping her fists in excitement.

"Tsk, a girl, huh. That's not gonna—"

"You fussy amateur!" Shinichi boomed. "Is that the extent of your fantasies?! Are you trying to tell me you can't change a girl into a boy in your mind's eye?!"

"…What…did you just say?!"

"If you really loved BL, you'd be able to pair a friggin' pencil and eraser together! Or turn a man into a woman! Entertain the possibilities of him getting pregnant and giving birth! Don't give me that bullshit! You can't even imagine a girl as a boy? Un-friggin'-believable."

"Um, Shinichi, I think standards in your country are out of whack…" Arian's face paled as she listened to him, but the dvergr chortled in response to his little pep talk.

"Heh-heh-heh. I guess I still have a long way to go… All right. I'll take you up on it and make the best BL manga!"

"Yeah! Attagirl! That's the spirit of a real BL fan!"

"I haven't agreed to this!" Arian protested frantically.

But he wasn't paying her any mind as he sauntered over to her without another word.

"Sh-Shinichi…?"

She could sense that he was different from his usual self. She took one, two steps back, banging into the wall behind her, preventing her from escaping his advances. Shinichi slammed his fist into the wall, supporting himself with one arm and leaning in.

"You might say no, but you're really into me, aren't you?"

"Y-yeah…"

He smirked devilishly, but his eyes were dead set on her. Arian's cheeks flushed red as she nodded slightly, yielding to him—

"Cut!" Mimolette screeched. "Cornering her into the wall is good, and your cocky lines are okay! But you!" She looked at Arian. "You can't just give in! You gotta build some tension in the scene. Up the ante! Resist his advances!"

"Say all you want, but I'm not sure I can reject him…"

"I'm sure you're unsatisfied about the way he treats you in some way or another, aren't ya? Look deep into your heart! And don't hold back! Tell him the truth—unapologetically!"

"……" Arian's expression clouded over with unexpected seriousness as she took Mimolette's pointers to heart, and she shoved Shinichi's chest, hard, with her two hands. "Stop it! I bet you say the same thing to the other girls!"

"What are you talking about?"

"Don't play dumb! I always see you hanging around her—giggling together. You don't even care about me!"

"…You're acting, right? This is all pretend, right?"

"Aaah! Wonderful! A conflict between lovers! An affair! I love it!"

Uh-oh. These accusations were all too real for Shinichi. He was starting to panic. In the background, the dvegr was getting riled up, giving them some more stage cues.

"All right, push him over!" Mimolette prompted.

"What?!"

"…This is all your fault, Shinichi." Arian swept her foot under his, and he came crashing down. She pounced on him, straddling him, tearing open his shirt with all her might, as he lay powerlessly under her. "I'll make my mark on your body! You won't be able to make eyes at someone else ever again!"

"Wait! Wait! Wait! Calm down! This is going too far!"

"Wooow—!" The dvergr whistled. "Switching positions? Reversing the top and bottom? Whew! I gotta say, words can't even begin to express my excitement! Oh, I curse how limited language is! How you betray me!"

"I think we'd call this a usurper— I mean, please stop!"

"Why won't you look at only me, Shinichi…?" murmured Arian as she brought her face closer until their lips, almost—

"—Having fun?" Celes asked, voice as frigid as the dead of winter, returning to the room after bathing Rino.

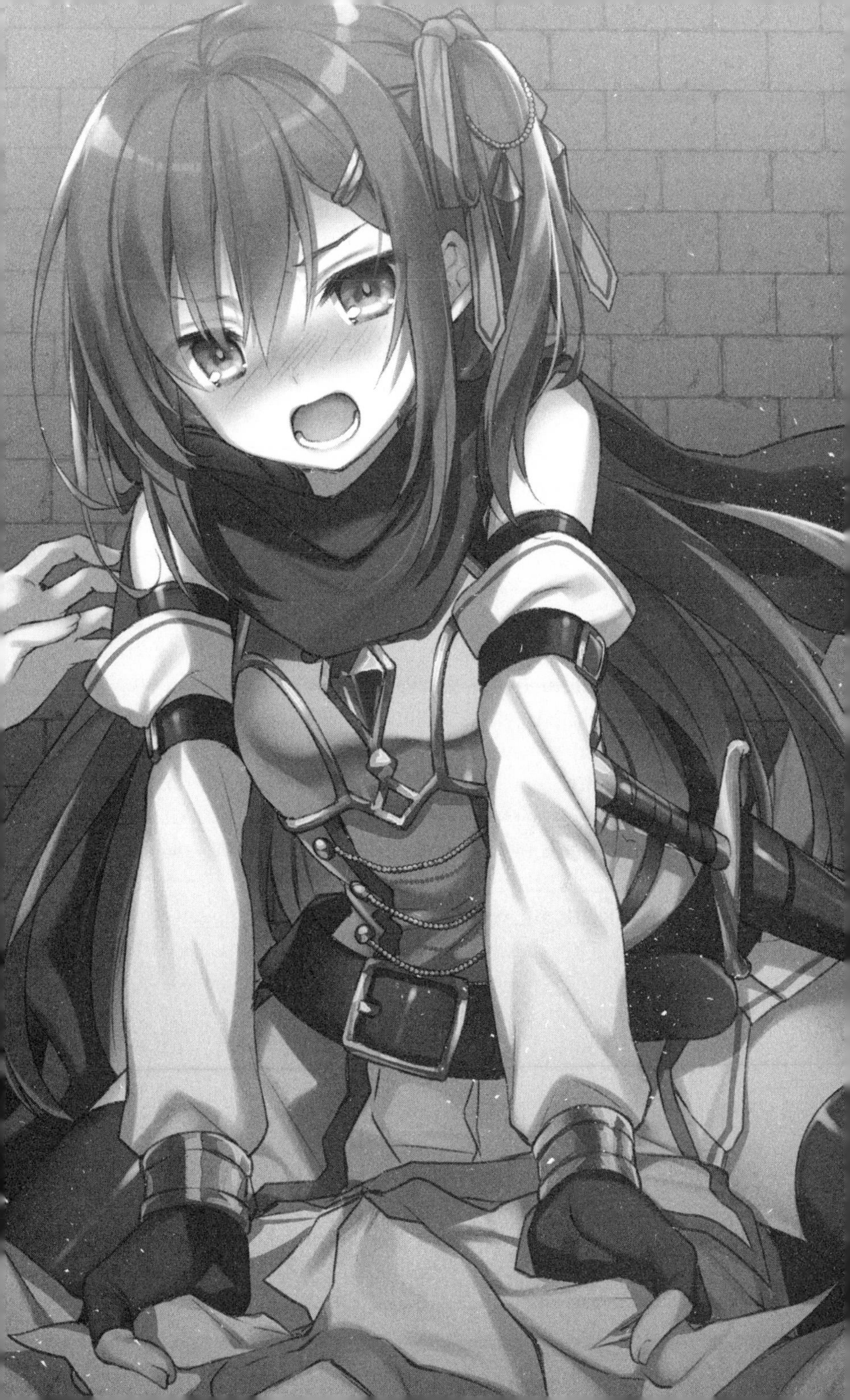

"Celes?! I-it's not! No! Aaaaah—!" Arian returned to her senses, totally startled at finding herself in a very compromising situation. She darted from the room, hiding her beet-red face.

"I believe this would make three times?" Celes let out a small sigh. She was unfortunately used to this sight by now.

She brusquely walked over to Shinichi as he lay in a heap on the floor.

"You saved me, Celes. Actually—"

"You can hold your excuses," she quipped, offering a hand to him as he wiped cold sweat from his brow.

Just as he was about to get up, Celes stamped his balls.

"—gh?!"

"You reap what you sow, right? I know who's to blame."

"Gah… That… might be true, but… Why are you ang—? Aaaaaagh—?!"

No mercy. Celes's foot came down again, leaving him bug-eyed and on the brink of fainting from the pain. She tossed him aside, pivoting sharply on her heels to leave the room.

"…You idiot," she whispered, leaving him with those words as he foamed from the mouth, twitching and convulsing.

There was one other person left in this room—

"Yes, yes, yes! Moan to me, charcoal! Dance with me, parchment! My gayest piece yet is ready to implode—!"

—the dvergr. With a flame burning in her eyes, she scribbled furiously, finishing off her sketches for a manga about boys with a dramatic flourish.

As he recalled these events, Shinichi's balls shrunk back into his body. But he managed to flash a villainous smirk in Vermeita's direction.

"Heh-heh-heh. I risked it all to act out the plot for this gem of a story arc. I bet it's your first time seeing something like this. One look, and it's enough to get you off, isn't it?"

"Th-this is—?!" gasped Vermeita, unable to form a full sentence.

An errant trail of blood trickled down her nose as she took in the drawings in all their glory. They depicted a tall, dashing young man with black hair cornered and straddled by an adorable redhead.

"You'll be able to read more BL manga in the future if you make a secret alliance with the demons. Not a bad deal, right?"

"You think I'd betray the church for these immodest materials? Try again!"

"Hmm... What exactly isn't to your liking?"

"For starters, the characters need to be younger; it would be so much better if they were young and pure with no clue about sexuality, you know, until they notice how *good* it feels to touch and prod each other; and then they become increasingly more sexual without knowing that it's wrong before slowly— Ack?!"

"Heh-heh-heh. Just as I would expect from a cardinal idolized by that flaming lesbian, Sanctina. You're into little gay boys? Kinky."

"Shall we rename her the Dirty Mother Cardinal?" Celes exhaled sharply, disappointed by her true identity.

Shinichi immediately began to pressure Vermeita. "So I wonder what'll happen if the world finds out about your wonderful little tastes?"

"If you do, I'll—"

"Hmm, if you activate these magic circles now, you'll eliminate us—along with the only existing copy of that manga."

"What?! I couldn't destroy such a beautiful story...!"

"Should I even bother to comment...?" Celes asked.

Shinichi gently laid his hand on Vermeita's shoulder; she was trembling lightly under his touch. "It'll be all right. It's fine if you want to cooperate with us in exchange for these steamy tales. It's a win-win situation."

"But I'm the cardinal. I'm supposed to be a role model. I can't betray the Goddess's teachings for such indecency..." A single tear rolled down her cheek as she battled with her inner shame.

In all honesty, she wasn't *that* worried about turning her back on the church. It would be much worse for her children to discover her secret desires and grow to resent her—or be disgusted by her tastes.

This type of shame wasn't exclusive to lovers of BL. There were lots of people with hidden preferences and desires, afraid that the world would look down on them for harboring lewd thoughts.

Shinichi faced her uncertainties and fears head-on. "Fine. There may be a few people who'd label you a creep. But consider this: Have you ever hurt anyone with your desires? Have you murdered anyone or stolen money?"

"Of course not! But..."

"I know: They'll look down on you even if it's not a crime. Listen, I hear ya. But let's put aside morals for now. We all have different perspectives, and we can't stop anyone from forming their opinions of us. That's why people tend to hide their innermost desires." Shinichi locked eyes with Vermeita. "But it doesn't matter if you're into little girls or boys! As long as it doesn't get out, it's totally okay!"

"It's totally okay?!"

"It doesn't matter how much you fantasize! As long as it's just a fantasy, it's not a crime!"

"It's not a crime?!"

"You're throwing out excuses like a red-handed criminal," Celes interrupted.

But Vermeita couldn't hear her and continued to quiver with uncertainty. "Does that mean I can look at two boys sharing a bed and fantasize about their conversations? *'You were a little rough, yesterday.' 'Shut up, you're embarrassing me.'* Are you telling me this is all okay?"

"Not guilty," Shinichi decreed.

"What if my dream is to become pope, make a school for boys, a choir of boys, and an entire church full of boys? What if I have ulterior motives to make a haven just for boys? To make more opportunities for them to fall in love with each other?"

"You didn't touch them. You didn't force them to fall in love. You're just creating an environment, which means you're... Not. Guilty."

"Ah...!" Vermeita fell to her knees, offering her prayers to Shinichi, as if he were a merciful deity, accepting all of her—including her sexual fantasies—gently in his arms. "I give up. I will make an alliance with the demons."

"Thank you. Love is our common language." He shot Celes a *sweet* smile, as if to tell her to back him up.

"This is too lewd for love," Celes commented, sighing for the umpteenth time.

And that marked the creation of a secret alliance between the demons and one of the cardinals—the Holy Mother Cardinal, Vermeita.

For a brief moment, Shinichi and Celes flew back to the castle of the Demon King to report back on this new development, teleporting back to the Holy City just as day broke.

But something in the city had changed overnight. The townspeople were uneasy and collectively heading closer to the center of the city.

"Excuse me. What's going on?" Shinichi asked a young boy walking by.

He offered a weak explanation, equally bewildered. "There's gonna be a big announcement at the Archbasilica. They asked everyone to come..."

"A big announcement?"

"I don't really know what it's for. We're not even close to the Advent Festival. It could be that His Holiness has..." It would be irreverent to say any more. He cut himself off short and wandered off.

"How should we proceed?" Celes asked.

"Erm, could you put Vermeita on the line with *Telepathy*?"

"I don't think that's wise. I do not know her very well, nor do I know her current whereabouts."

"Right. I imagine she's left the orphanage to go straight to the Arch-basilica, but…"

It would certainly be fastest to ask her directly. But if that wasn't possible, he needed to come up with another plan.

After a while, he started to move with the flow of the crowd, follow-ing their lead. "Let's go see what's happening. I can't imagine Vermeita has already betrayed us. She'd never use such a huge event to trap us, I think."

"Understood."

The two headed to the heart of the Holy City, right to the front of the Archbasilica—a large, empty square to host ceremonies and festivals.

Tens of thousands of people were crowded in the space, milling around, heads dipping and ducking like bobbing potatoes in a sink.

Shinichi didn't like the thought of being caught up in a wave of people. That could be potentially hazardous, since his reaction time would be significantly delayed. Instead, the pair stood in the shadows of a distant building, where he asked Celes to cast *Telescope* to observe the entire ordeal.

"Huh. I wonder what's gonna happen," he muttered.

The clamorous crowd of spectators hushed, and a series of figures began to appear on the balcony of the Archbasilica.

There were only three of the four cardinals: the Agreeable Cardi-nal, the Materialistic Cardinal, and the Holy Mother Cardinal. For no apparent reason, the Elderly Cardinal was nowhere to be found.

This riled up the audience, as their voices rose up in surprise and suspicion. In the midst of their chaos, Vermeita stepped forward to speak on behalf of the rest.

"I would like to share some unfortunate news. Our longtime spir-itual guide, Cardinal Cronklum, retired from his position yesterday, choosing to return to a simpler life."

"""…Huuuh?!""" It took the crowd a full beat to make sense of her announcement. They started to blubber and burst out in confusion.

In the past, members of the church stepped down when they became too old to perform their duties. This was true for those chosen as undying heroes, too. The pope was the only exception to this rule.

But everyone knew that Cronklum was in good health. It was true that he was in his seventies and jeeringly called the Elderly Cardinal, but he was still lively enough to surround himself with multiple lovers. He'd been so close to becoming the next pope. It was way too sudden for him to abandon his position and go back to the simple life, or whatever.

Shinichi wasn't quite as surprised as the rest of the onlookers, but he'd be lying if he said he wasn't confused. "Do you think he was forced to resign over the whole Sanctina thing? I feel like it's too early for that..."

But there wasn't enough time for him to form his thoughts. Vermeita spoke again. "And in Cronklum's stead, we'd like to welcome a new cardinal to the church."

She gestured to the side, and a man took his time to step forward onto the balcony.

When they saw his full figure, Shinichi and Celes's eyes nearly popped out of their heads.

"Why the hell is he...?!"

It was a man in his early thirties, smiling serenely without a hint of a dark or turbulent personality. In the robes of a cardinal, his dress was more opulent than in the past, but he was unmistakable.

There was no way they'd confuse him with anyone else.

This was the man who'd bullied the king of Boar Kingdom into dispatching the troops upon demonkind without so much as an attempt to investigate or reconcile their differences. It wouldn't be a stretch to label him as the person responsible for lighting the fires of war.

"Please give your warmest welcomes to Cardinal Hube."

There was a short pause where Vermeita seemed to tense her jaw.

It was followed by a smattering of applause. The crowd was in a state of shock. Shinichi and Celes were unable to process what was happening before their eyes, frozen in place as if they were statues carved from stone.

A few hours before the announcement of the new cardinal, a young priest let out a heavy sigh. He'd been charged with guarding the dungeon below the Archbasilica, aptly named the Pit of Divine Punishment.

"Hey, it's about time to do the rounds," one of his colleagues called out.

"Oh man. How 'bout you go for me this time? Drinks on me later."

"No way in hell. I'm not about to walk around this place at night."

Not that it mattered if it was night or day. It could very well be either, since no light ever reached depths of the Pit. But there'd been rumors circulating that the ghosts of heroes past haunted the place, roaming around at night. It was far too eerie for him.

"*Haaah.* I don't wanna go," the young priest protested dejectedly, but he obediently left the guardroom and descended the stairs farther underground.

It wasn't a real problem since the majority of the imprisoned heroes were rendered harmless after they'd endured great psychological torment. But they had been some of the most gifted fighters of all time before their fall.

If they managed to snap back to their senses, they could easily slam through the wrought-iron doors or dig their way through the walls with a *Tunnel* spell. That was why these regular rounds were critical—especially for those on the highest floor, those who managed to cling to their sanity. They were the most dangerous of all.

"Dammit, I wish they'd just transfer me already." He shuddered at the beastly howls of the insane, ricocheting down the halls.

He stopped at every cell and peered through the small window on the iron doors to check on the prisoners. To the relief of the priest, most of them were sleeping quietly, with the exception of one.

He halted in his tracks when he heard a voice.

"Y-you…? Can you really be…? Ah…!"

It rang out of the closed cell of their newest prisoner, the ex-bishop of Boar Kingdom—Hube.

"Y-yes… I'm incredibly grateful… Everything will be as you intend!"

He was the only person in his cell, but it sounded as if he was having a conversation. His energetic chattering spilled through the halls.

Oh, how pitiful. He couldn't handle this, huh?

The Pit of Divine Punishment housed some of the most heart-wrenching groans and screams. The turnover rate for the guards was high; many were unable to withstand it.

It wasn't all that surprising for a prisoner to have a breakdown after they'd been subjected to that noise twenty-four seven.

Well, I suppose he'll be happier that way. Better that than suffering through this hell for who-knows-how-many years. As the young priest continued this thought, he peeked through the window of the cell. That's when the iron door was blasted from the inside out.

"Gah—!"

The door flew across the hall, taking the priest with it and crashing hard into a wall. Shrieking in agony, he lay in a crumpled heap on the ground.

As he started to slip from consciousness, he saw the face of the man stepping calmly out of his cell. It wasn't the face of a man suffering from confusion or insanity. It housed a smile as bright and breezy as the sky on a sunny day.

"Emergency…situation… Hube has escaped…" With the last of his remaining strength, the young priest sent a telepathic message to his colleagues. Then he passed out.

Within a minute, a squad of heavily armed holy warriors sprang down to the upper floor of the Pit. But Hube was nowhere to be found, vanished into the night.

"He's not here! Has he already escaped the Pit?!"

"Get the patrols outside! We can't let him get away!"

"Wait, there's no magical residue left of the *Tunnel* or *Teleport* spell. He should still be inside."

"But he's not in his cell. Could he have gone farther down...?"

But why would he run deeper into the Pit when it clearly didn't have an escape route? The holy warriors weren't certain of the reasons, but they hustled down the stairs, trudging deeper into the Pit, dashing onto the floor above the torture room, the lowest level of them all.

That was where they spotted the former bishop. His back was turned to them.

"Don't move! There's nowhere to run!" boomed the squad captain of the holy warriors, pointing his halberd at Hube. "You should have stayed in your cell! I can't believe you'd act so foolishly."

These attempted escapees were deemed high risk. They were made powerless—in other words, psychologically tortured to the point of insanity. The squad captain wasn't without some sympathy for these people, but he intended to fulfill his duty and signaled for his squad to circle around Hube.

But they were far too late.

"...Heh."

No sooner had he turned around with a genial smile on his face than chains of light snapped out of thin air, tightly binding each of the holy warriors.

"Huh, a *Photon Bind*?!" yelped the squad captain.

In a hurry, they cast *Dispel*, but its iron grip wouldn't budge an inch.

"This is insane! How can he cast such a powerful spell on everyone without reciting an incantation...!"

The squad captain and Hube should have had comparable magical strength. After all, the captain had similar magical skill to the average bishop.

But he couldn't wiggle out of this binding spell, even though it should have been weaker without an incantation. In other words, the difference between the two was like a newborn baby and a grown-ass adult.

"Impossible! How did he get so strong in such a short time—? Ack?!"

There was one possibility. It raced in the back of his head.

It had been a miracle: a certain young man, a humble woodcutter, who'd transformed into a formidable magic user overnight.

"N-no... It can't be...?!"

"...Ha-ha." Hube chuckled at the squad captain, who was quivering upon this realization.

Sauntering to the nearby iron door, Hube cast *Unlock* without an incantation, opening the door that'd been shut for the past few decades.

The prisoner inside let out whoops of excitement and came tumbling from the room.

"Aaaahoooa—!" Saliva spewed from the corner of the elderly man's mouth as he sputtered, as if he were a rabid dog ready to attack. Hube stood directly in front of him, stopping him with one swift motion, and lifting him toward the ceiling.

"You poor criminal. I'll put an end to your suffering now." He began to cast his spell as the raging man tried to claw free from his grasp. "Forget all your sins. *Uninstall*."

The wave of magic pulsed from his palm into the man's brain, burning through neuron after neuron.

"Ah..." For a moment, the man made a sound as if he had suddenly regained his sanity, but then he seemed to lose all the energy from his body and hung limply in Hube's arms.

But Hube wasn't done yet. "You are now the obedient vanguard of the Goddess. *Install*."

The elderly man's brain started as a blank slate, and new information was being etched into it.

"Ah, ah, ah." As if shocked by electricity coursing through his nervous system, he convulsed a few times then stopped moving.

Hube released his grip on the man, and he held himself up as his feet landed on the ground, spine straight. The man's face was tense, put together. It didn't carry any semblance of the unrestrained beast from before. At the same time, his expression was completely blank: It held no joy, no anger, no fear.

"Wh-what…? What have you done?!" The squad captain was unable to process anything. He only knew that this was something absolutely horrifying.

Hube calmly turned to the shrieking, pale-faced captain. "Will you all join me? Or will you become the Goddess's vanguard?" he threatened.

They had their choice: join him willingly or be brainwashed. No other options. There wasn't even room to resist. Trembling from fear and humiliation, they nodded respectfully. To this, Hube smiled, satisfied.

"That's all."

As soon as he said that, the chains of light dissipated. But no one tried to run. If they did, they'd be caught instantly, and their minds would be erased—just look at that elderly guy. They shook and emptied their bladders at the thought.

"Well then, open the doors please."

The captain hurriedly unlocked them. Hube stopped the escaped prisoners one by one, erasing their minds so that all that remained was the empty vessels of their bodies—tools for the gods.

After their top-secret discussion came to a close and the advisor of the Demon King took his leave, Vermeita read, reread, and re-reread the

BL manga before finally climbing into bed. But that didn't last long. She was rudely awakened by a telepathic message.

"Cardinal Vermeita. Bad news. Please come to the Archbasilica as quickly as possible!"

The voice belonged to the bishop in charge of security at the Archbasilica. The fact that he was contacting the cardinals directly meant that this situation was urgent. Vermeita leaped from her bed and threw on her cardinal robes over her thin nightgown, picking up her well-loved iron cane and dashing from the orphanage.

"What's happened?"

"H-Hube has escaped from the prison, releasing the other prisoners so they'll join him. Even the guards have his back…"

"…I'm sorry. What?"

"Hube has escaped, and he's leading a revolt!"

The hysterical scream echoed in her mind. She furrowed her brow and forced more strength into her legs to run.

"Okay, so Hube has escaped. But I don't understand how he got the guards to join him, much less the mentally ill prisoners. How did he manage that?"

"I have no idea!! Please hurry, hurry, and save us! If you don't—ah?!"

The telepathic connection cut out after that final scream. Vermeita felt sweat drip uncomfortably down her back, but she strengthened herself with *Physical Enchantment*, feet pounding through the night, running faster than an arrow.

Just as she arrived in front of the Archbasilica, three shadows descended from the sky.

"Ah, youngsters. So full of energy."

"Indeed. We hardly have the energy left to run here."

"My belly has gotten so heavy, too heavy. The girls are always harping on me to lose weight, but I'm just not up to it."

The Elderly Cardinal. The Agreeable Cardinal. The Materialistic Cardinal.

The three chattered pointlessly as they released their *Fly* spells and landed softly on the ground, but their faces mirrored Vermeita's—full of unchecked concern.

"Well then, shall we go see the face of the foolish escapee?" Cronklum suggested as he led the four into the Archbasilica.

Inside, it was uncomfortably quiet. Not a single escaped prisoner or a priest to be found.

"......"

Their feet silently shuffled forward, carrying them to the prayer room in the center of the building. Beyond its heavy doors, they found the person in question surrounded by a crowd.

"I've been waiting, cardinals." At a leisurely pace, Hube turned from the statue of the Goddess upon finishing offering his prayers.

A warm smile pulled at his face. It was as if he was a different man from the one who'd spewed hysterical fury and antagonism when he'd been dragged out of this exact same room.

But upon closer inspection, there was something dark and murky that glinted in his eyes. It manifested in the looks of the holy warriors around him, as their expressions showed nothing short of sheer terror.

What on Earth...? Vermeita couldn't get a good read on the situation as she looked from face to face of the obedient holy warriors and the group of people directly facing them: the former heroes who'd been psychologically broken and imprisoned for the heinous crimes.

Their faces reminded her of dolls, completely devoid of emotion as they stood stock-still at attention, like a line of toy soldiers. Every fiber of Vermeita's being was screaming at her to run, and while she fought to control her instincts, Cronklum took a heroic step forward.

"Hube, what exactly are you trying to do?"

"Oh, isn't it obvious?" Hube spread his hands with a rapturous expression on his face. "I vow to eliminate the evil demons and all the sinful humans on their side from this world. That's the will of the Goddess Elazonia!"

"......"

It was clear that they weren't on the same page. Cronklum muttered under his breath, "I guess you've finally cracked..." He let out a long sigh. "Yes, you're right. That is the Goddess's will. But it is not a duty for a criminal to take on. Return to the prison. Go on. *Photon Bind.*"

The chains of light reached out to ensnare Hube's body—and shattered into fragments of light.

"What in the—?!"

"It's all futile. There's no one in this world who can capture me now." In a dramatic gesture, he showed the backs of his hands. "For I've been chosen by the Goddess Elazonia as the true messiah!"

He revealed the shining golden symbol of the Goddess on the backs of both hands.

"What's that supposed to mean?!" shouted Cronklum in confusion.

"Don't you understand? Fine, let me demonstrate on you."

As he chanted, Hube thrust both glowing hands in the cardinal's direction. He spoke as if to clear away his deep-seated resentment, which had brewed for as long as he was locked away in the dark prison.

"—You're not fit to be a hero."

As Hube's voice echoed through the room, Cronklum's right hand started to burn, as if seared by a branding iron, and the symbol slowly peeled itself off from his skin. A throbbing, excruciating pain overcame his senses.

"GAAAAAAAAH—!" His screams filled the chambers as the symbol completely flaked off his hand, scattering into a million tiny embers of light before disappearing to the heavens.

That was the moment an undying hero—one with protection from the Goddess—fell and became a simple old man.

"Th-that's impossible; m-my undying status..."

"Thank you for your service, Cronklum." Hube addressed him without his title.

The old man crumpled feebly to the ground.

Then Hube turned his attention to the three remaining cardinals, frozen in place. "Well, then. Would you all be so kind as to assist me?"

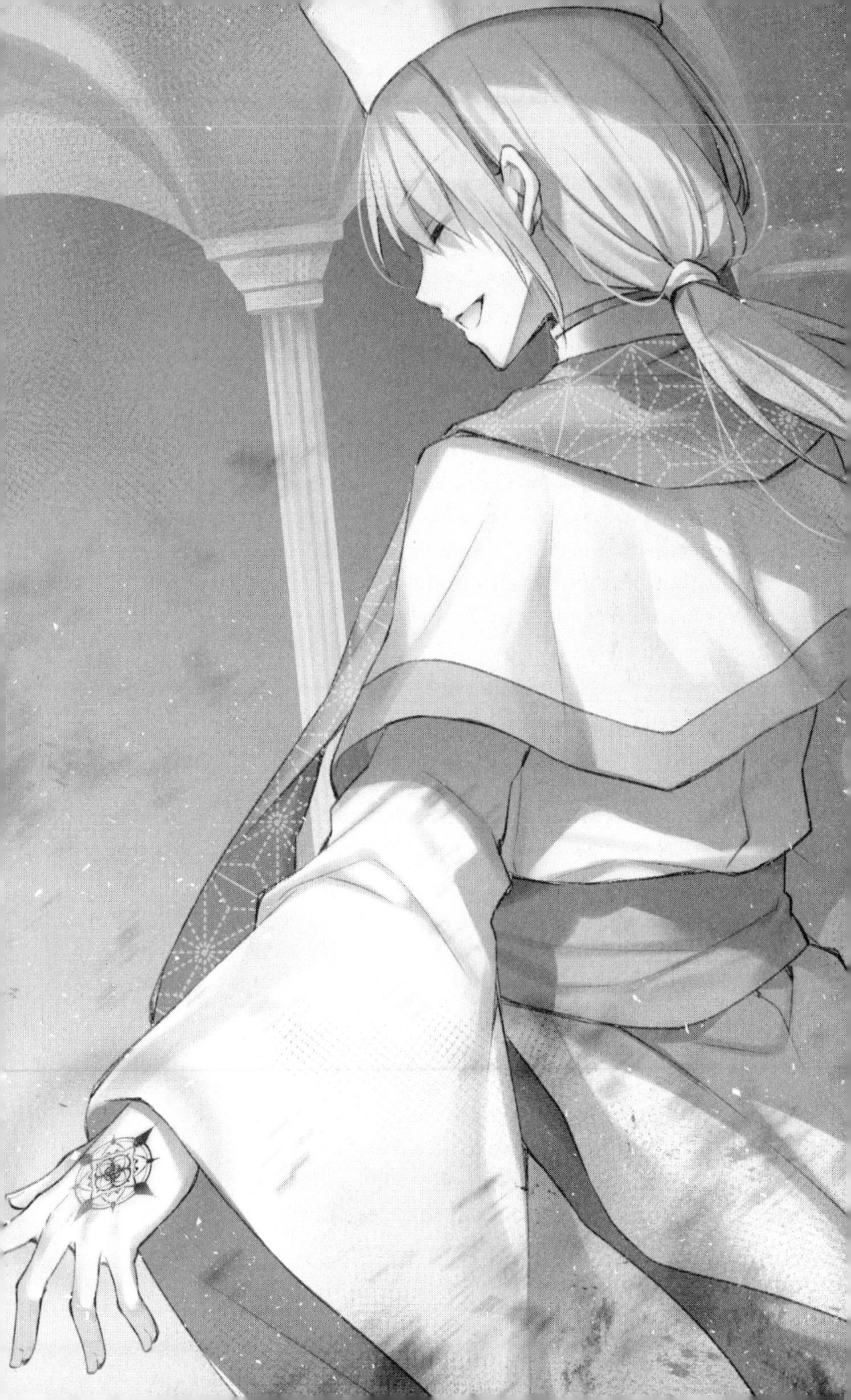

At this point, it wasn't a question. It was a thinly veiled threat under the guise of a command.

He had the power to remove their right to receive infinite resurrections, which was exclusively granted to the Goddess's chosen few. The man in front of them was like the first pope, Eument— No, he might have been stronger than him. Faced with his power, they had no choice but to accept him as the messiah.

Vermeita clenched her jaws to keep them from chattering in fear. Along with the other two cardinals, she lowered herself to a knee and bowed her head.

Is he really the messiah? No, if he's using violence to control people, he's like the—

She couldn't let these words slip out. She had to keep them in.

—He's like the Demon King, she'd wanted to say.

Back to the public announcement.

Shinichi was frozen from shock as he looked at Hube, who'd been appointed as the new cardinal. The rest of the onlookers exhibited a similar uneasiness, chattering nervously among themselves.

"Anyone remember who this 'Hube' guy is?"

"I feel like there was a bishop that went by that name…"

"Oh yeah. I think he was responsible for some region, but I heard he was a huge dud."

Other than members of the clergy and merchants—who were always up-to-date on the latest news—the average city dweller hadn't known much about Hube, including his name. Of all people, why had *this* man been suddenly promoted to the rank of cardinal?

Hube attempted to quell the confusion that rang through the crowd. "Brothers and sisters, there is only one reason why I have been made cardinal. And that's to enact the Goddess Elazonia's will... In other words, wipe the demons in the western lands of Dog Valley from the face of this world!"

""""......""""" The spectators were further confused by his fanatical speech.

"Defeating the demons, well yeah... That's a given."

"I mean, is it even true that these legendary demons or whatever have come to this world?"

"Yeah, they definitely exist. They crushed the troops of Boar Kingdom and even defeated a few heroes."

"Oh, that's right! I'm pretty sure Hube was originally the bishop in Boar Kingdom, but I thought he was arrested for doing indecent things to that hero, Red..."

As the crowd started to murmur about his terrible reputation, the onlooker's glances turned increasingly icy cold at Hube. Not that he noticed. He kept yakking on, as if conversing with the Goddess, invisible to their eyes.

"I understand that you're afraid. The demons are far more powerful than humans. Evil! Cunning! Cruel!" By the way his voice quivered in fury, one could only think he had a certain twisted bastard in mind. He gestured grandly. "But have no fear! We are protected by the mighty grace of our Lady Elazonia!"

With that, thousands of members of the church filed out of the Archbasilica, forming ranks in front of the crowd. Their faces didn't show ambition and bravery: They showed deep unease and disapproval.

"Why is this criminal...?"

"You saw, didn't you? Everyone on duty last night was standing there trembling. I don't know what happened, but I know we shouldn't resist."

They didn't know the details of the night before, but the cardinals had ordered them, which left them no other options but to go along with whatever this was.

Hube turned to the uncertain clergy members. "Crusaders for our

Goddess Elazonia! You will now receive an undying body so that we may destroy the evil demons— You are fit to be heroes!"

A blinding light was unleashed from his hands, bursting forward from the symbols of the Goddess. It coursed through the air, breaking off into infinite new iterations of itself, melding into the hands of the clergy.

"Ack?! Is this the proof of a hero?"

"No way. Does that mean we're heroes now, too…?"

They'd longed for this divine privilege, but they were afraid to ask for her blessing and risk rejection. There were some that had tried and failed.

But now they were all heroes. This was one source of their bewilderment. The other was that it had not been Goddess Elazonia who had granted them this blessing—but a new cardinal.

"To endow this proof onto us… Only the first pope, Eument, could do such a thing…"

"Does that mean that Hube is…I mean, *Cardinal* Hube has been given the Goddess's power? Does that make him the messiah?!"

A single cry turned into a buzz, then a chatter that spread through the thousands of clergymen, until it became a roar among the tens of thousands of onlookers. Once everyone had finally grasped the meaning of the miracle before their eyes, Hube calmly addressed the crowd once again.

"The chosen few. The new heroes. Death is beyond you! In the spirit of the Goddess Elazonia banishing the Evil God into the depths of the earth, we, too, will defeat the evil demons!"

""""Yeah… Yeeaaah!""""

"This is a battle for holiness… Yes, a crusade!"

""""Whooooooooooa—!""""

The confused murmurs had long disappeared, replaced with an earth-shattering cheer. In the face of this historic moment, the only people who didn't share that joy were the three cardinals, and of course, Shinichi and Celes, who were tucked away in the shadows of a building.

"That's insane… Thousands and thousands of heroes? You've got to be kidding me..." Even he couldn't have predicted Hube's return to power and the birth of the army of heroes. "I'd thought about what we would do if we couldn't get a cardinal to work with us, but what the hell are we gonna do about this...?"

He'd managed to turn two heroes, Arian and Sanctina, but each one took a number of days to persuade to switch sides. Now he had to multiply that by thousands, and he couldn't be sure that their numbers wouldn't grow even more.

"I was able to break Ruzal and his guys—five in one go—but that was dumb luck. Even if I could manage ten per day..."

It would take them twenty days to walk from the Holy City to Dog Valley and the Demon King's castle. To move thousands of soldiers, they'd need to secure food, water, and shelter. That would slow down their advances considerably.

But that wasn't the case for their newest enemy: Every member was a priest or holy warrior. They could use *Physical Enchantment* spells and treat themselves with magic. The biggest problem of all was that they were undying heroes. They would be able to trudge through this hellish march.

"Eh, let's just say it takes them twenty days. Rough estimate. Even if I managed to do ten people a day, that's only two hundred... It's impossible. There's nothing I can do."

After he'd rationally calculated the situation, he knew with certainty that doom was coming—and fast. His back slid down the wall of the building, and he crumpled to the ground.

These newfound heroes were weaker than the usual ones, as they wielded the strength and capacity of the average priest. A group of a few dozen wasn't enough to take on Arian or Sanctina, even if they worked alone.

But there were thousands upon thousands...upward of ten thousand. And they'd all be ready to attack.

"I knew war was all about having the largest troop, but..."

But the almighty Blue Demon King would be able defeat a few

thousand men, easy. After all, he'd blasted away three thousand soldiers from Boar Kingdom in one fell swoop. What difference did one, maybe two, times make?

But the third time? The fourth? The fifth? They could come back to attack infinite times: an army of zombies springing back from the dead. It was only a matter of time until the demons were defeated.

"Is our only option to retreat to the demon world? But that'd mean leaving behind the people of Tigris Kingdom..."

They'd be branded heretics, allies of the demons—starting with the captain, King Sieg, down to all the other jolly miners and exuberant children. The church would slaughter everyone that Shinichi had gotten to know through Rino's live performances.

He needed to quash this horde of heroes. He'd do whatever it took to stop them. But he couldn't conjure a single strategy, even as he racked through every inch of his brain.

"What are we going to do...? What should we do...?!" Shinichi cradled his head in his hands, crushed under the full weight of his responsibility. In a frenzy, he desperately tried to think of a plan. But the more he panicked, the less he could think.

A shadow cast over him as he writhed in torment.

He looked up to see the maid towering over him, hiking up the hem of her skirt in both hands. "Celes...?"

Before he could follow up, she lifted her right foot and slammed it into the wall behind him, grazing his cheek as her shoe sailed past it.

"Ack?! You *trying* to kill me?!"

"Keep up your spineless whining, you freeloader, and I'll toss your corpse to the *parbeguts*."

"Hold up, do *parbeguts* eat people?!" he screeched, voice cranking up a notch.

He'd heard its name being thrown around a few times, but he still hadn't cast eyes on this mystery animal.

Seeing he'd returned to his normal self, Celes cracked some semblance of a smile before glancing away. "Please try not to look so uncool."

—Put on that sinister smirk of yours and solve this problem. That's what I want to see. She didn't have to say as much, but color crept into her cheeks anyway as she sulked.

Shinichi forgot his worries for a moment as he was a little charmed by this sight.

"...Celes, I can see your panties."

"I'm letting you see them." She was acting a little too bashful for that bold proclamation, slipping her foot off the wall and dusting off pieces of errant brick from her shoe. "Now that I've paid my dues, I need you to hurry up and deliver some of your dirty tricks."

"Couldn't you have come up with something hotter?"

"Aren't they red-hot today?"

"That's not what I meant! And side note, nothing's better than white panties against olive skin! Mmm! That contrast!" Shinichi couldn't keep himself from laughing at their usual sexual schtick. "Heh-heh-heh, you're right. It's not like me to get pushed into a corner in a panic. I should be the one doing all the cornering. 'Cause I'm the advisor for the Blue Demon King, Shinichi Sotoyama."

"And that's the bare truth."

"Seriously? A pun?" yelped Shinichi as he shuddered at her joke, but his senses had come back to him and the gears in his mind started to move. "We don't have time to take down the heroes one by one... Could we break them all at once? Nah. I won't be able to break them with something half-assed, since their morale is, like, off the charts... Plus, they can kill themselves and escape, so we can't imprison them anywhere..."

He shot a quick glance at Hube, standing over them on the balcony, and then at the new heroes in the crowd as they continued to cheer wildly. Shinichi shook his head.

"It's impossible. There's no way to defeat an army of heroes." But the moment he muttered that, the corners of his mouth twitched up into a diabolical grin. "If there's no way to defeat them...then we don't need to beat them."

"I'm guessing you've come up with something." She knew that much, even though she couldn't solve his riddle-like words, as she broke into a smile.

He smirked back. "Let's give that pedo-Cardinal Hube and his motley crew something to cry about. They've bitten off more than he can chew. But first—"

"First?"

"Could ya fix that wall with magic?"

"…Forgive me." Celes's face burned as he pointed to the wall, a huge chunk missing from the sheer force of her foot.

The crowd still hadn't died down when Hube spun around to leave the balcony, tailed silently by the other three cardinals. Upon returning to the prayer room, Hube hunkered down in the seat in the middle of the room with dramatic flair. It was the chair of the bedridden pope.

"Cardinal Snobe, prepare the necessary resources to mobilize the army."

"Yes, sir."

"This crusade may be an offering for the Goddess, but the church's coffers still belong to her. Do you understand what I'm trying to say?"

"…Of course." The Materialistic Cardinal bowed his head in order to hide the visible displeasure in his eyes.

Hube was implying that he should shell out his personal funds to pay for the food and lodging and weapons to equip thousands of soldiers— every little thing between here and Dog Valley. It wouldn't be impossible for Snobe to cover these costs. His pockets were lined deep enough. But he'd have to live frugally in the future to compensate for his losses.

He wouldn't have minded if he were spoiling his mistresses with lavish gifts. But for this loathsome scum? He didn't want to waste a single copper coin.

Snobe thought about Cronklum, overcome with shock when his status as a hero was stripped from him. In an instant, he'd become older, aged considerably and half-senile. With these threats in mind, his only possible choice was to comply.

"Cardinal Effectus, I would like you to oversee the Holy City in my stead."

"Indeed," replied Effectus.

"And focus on the wretches attempting to sleep with the wives and girlfriends of other men. Make sure they're handled accordingly. We can't have anyone act immorally."

"Leave it to me." Unlike Snobe, the Agreeable Cardinal was eager to accept these orders.

As a blind follower of the Goddess's teachings, Effectus regarded Hube as the second coming of Eument. Hube's words may as well have been words from the Goddess's own mouth. With a personal goal of enforcing public morals, Effectus had no interest in love affairs and a particular dislike of philanderers like the Materialistic Cardinal.

"Thank you for your help." Hube got out of his chair and sauntered out of the prayer room without so much as a word to Vermeita.

He saw all women as filthy traitors. Maybe.

Ha-ha-ha. If we weren't in such a pickle, I really could have enjoyed this situation...

Vermeita smirked over her dirty fantasies even under these tense circumstances. But she desperately needed this escape. Backed into a corner, she couldn't have kept her cool without her lewd thoughts. *He isn't just able to take away a hero's status. He can grant it, too... There's nothing anyone can do to stand against him.*

It wouldn't be an exaggeration to claim that the church was able to maintain its power and control with the support of these undying heroes. It was the reason the Goddess's teachings traversed the continent at breakneck speed. It gave the bishops and cardinals in the upper ranks confidence. It granted a feeling of complete security.

Once the chosen few were blessed with this gift, they hadn't needed to fear that it could be taken away. Other than reaching the end of their natural life span, there was no way they could die.

Who could ever stand against the terror of having that stripped away?

And then there's those prisoners and their empty minds…

Expressionless as dolls, they never spoke a word, listening to Hube's every command and following orders obediently. Shivers ran down Vermeita's spine whenever she caught sight of those living marionettes. Even their tormented minds had been ripped away from them.

If Hube keeps going and becomes pope, there is a chance that will happen to everyone in the Holy City…

Any dissenters would have their minds erased. It would turn into a city full of slaves to the Goddess. How would that be any different from the undead milling around the city of the deceased?

We have to do something…

If they didn't, the world would begin to deny her even the purest, honest love between two boys. There wouldn't be a shred of anything undignified in sight.

Humans are ugly and rotten creatures… Can you call something "living" if it isn't?

Vermeita left the prayer room. Someone had to do something to stop Hube, but who could stand against him, especially as the supposed messenger of the Goddess? She didn't have a single clue. Her feet carried her forward. Eventually, she realized that she'd arrived at the orphanage on the outskirts of the city.

"Welcome home, Mother!"

"It's nice to be back." Trying her hardest to hide her dark fears, she broke into a smile at the children's beaming faces as they ran up to greet her.

The eldest girl walked up hesitantly. "Mother, this was delivered while you were gone…" She held out an envelope with the name Manju scrawled on the back.

"Thank you." Vermeita took it from her with a smile, stopping her quivers from erupting to the surface. To prevent the children from suspecting anything, she took her time to hug each one tightly before heading to her room.

She locked the door behind her, finally ripping open the envelope when she was alone. The letter was packed with words in a neat, graceful script, making her think the dark elf had written as the boy dictated.

"...I see." As she read through it, a smile slipped onto her face, chasing away her brooding expression. "No intentions of giving up, huh, even in the face of thousands of heroes."

The letter didn't contain minute details of their plan, which made it difficult to gauge if their strategies would be successful. They must have taken this extra precaution out of suspicion that Vermeita would turn on them. But with Hube on his way to world domination, she was willing to take this gamble.

"Even if they defeat demonkind, it won't make my current situation any worse than it already is."

After all, she was only responsible for assisting with the cleanup, which meant she wouldn't interact with Hube directly or incur his wrath if things went south. She had nothing to lose even if she accepted the directions in the letter.

"But I do want the demons to live. Otherwise, I wouldn't be able to read Ms. Mimolette's newest piece. Hee-hee-hee."

Vermeita took the BL manga out of its hiding spot in her desk, a rotten smile spreading out.

Meanwhile, as thousands of heroes were dispatched from the Holy City, hordes of people were ramming their way into the cathedral in Tigris Kingdom, far to the north.

"No need to rush. Please proceed slowly. There's plenty to go around!"

"You there! No cutting! Join the line at the end where you see the sign!" With Arian and a group of Rino's fanboys skillfully directing throngs of people into neat lines, they were able to prevent any serious brawls from breaking out. In any case, the crowd couldn't hide their obvious anticipation as they moved forward in the long line.

It led to the prayer room deep inside the cathedral, right to the massive crystal—the national treasure of Tigris Kingdom, a magic conductor called the Tears of Matteral. One by one, they approached this huge hunk of rock, making contact to pour their magic into it.

"Woah! That made me dizzier than I thought it would..." A young man walked unsteadily, unsure of his footing after he was drained of his magic.

"Are you all right? Should I cast a little healing spell?" Rino asked, concern coating her voice.

"Nah, I'll be all right." He flashed her a smile, grounding himself down through his toes and heading toward the back of the room.

There, Celes stood in front of a mountain of gold, handing a piece to each person for their participation. "Thank you for your help. Please make sure to get plenty of rest today." She placed a nugget in his hand.

"I—I will! I can't believe you're giving us so much..." It was equivalent to two days' pay for hard labor in the mines. He was almost drunk off his excitement.

Though he would have trouble moving about for the greater half of the day, this was more than enough compensation for his troubles.

"Wow! If it's this easy to make money, I might just come back tomorrow." He exited the rear door, ecstatic.

There were those who came to make a little extra cash, like the young man. Others were fans of Rino. Together, they formed a long line that snaked out the doors of the cathedral.

The Tears of Matteral was beginning to shine luminously, eagerly gulping down magical energy from the people in line. Sanctina gazed up at it with a complicated expression on her face.

"I know this is a testament to Rino's charisma, but it's just so different from when I..." Her eyebrows scrunched as she remembered her own tribulations when she'd been tasked with gathering magic. Instead of a line out the door, people hadn't come at all.

Shinichi approached her, though he wasn't trying to console her. "Well, in this particular case, money has a lot of power. Either way, if you want to receive, you have to give first."

"Give first... You're right, I'm still lacking in that area."

As a saint, she'd always been treated with respect without giving anything in return. Over time, she had started to take that respect for granted, forgetting this most basic rule. She nodded sheepishly at her own shortcomings. "I guess I can start by giving my panties to Rino."

"...I'm seriously gonna feed you to the pigs if you take things too far," Shinichi warned.

"But if that pig is served to Rino, I'll be indirectly ingested by her."

"That's not the same as an indirect kiss!" Shinichi shuddered.

They say that love makes you stronger. In the case of this particular pedo-lesbian, it seemed to have made her mentally tougher—and not in a good way.

As he walked away, a cheery voice called out to him. "Sir Shinichi, thy plan doth appear to be proceeding well."

"Captain. It's going well, thanks to you." Shinichi grinned at the approaching young man in the shape of a marshmallow: He just so happened to be a huge fan of Rino—and King Sieg of Tigris. "Are you sure it's all right for us to use the Tears of Matteral? It is your national treasure after all."

"No worries, good friend. If I am truthful, we only made it a national treasure as it is rare. We have no real use for it."

It was a pain to attempt to gather magical energy from tens of thousands of people, not to mention the fact that they'd need a very powerful magic user on par with Sanctina to unleash its power. In reality, it just sat around gathering dust.

"Thou hast provided a significant payment for its use." Sieg eyed the mountain of gold, guarded dutifully by Celes.

When the people prospered, the kingdom followed suit. Plus, Shinichi had agreed to give any remaining gold directly to the kingdom afterward.

"Instead, I should inquire of thee, can thou truly afford this expenditure?"

"It's cleaned out the Demon King's wallet, but no pain, no gain, right?"

Shinichi's master had approved of this plan, boasting, "I'll secure more if it's not enough," and returning to the demon world to seek gold deposits in the mountains.

"Then all is well. Also, *that thing* hast been completed. Dost thou wish to view it?"

"Ah, it's done already? Should have expected as much from a mining country."

"The Matteral Mountains doth provide many blessings."

As they chatted, the pair left the cathedral, heading toward the castle. But instead of making their way to the castle proper, they passed through the gates to turn toward a small stone building near the wall. Used to store weapons for emergencies, it had been coated with a thick layer of dust for a long time.

But now a number of magic users were gathered together as they looked at something with uncertainty.

"Sir Shinichi, thank you for coming." Dritem, the stern-faced head court mage, bowed his head upon seeing Shinichi and King Sieg enter the room.

"No need for formalities. Can I see it?" Shinichi asked eagerly.

"Of course. Here it is." With a nod, Dritem carefully offered a small bowl. Inside was black powder.

"Ah, that looks about right." Impressed with their work, Shinichi carefully scooped an amount of the powder on the tip of his little finger and placed it on the stone floor. Then—

"*Fire.*"

The moment the tiny fire flashed from his palm, the black powder ignited in a grand explosion.

"Success! That's the stuff—black gunpowder!" His eyes twinkled at the sight of the first explosive to be created by humanity: gunpowder, a mixture of charcoal, sulfur, and potassium nitrate.

"No matter how many times I see it, I'm still shocked that this kind of explosion can be created without magic." Dritem had prepared the gunpowder himself upon receiving the ingredients and instructions from Shinichi. But he still had a hard time believing it as he looked at the mark left on the floor from the explosion.

Sieg was the only one there who didn't seem happy as he gazed at the gunpowder with a concerned expression.

"...Sir Shinichi, dost thou truly believe thou should teach us these secrets?"

"Quick as always, Captain. You've already predicted the potential dangers of these explosives."

"What do you mean?" asked Dritem, unable to pick up the undercurrent of their exchange.

It wasn't because he was a blubbering fool. It was because he was a magic user, which meant he had little use for this new discovery.

On the other hand, Sieg was a man of authority—and more importantly, an extraordinarily average man with no particular powers. That was exactly why he could see the unrealized potential of this powder.

"If a man hath access to these explosives, even if he was not a magic user, he wouldst be able to split hard stone. I do believe it to be an advantageous material. However, it hath potential to become a most fearsome weapon."

"Exactly. This can give the average person firepower to rival a magic user. Think of it as a magic powder." Shinichi broke into a daring smile as he gave a brief description of weapons with gunpowder, using the construction of grenades and matchlock guns as an example.

"You're telling me it shoots out small balls of lead?" asked Dritem incredulously.

"Faster and stronger than an arrow. Early iterations of guns won't be any better than a ballista, but as you continue to refine them, they could probably rival a magic arrow."

"Meaning an explosion that scatters iron fragments...," said Sieg.

"Leaving aside range and accuracy, a foot soldier with a grenade would basically be carrying around the firepower of a *Fireball* spell."

Dritem and Sieg hadn't seen that with their own eyes, and without a point of reference, it was hard to gauge its strength. Either way, they knew that the explosive spell was dangerous.

"A normal soldier equal to a magic user... I would be happy to strengthen our military, but as a magic user, I'm not sure how I feel about it," Dritem admitted.

"More importantly, I fear that the world wouldst become a dangerous place if every man couldst use it."

"Exactly. That's why I had you make it secretly in this storage shed."

Any normal farmer with no formal training could kill as easily as a trained solider. It was the same with those who lacked physical strength, women, and children. That was the scariest thing about weapons that used gunpowder.

It was surprisingly difficult to subdue an armor-clad enemy welding a shield requiring brute force to cut through it or long hours of training to duck under and pierce through the edges of the armor. Neither were skills that could be obtained overnight.

It was a similar case for arrows: It required high levels of physical strength to pull the heavy bowstring and skill to hit a target in the distance.

But with guns, all one needed to do was load it up with ammo and pull the trigger, making a ten-year-old child capable of killing a soldier who'd been training for ten years.

"With a sword, you have to live with the sensation of slicing through the meaty body of your opponent and getting drenched in their blood. There's a certain disgust that follows it, averting most from the act of murdering someone. But you get to disconnect from that when you use a gun—or so I've heard. Wonder if that's actually true," Shinichi said, shrugging his shoulders and speaking in increasingly vague terms.

Everything he knew he learned from books, and he'd definitely never shot and killed someone, so any psychological effects were pure conjecture.

"Anyway, I make these weapons sound really scary, but gunpower can be useful. I guess the only weakness is that you'll burn through your money pretty fast—unlike magic users, you know, 'cause they can get their magical power back from resting enough."

Though an added bonus was that gunpower could be stored for extended periods of time, unlike magic, as long as it's in a dry place.

"Long story short, it all comes down to obtaining high-quality guns. You don't have to rely on swordsmanship or magical strength anymore. That means the victor of any war is decided by money."

As things were, economic strength was already tied to military prowess: It placed limits on the quantity of armor and weaponry that a country was capable of procuring. More than that, they would need money to feed soldiers—the more, the better. But this relationship would accelerate exponentially once explosives were added to the equation.

Shinichi was steering the conversation too far away from Sieg's understanding of the world. Even Sieg couldn't be on the same page as Shinichi. But he hadn't lost his concerned expression.

"...Sir Shinichi, dost thou truly believe thou should teach us—humans—about explosives?"

Shinichi noticed that his question was almost exactly the same—except for one part—and he could feel an evil smile stretch across his face.

"It's not a problem. You see, these explosives aren't effective against demons, though it's a different story for wars between humans, I guess."

Take Arian for example. As a half dragon with superhuman strength, she'd never be hit with a bullet. Even in the case that it did hit her, it would never deliver a fatal blow.

Plus, while it was difficult to stop an oncoming projectile head-on, it would be easy to change its trajectory by applying force sideways. That's why any magic users on par with Celes could use the wind to blow aside arrows with the spell *Missile Protection.* It'd have the exact same effect on bullets.

As for the Blue Demon King? He outclassed Arian's physical strength and Celes's magical abilities, meaning nothing less than the cannon on a battleship would be effective against him.

"You won't be able to create the kind of firearms that could take down the Demon King for five hundred years, at least. And by that time, we'll all have died from old age so it's not gonna be a problem for us."

He couldn't care less if there were a bunch of causalities at the hands of these new explosives *after* he was dead. And since those people could be resurrected, death wasn't as final in this world as it was on Earth anyway. If that hadn't been the case, he wouldn't have been so laid-back about the idea of introducing explosives to them.

"Thou art dirty..." Even Sieg couldn't believe Shinichi's lack of accountability.

Beaming broadly, Shinichi seemed heedless of his misgivings. "It's not like I *want* wars to start. But I'm hoping these explosives will kick-start some scientific development. Otherwise, humankind will eventually stagnate."

This world had enough technological advancement to rival the medieval period on Earth. But their magical capabilities put them at an advantage, since medical treatments were far beyond that of the twenty-first century. The problem was the death rate was in a sharp decline, particularly in the past three hundred years since the church rose to power as an organized healing collective.

"People aren't dying. The human population is gonna keep increasing. But there won't be enough food stores to feed them all. At a certain point, the world is gonna tip into a cannibalistic hell of ravenous humans or a society with stringent rules and regulations, capping the number of children per household."

This problem was already manifesting in Vermeita's orphanage; it was filled to the brim with abandoned children, left behind because their families couldn't feed them. It hadn't exploded into a massive issue—yet—because the people of this world were lucky enough to have potatoes, which basically hacked the food pyramid.

"There could be a policy that encourages couples of the same gender to prevent any more births. There's already one dirty-minded lady who would be more than happy to oblige. If we want our children to be healthy and happy, we have to improve technology that increases crop yield."

There was some knowledge about science in this world, but its progress had been held back by the existence of magic, since it could do anything and everything. In order to break free from this cycle, Shinichi handed them something that could theoretically surpass magic—information about gunpowder—with that hope that it would catalyze innovation.

"Hmm, thou dost see far into the future, Sir Shinichi." This made an impression on Sieg.

Shinichi responded with an embarrassed smile. *Well, I am sort of cheating.*

The twenty-first century basically had the answers to everything. All he needed to do was work backward in order to figure out the question. But it was still too early to tell Sieg that.

"We probably won't see serious food shortages for another hundred years, so no rush. All I'm hoping is that you'll start to look into science a bit more and rely a little less on magic."

His dreams might be dashed, but he still loved science. Seeing its advancement was one of his greatest hopes.

Sieg slapped his jiggly belly upon considering this serious request. "Understood. For the moment, however, dost thou wish us to prepare large quantities of this explosive?"

"Yeah, we won't have scientific advancement—let alone a future—if we don't fend off the army of heroes."

Shinichi was about to leave, but Sieg seemed to remember something, stopping him in his tracks. "On another note, thine incubus hast bade me to inform thee that 'over half of the holy warriors have realized their love for me!' …Dost thou wish to see?"

"…Nah, I'm not into that kind of thing." Shinichi's face turned pale at the thought of the disheveled warriors, as they continue to be brainwashed by the incubus, and he made his way away from the stone shed at long last.

Led by Hube, the army of heroes was nearing the halfway point to the Demon King's castle.

Meanwhile, led by the dvergr blacksmith Ivan, the demons gathered in front of the castle, working on putting together some huge structure.

"Good. Now I want you to keep the obsidian slab… Hey! Sirloin! Didn't I tell you that number thirty-one should be two over from the right?!"

"*Oink.* This is too complicated! I can't put it together, *oink!*"

As the dvergr reprimanded the whining orc, Shinichi wormed in between them, a jug in one hand. "Looks like you're having fun, Boss."

"Who ya callin' Boss?!" shouted Ivan, but he accepted the jug filled with cool ale from the Tigris Kingdom and gulped it down in one swig. "The dvergrs hate bright places, ya know! But you've got me working all day under this infernal red sun. If it weren't for this ale, I'd have gone and tossed you in the furnace just now!"

"Ah-ha-ha, sorry, sorry." Shinichi chuckled as he looked up at the thing under construction. "You've done a great job, turning my scribbly designs into this."

"Hmph, I may specialize in blacksmithing, but we are a crafting people second to none." He puffed up his chest proudly and gazed at his work with Shinichi. "But you've got me making something interesting again. Maybe next time, I'll try my hand at designing."

"Oh, did this pique your interest?"

"Uh-huh. I've made good progress making a sword that surpasses His Highness. It may be time to shop around for a new hobby."

"Uh, blacksmithing is your hobby...? I'm guessing the sword thing is going well?"

"It is. With your method, I was able to forge a blade that can cut His Highness's skin. But I made it a tad too hard, so it was brittle and broke after one strike."

"Ah right. There's that problem." Shinichi tilted his head to the heavens. He'd totally forgotten about that. "Even though diamonds are the hardest substance in the natural world, they break pretty easily if you apply force that's parallel to the lattice structure..."

"That's why I had the idea of keeping the cutting edge of the blade hard and sharp while making the inside flexible so it can bend. But that's been difficult."

"Hard on the outside, flexible on the inside. That's the same as Japanese swords." Shinichi nodded, impressed that all experts drew the same conclusions, regardless of their homeworld.

He heard Arian's voice ring out cheerfully. "Dinner's ready—!"

With Celes, she carried out a massive pot, and all the demons immediately stopped working and dashed over to them.

"Phew, I've been waiting for this, *moo!*"

"The soup of the day is made with goat meat from Tigris."

"*Oink*?! Hot soup in this sweltering weather?"

"If that's how you feel, I'll take your share, *moo.*"

"I never said I wouldn't eat it, *oink!*"

While the orc-and-minotaur duo continued to make a fuss, the demons smacked their lips at the taste of the delectable ingredients from the human world. As Shinichi watched over them with a smile, Arian ladled some soup into a bowl, handing it to him.

"Here, Shinichi. Eat up."

"Oh, thanks." He took one sip from his spoon before his face hardened. "Arian, I should have asked this sooner, but are you sure you're okay if I defeat him?"

"Hmm? ...Oh, yeah." Her momentary confusion lifted when she realized he was referring to Hube. She nodded, but there was an inexplicable sadness in her eyes. "I still haven't forgotten all he did for me. But there are a lot of things here that I don't want to lose." As she gazed at the demons scarfing down their meal in merriment, her eyes crinkled.

This was a safe place for her. She could live peacefully without facing any discrimination for being a half dragon. And most importantly, there was the kind, albeit twisted, young man who had led her here—

"I'll fight against the bishop even if people think I'm a thankless brat." She peeked up at him shyly, wondering if he'd be displeased that she was a bad girl.

But he just flashed back his usual evil smile. "Heh-heh-heh, sweet. As people say, 'Betrayal is a girl's best friend.' 'Every rose has its thorns.' A good girl with a bad streak is honestly kinda hot."

"A hot girl with a bad streak...hee-hee-hee," Arian giggled innocently, looking the absolute opposite of a bad girl. This was the first time that someone had called her that: All her life, she'd played the act of a good girl, as if to compensate for being a half dragon.

Shinichi couldn't help but loosen his mouth into a smile at her cuteness, but just as soon as he did, he felt a murderous glare creep up behind him. When he dared to turn around, he saw Celes, eyes icy and face expressionless as she held the massive pot of soup over her head.

"Um, Celes. Am I safe to assume you aren't gonna dump that pot of hot soup on my head?"

"Of course not. That would be disrespectful to Sir Goat Meat."

"No concern for me?!" countered Shinichi loudly.

Meanwhile, Celes seemed to come to her senses, puzzled by her outburst as she lowered the pot.

Arian's smile vanished as she eyed the maid. "Celes..."

"Miss Arian..."

In between their abruptly serious expressions, he could feel their gazes sharpen. A moment later, Arian laughed nervously and Celes sighed in resignation.

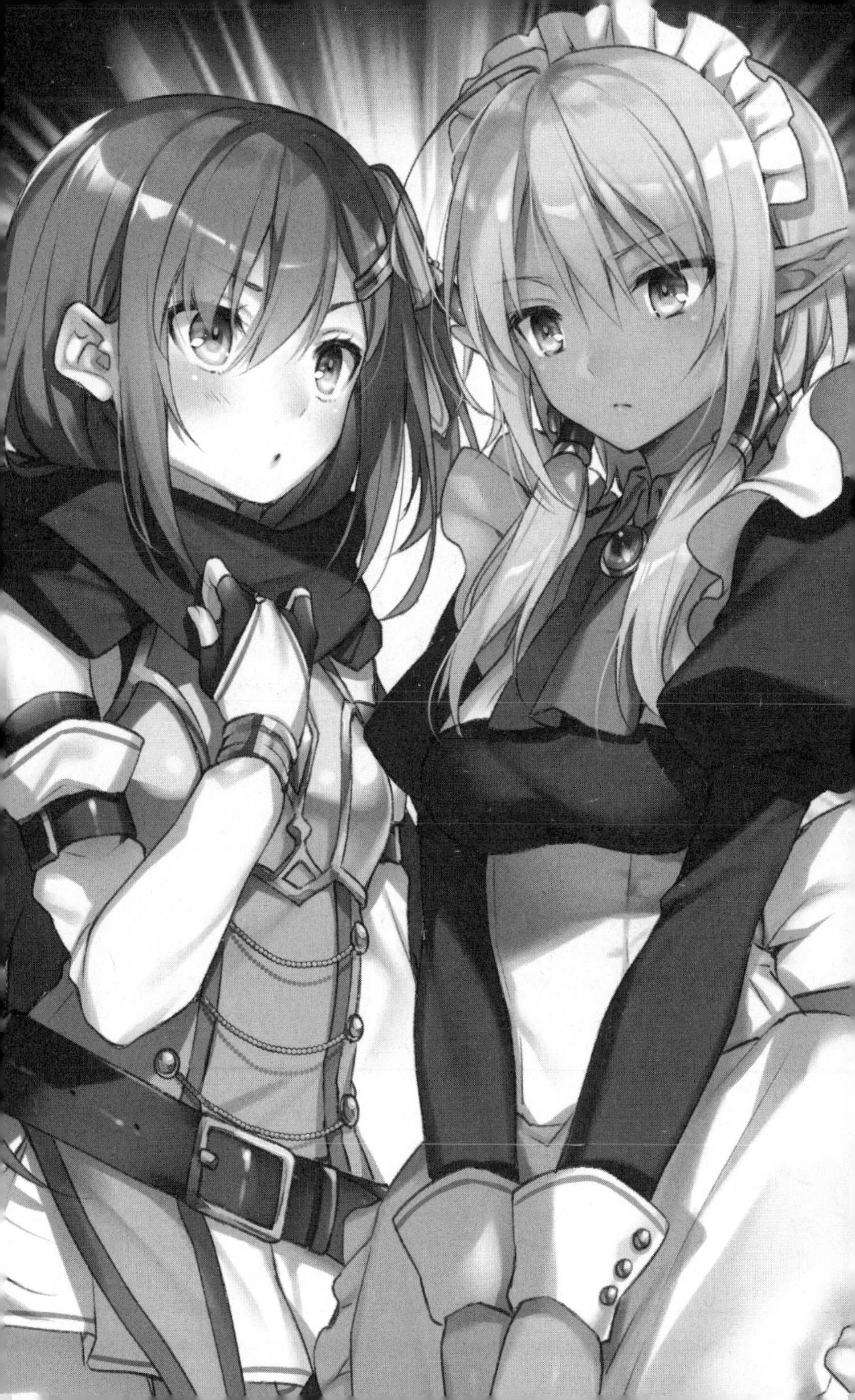

"Um, what just happened...?" asked Shinichi, but the girls just shook their heads.

"Nothing happened, *this time*," Arian emphasized.

"Yes, not *now*," Celes echoed.

"Uh, right..." Shinichi wasn't so dense that he couldn't piece together what had happened between the pair. All he could do was nod and quietly go along with it.

The orc and minotaur came running up to the big pot, entirely unaware of the strange tension among the three.

"It was delicious, *moo*! If I get used to food this good, I'll never be able to go back to the demon world."

"Shinichi, that's why you have to beat the heroes, no matter what, *oink*!"

"Leave it to me."

As the demons beamed and went in for seconds, Shinichi smiled and nodded, renewing his vows to protect his country of jollity—which was finally starting to take shape—from the invaders that went by the name of *heroes*.

It had been nineteen days since the army of heroes departed the Holy City, and they set up camp at the mouth of Dog Valley. As they traversed the land, more members of the clergy and monster hunters tagged along upon hearing the rumors. Hube indiscriminately granted all of them the status of hero. Their numbers had swelled to ten thousand men.

"Tomorrow will mark the start of our crusade against those diabolical creatures. Rest well tonight. Your bodies must be exhausted from the long trip," Hube announced.

""""Yes, sir!"""" replied the soldiers.

"We cannot, however, let our guard down. The demons are not above launching an ambush in the night."

""""Yes, Cardinal Hube!"""""

Upon seeing the army respectfully take a knee, Hube nodded in satisfaction before retiring to his tent for the evening, followed by the mechanic footsteps of the emotionless prisoners-turned-dolls. The moment they were out of sight, the heroes released the tension in their shoulders.

"Man, I was excited to come 'cause I heard I could become a hero and get famous for having defeated the demons, but..."

"That cardinal-in-charge's got those creepy guys tailing him. I don't really get his deal."

The heroes grumbling about the uncanniness of this entire operation were the newbies, the ones who'd joined the army partway through its march. They should have been reprimanded by the clergy, since they'd been in this position since the beginning. But they didn't step in, letting it go and adopting similarly dour expressions as the newcomers.

"I've heard people saying he's the second coming of Eument, but if you think about it logically..."

"I thought he was thrown in jail for that scandal. Why would he be given the Goddess's power?"

"Speaking of jail, I'm pretty sure his human dolls were all prisoners in the Pit of Divine Punishment. I remember seeing some of them."

Their physical exhaustion from the long journey was chipping away at their initial fervor. And because these priests and priestesses were intimately familiar with the inner workings of the church, uncertainty and suspicion were beginning to harden in their chests.

"Either way, if we defeat the Demon King tomorrow, it'll all be over— What's that?"

"Something wrong?"

"Nothing. I just thought I felt a magical current..." The middle-aged priest examined his surroundings, but he didn't see anything suspicious in Dog Valley and his dimly lit surroundings.

"You don't think Cardinal Hube's using *Wire Tap* to listen to our conversations, do you…?"

"Shit, don't say that! If it were true, we'll be turned into one of his dolls."

"Maybe it's a demon ambush. Well, no point sitting around speculating. Let's look around then get some sleep." At the suggestion of the oldest priest, the others complied, scanning around.

It never occurred to them that it might be a maid flying high in the sky, cloaked in darkness with an *Illusion* spell and using *Wire Tap* to listen to them.

While the army of heroes was wrestling with their doubts, Hube was alone in his tent with a merry smile playing on his lips. "Soon. Soon, I will destroy that bastard heretic… Heh-heh-heh!"

He imagined the despair on the boy's face as he tore the Goddess's symbol from the redhead, stripping her of her status and shredding her to bits. Or maybe he should do it the other way. He'd put the boy through a horrific torture fest and force her to cry and beg for forgiveness. That might be more fun.

"Ah, I can't wait!" Hube stared lovingly at the two symbols branded on the backs of both hands, filled with fiendish amusement—a far cry from the usual appearance of a man of the cloth.

Those symbols had given him the right to grant the status of hero and to take it away—and a portion of the Goddess's power, the magical strength of a hundred bishops. While this was unheard of, it still wasn't enough to defeat the Demon King single-handedly. And there was the additional problem of depleting one's supply. That's why he'd taken great pains to gather ten thousand heroes.

"My Divine Goddess Elazonia, I will ensure your holy will is done. You have saved me, and my life is yours. I will sacrifice it as many times as necessary!"

He would die and die again if it meant weakening the Demon King.

He'd die until that behemoth fell before the heroes' blades, and then he'd wipe the demons and that heretical boy from this world.

Their military strategy was to wage an infinite war. There was no reason they would lose. All the heroes in the army believed this.

But they didn't realize that the first heroes to go against the Demon King in Ruzal's party had used the same strategy.

They didn't realize that that was why the Twisted Advisor had been summoned in the first place.

On the morning of the twentieth day, the dim sky was still cloaked in mist when the earth shook violently, and the ten thousand warriors leaped up from their slumber.

"Wh-what's happening?!"

They heard a heavy thud as something enormous approached through the fog.

"I-is that—?!"

They stood in utter disbelief as it emerged from the mist—a figure so massive they had to crane their necks to look at its face. Its Herculean arms and legs were thicker than tree trunks. Its blue skin was harder than steel, and horns sprouted from either side of its head before curving up toward the sky and ending in sharp points. As if to cockily suggest any actual armor was unnecessary, he wore only a loincloth and cloak. All this gave the imposing specimen the appearance of the physical manifestation of raw, furious force. But there was something oddly marvelous about the way his muscles curved around his monstrous body.

"It's the Demon King…!"

The heroes stood frozen in front of his overwhelming presence, but Blue Demon King Ludabite made no attempts at a surprise attack. Instead, he stood tall and folded his arms, as if to say, *Get a move on. Prepare yourselves and come at me.*

The heroes scrambled to arm themselves and assume battle formation. Hube and his doll squad swiftly appeared at the army's fore.

"Well, well, well. Very kind of you to come out to be killed. I was worried you might have fled back to the demon world."

"You must be their leader." The Demon King didn't respond to his provocation. Then, bizarrely, he quietly addressed the ten thousand heroes. "Flee, soldiers. We broke through the earth's surface to eat well. That was the nature of our mission. We have no desire to fight you."

"...Eat well?"

This came as a disappointment to the heroes. Weren't the demons trying their hand at world domination or destroying the human race?

Hube roared back at the King in an attempt to cut over these thoughts. "Silence, you foul demon! You diabolical beast, standing in the way of her teachings! Your countless acts of evil by deploying that boy will never be forgiven—even if you were to take your own life!"

"...That boy?" murmured some of the heroes with mounting uncertainty as they looked at the young cardinal. They weren't aware of the Twisted Advisor.

In order to brush aside the doubts, Hube waged war. "We will not lower ourselves to speak with these corrupt beasts! Prove yourselves in battle as heroes of the Goddess!"

""""Uh, YEEEEAH!"""" The heroes managed to shake off their doubts, roaring into a battle cry as they charged the Demon King.

"Fools... Arrows of light, pierce their hearts, *Homing Rain*," the Demon King chanted, pitching an orb of light into the sky. Exploding into shards of light, they continued to shatter until they formed three thousand magic arrows, capable of piercing through steel.

"AH?!" The army let out a scream of terror as they saw the thousands of arrows aiming toward their hearts, but—

"Lady Elazonia, please grant these soldiers your protection, *Shield of Protection*." Hube formed a massive shield of light over the heroes, repelling the arrows.

"Hmm, not bad," the Demon King noted with a bit of respect,

knowing that each individual arrow was weak, but there was strength in numbers: Repelling three thousand arrows would take a considerable amount of power. "But I can tell this strength isn't all you."

Furrowing his brow, the Demon King could sense traces of an alternative source to Hube's magic—as if he was drawing power from a magic conductor. How boring. That said, he had no intensions of holding back.

"Pierce them, *Land Bite*."

Sharp earthen teeth erupted from the ground, snapping up at the feet of the heroes—where the *Protection* spell was the least effective. Piercing through their soles to their thighs, tearing all the way up to their stomachs, thirty heroes in the front of the charge were brutally gutted in the blink of an eye.

"Agh! Gah!"

"Gack!"

At the heartrending sight of their peers hacking up blood and sinew, the heroes behind them stopped dead in their tracks.

But Hube wasted no time to scold them, raising his voice an octave. "Have no fear! We've been granted the Goddess's protection! We are the undying heroes!"

"Y-yeah, that's right!" Catching a glimpse of her symbol etched into the backs of their hands, the heroes gathered their courage, steadying themselves before charging toward the Demon King for the second time.

"Let's go!"

"Scorching flames ignite, *Fireball!*" chanted twenty magic users as the fire blasted in front of them, smothering the Demon King out of sight.

He waved his hand. *"Reflection Wind."*

A powerful gale burst forward, flinging back the balls of fire.

"Huh… Gyah!" With the heroes just managing to regroup post-incantation, they weren't able to dodge the attack, burning straight to a crisp from their own spell.

To the comfort of the other heroes, however, they witnessed these corpses vanish from the field.

"Don't be afraid! We can't die!"

"Yeah! We're undefeatable!"

Even without a physical body, they were consoled by the fact that they'd be resurrected at a nearby church—no matter what happened to them. Witnessing this miracle in the flesh reaffirmed that, encouraging them to toss aside their baseless fears of death.

"Onward, slay him!"

"Don't falter! Even if your attacks are ineffective! We'll keep doing this until the enemy falls!"

The horde surged forward, pushing through even as their spells backfired, their swords snapped, and their peers were cleft in two.

"...Maggots." As the Demon King flung them off his body, his eyes blazed scornfully.

He'd always revered brave warriors, undaunted by the prospect of death, even the weak ones. After all, there was a time when he'd been nothing more than a weed, before he'd become the all-powerful Blue Demon King. It took trial and error, defeat after defeat. But he'd trained hard, fought harder, trained, fought, trained, fought—until he made it to this present moment.

Of course, he'd been granted a massive advantage. He had a natural-born knack for it.

It would be impossible for any human to push themselves hard enough, hacking up blood from their strenuous efforts, to scratch him. And yet, there were some who continued to strive forward, refusing to fold under the pressure and pain—the ones that the Blue Demon King himself would acknowledge as strongmen. Their species or social status didn't matter. The Demon King revered them regardless.

But the heroes here were nothing more than a swarm of giant ants. He felt nothing short of disgust toward them.

They're not strongmen. They're barely even alive.

A fearless warrior wasn't the same as a warrior without fear of death.

The former was a true warrior, absolutely petrified of death, who actively chose not to yield to their anxieties—to protect things worth fighting for. A real hero held his sword in shaking hands, planted his feet, and refused to budge. But these "heroes" in front of him were cowards. They were so scared of "death" that they retreated, becoming the "undead."

"So irritating." The Demon King squished one of the hero's heads in with his fist.

A strongman shrouded in the possibility of death. The cowards who ran away from it. Their battle raged on for the course of an hour.

At the start of the battle, the army had ten thousand men—by now, it'd been cut in half. And yet, there wasn't so much as a little scrape on the Demon King, though his breaths turned into pants, more laborious than before.

Hube smirked to himself. *I thought we'd need to repeat this two or three times, but if things go well, we could kill him off today.*

He'd used up almost all of his divine gifts, the Goddess's magic, but he knew he had just about enough to cast a high-level spell—*Holy Torrent.* He could end this battle right here, right now, once the five thousand heroes wore the fiend down, chipping away at his power bit by bit. When all his men were finally torn apart, he'd unleash this spell.

"This is the moment! This is when we destroy the evil Demon King!"

""""Aaaah—!""""

They'd lost count of their attacks, but they obligingly charged again. They had no way of knowing they were pawns—to be used, abused, and tossed away.

But their advances were cut short by the boisterous sound of laughter echoing across the length of the entire battlefield.

"Heh-heh-heh, ha-ha-ha, MWA-HA-HA-HA!"

"That voice!"

It was a superb three-level laugh, signaling the arrival of a villain. Hube's eyes narrowed. "You heretical bastard! Show yourself!"

"Heh-heh-heh, I wasn't hiding to begin with," rained down a derisive voice from the sky above.

They looked up to find a boy in a white mask with a painted smile, floating in the air along with a dark, elven maid against the backdrop of blue. Hube glared up at them with a fearless grin.

"Ha! Ha-ha-ha, you might have come to save your master from his peril, but you're too late! I'm going to have you suffer the most gruesome death, along with the Demon King! I'll personally see to it! And have no fear—she'll be sent to hell with you!"

"Cardinal Hube...?" As the cardinal switched out of his usual demeanor, waves of perplexity washed over the army.

But the boy in the white mask chuckled again, expecting his dramatic speech. "Ha-ha-ha, you're calling me the faithful advisor to His Highness—no, to the Blue Demon King? It's all an act."

"What?!" the heroes yelped back.

He drew out a second mask, layering it over the first: pitch-black with a single red eye in the center. Even without any context, it looked diabolical.

"I'm a faithful servant of Elazok, the God of Evil. I'm their unholy priest, known as the True One!"

With that, the boy in the black mask—Shinichi—let out another depraved laugh.

"I've never heard of Elazok!"

"The name sounds a bit like Elazonia. Is there a connection?"

"Wait, is that the Evil God that Lady Elazonia sealed away...?"

"What, does that mean the sealed Evil God has returned?!"

In a panic, the heroes took this humongous lie at face value, amusing Shinichi to the point that he had to hold in his laughter behind his mask.

"Heh-heh-heh. Just as they say: 'He who believes in the existence of god doesn't doubt the existence of evil.' Amazing."

"Is this really an appropriate time to laugh?" Celes poked Shinichi from behind, jerking her head toward Hube.

"You heretic! Stop your pathetic jokes and attempts to deceive us!" Hube refused to believe him, especially because he'd already been burned once before by Shinichi's tricks.

But that didn't stop the heroes from milling around, completely baffled. Shinichi's appearance was that ghastly and hellish. And he wasn't about to take any chances and let that confusion abate. He laid out his next move.

"Heh-heh-heh, you don't believe me? Well then, how about I show you the power of Elazok?"

Celes recited an incantation. "Appear before us, *Apport*."

It was a fairly low-level spell that teleported something to your location. But in this case, this "something" was completely out of left field.

"Wh-what is that?!"

The space in front of the heroes cracked in two, as if ripping it by the seams, and let a colossal silhouette slowly crawl out.

Its hind legs were large enough to crush a two-story house; countless broken swords sprouted from its curling tail. Its entire body was encased in hard obsidian. On its back were two mysterious pipes where wings should have been. Its maw was large enough to swallow a human whole, flashing fangs stained red as if they'd been dyed in blood. Its sinister eyes were the same crimson color, and it looked down at the heroes, insect-size compared with this mammoth.

It was unmistakable. It was the most powerful of monsters, the killer of gods.

"A dragon?!" The heroes let out shrieks of terror.

The dragon mockingly let out an earth-shattering roar. The men had no way of telling that Shinichi was behind this whole thing, modifying his voice with magic.

"This is insane! The Evil Dragon has been brought to life...?!"

"Heh-heh-heh. Unfortunately, this little guy isn't our lord, the Black Dragon."

"What?!" The army let out another yelp for the umpteenth time.

Shinichi explained with dramatic flair. "This is one of the Four Unholy Dragons who answer to the Black Dragon, meet the Black Boulder Dragon, Hellsaur!"

"Black Boulder Dragon, Hellsaur?!"

Its name was somewhere between half-assed and childish. It low-key deserved to be the butt of some jokes, but creativity in this world could use a bit more work.

"Heh-heh-heh, Hellsaur is the smallest of the Four Unholy Dragons, but he's plenty to kill you fools—along with the Demon King in his weakened state."

"Wha—? Kill the Demon King?!" They croaked back.

Even Hube was bug-eyed this time.

"Yes. My orders are to eliminate Elazok's sworn enemy, the Blue Demon King Ludabite."

"What do you mean? Aren't the demons working for the Evil God?!"

"I have no idea what you're talking about. Elazok and the demons have never worked together."

"Does that mean the holy book is a lie…?"

"You see, Elazok had been kind over the years, overlooking the demons if they chose to stay in their lane, tucked away in their corner of the demon world. But what do you know? Ludabite has been attempting to form relations with the humans to feed his daughter some good food. As a faithful follower of Elazok, I cannot forgive this! As the divine will of Elazok is to eliminate all of humankind!" Shinichi pointed angrily at the Demon King.

"Wh-what the hell…?" The heroes were grasping at straws, but even that was too much. They were completely bewildered.

Hube tried to dispel their confusion by shouting over him. "You cannot fool us by your meaningless lies, you idolater!"

Well, he was right about that. Elazok was nothing more than a figment of Shinichi's imagination.

But Hube's men were already growing so suspicious of him that

they doubted his proclamation. Plus, his opponent was willing to go
real low.

"Heh-heh-heh. Hube, you've already done so well. No need to put on
your act any longer."

"What are you saying?!" Hube screeched.

"What does he mean? Does Cardinal Hube know that unholy
priest?"

To the befuddled lot, Shinichi cooed, babying them as he lied
through his teeth. "Heh-heh-heh, it was just a simple trick. Hube is
another unholy priest for Elazok!"

""""Whaaat—?!"""""

"He made you into fake heroes and dragged you here so that you
would sacrifice yourselves and weaken the Demon King!"

""""Whaaaaaaaaaaaaaaaaaaaaat—?!"""""

The heroes were so disoriented by this news that they could only
shout back. Their jaws went slack in shock, locked open as if they were
scarecrows.

Hube denied Shinichi's claims. "Don't take in these absurd claims!
My power is holy, granted to me by the Goddess Elazonia!"

"We know. That was your role. But there really isn't any need to hide
it any longer, Hube. Your fake heroes have served their purpose well."

"You bastard! How low will you go...? Listen up, all. You cannot
let yourself be deceived by this heretic's lies!" But his actions so far
had been too suspicious to allow him to convince them of his innocence now.

"I thought it was weird that a criminal would be chosen as the second coming of Pope Eument—you know, as the messiah."

"And what he did to those emotionless doll people? The Goddess
would never approve of that."

"It was all to mislead us. How unforgivable!"

They weren't idiots. That wasn't the driving force behind their
flip-flopping ideas about Hube.

It was more convenient to see Hube as an agent of the Evil God than to face their own jealously toward him for rising into power. It was easier than addressing their envy of his position as cardinal, backed by the Goddess's strength.

But that also meant that they weren't so foolish as to miss the holes in his argument.

"W-wait. But we're heroes, aren't we?!"

"Yeah, only the Goddess can grant the gift of infinite resurrection!" A hero raised his hand to display the symbol of the Goddess—proof that Hube couldn't be an agent of evil.

Shinichi had predicted this argument would come up. "Heh-heh-heh, you really think Elazok couldn't imitate this 'Goddess-exclusive' right?"

"What?!"

"Sure, this marks your status as heroes. If you die, you'll be resurrected at a nearby church. It'll work once—maybe twice. But the third time? The fourth?"

"What, so is it really true that we're fake heroes…?" Even the most resistant of the bunch started to waver in their conviction.

From the looks of it, it seemed that their fallen soldiers were magically transported to a church for resurrection. There were a few men mixed in the bunch that were so mistrusting of their newfound status that they secretly killed themselves just to test it out.

But there wasn't anyone crazy enough to test just how many times they could be brought back to life. To top it off, no one had any definitive proof of Hube's innocence. The heroes regarded him with mounting cynicism.

"How long are you just going to stand there?! Quick! Kill the heretic!"

But Hube's desperate instructions grounded their suspicions even further.

If anyone had considered the situation more rationally, they would have noticed a few holes in Shinichi's claims and actions: If his real goal was the defeat of the Demon King—plus the heroes—wouldn't it have been better for him to wait longer before appearing when they were both considerably weakened? And was it necessary to reveal Hube's "true" nature if they were working as a team?

A devilish whisper ran through the crowd, preventing them from thinking about it further.

"—*He's a traitor.*"

A voice buzzed in their ears, a voice they didn't recognize.

"—*A fake messiah.*"

It was Shinichi. He'd altered its sound, and Celes used her magic to project his voice into the crowd.

"—*An agent of evil.*"

It was a piss-poor strategy. It could be seen through, if only one thought it through.

"—*We can't forgive him.*"

But these so-called heroes were cowards, terrified of death. They'd been pulled out of the peak of their battle, just when things were on their side, and tossed callously into this state of skepticism. It was easier to go along with someone else's claims than think for themselves.

"—*Kill him.*"

"Traitor!" bellowed one particularly hot-blooded fool, letting out a battle cry as he charged toward Hube.

"—gh!" Hube instantly raised his hand and cast a *Force* spell without bothering with an incantation. Thanks to the Goddess's divine power, his invisible bullet was far stronger than usual, tearing through the dissenter's body with one critical hit.

"Ah..." Hube realized his mistake too late.

No sooner had the corpse disappeared than the remaining heroes rushed him with the intent to kill.

"This traitor's done for!"

"He was an unholy priest from the beginning! He lied to us!"

Eyes bloodshot with rage, they brandished their weapons. They were at the point of no return. Words wouldn't be enough to placate them.

Hube gave an order to his faithful, will-less dolls. "You, slow them down!"

"......" Wordlessly, the ex-prisoners trudged forward, facing the oncoming heroes head-on. Hube turned his tail and sprinted.

"You can't run, you traitor!"

"You! You friggin' heretic—!" As the heroes pursued him from behind, Hube looked up, spitting curses at the boy observing the scene from the sky. With his remaining magic, Hube used his *Physical Enchantment* to strengthen his body as he ran.

As Shinichi looked at the pathetic sight, he smirked behind his mask. "What an idiot. He could have proved his innocence by sacrificing himself, or he could have ignored me and continued attacking. There were so many ways he could've broken down my plan."

But he hadn't. That was because Hube had a secret phobia, scarring the back of his heart. It was so far in there that he didn't even realize it was there—a fear of Shinichi.

He was so terrified that he'd never win against this demonic boy, no matter what Hube threw at him. That boy had robbed him of everything. Hube's wrath was another way for him to project his fears of Shinichi instead of facing or processing them head-on.

"Heh-heh-heh. Guess he's also one of those scaredy-cats that chose to run from death."

"You're the sickest person in the world," Celes spat, as she looked down at the hellish landscape of the former prisoners and heroes killing one another in a brutal bloodbath.

Shinichi cracked his signature smile. "What're you talking about? We're just getting started."

With that, they landed on the head of the Black Boulder Dragon— patiently waiting for its turn. Well, it was actually a dragon-shaped golem that the demons had worked hard to build. Shinichi opened the hatch on its head, leading to the cockpit and engine section where the massive magic conductor, the Tears of Matteral, was gleaming brightly.

"You coming, Celes?"

"I'm not particularly interested in reaching climax in a golem."

"Someone's in a good mood," he noted, relieved that the dark elf could still find it in herself to make these dirty jokes before turning to address the heroes. They'd just about finished off the former prisoners. "Mwa-ha-hah, you fools! I will not allow you to pursue my companion, Hube. You die here!"

As Shinichi boomed, Celes got the Black Boulder Dragon to move by using the magic in the Tears of Matteral.

As the heroes looked on in confusion, the two pipes on the dragon's back leveled onto them—two cannons carved from obsidian and strengthened with a *Protection* spell. Then—

"Fire!"

With an ear-piercing roar, each cannon spewed out two thousand tiny iron balls—no more than half an inch in diameter each. Gunpowder had been packed into this cannon for this very moment. Together, the cannons launched four thousand bullets. The iron rain—call it *buckshot*—turned two hundred heroes into mincemeat in one fatal blow.

"Wh-what the hell was that sound?!"

"I didn't feel any magic! How'd they do that without it?!"

The heroes found themselves devolving into panicked chaos yet again. Shinichi gave Celes her order. "Do it."

"Understood," she replied. "Black Dragon who rules below the surface, the embodiment of strength, grant me a sliver of your breath, scorch your enemies until no ash remains—"

She conjured the largest powerful image to her mind's capacity, drawing on the magic of tens of thousands of people stored in the massive magic conductor. With that, she modified reality to match her imagination, clicking it in place with an incantation.

"—False Dragon Breath!"

Her hands were positioned to make it appear as if the black flames flared out of the mouth of the dragon—laying waste to wide swaths of land in a deadly blast. The dirt was peeled from the earth; chunks of mountains went missing; human bodies were torn apart down to their very atoms.

By the time the torrent of black flame subsided, the army of 4,700 heroes had been cut in half.

"Wow..." Even though he'd been the one to order it, a cold sweat streaked down Shinichi's brow at the horrific sight.

There are no words to describe the utter despair the heroes felt at witnessing such destructive power.

"It's over... We can't win, even if we can't die, even if we keep coming back forever..."

Their swords fell from their trembling hands, and their knees gave out.

It didn't matter if their corporeal body wouldn't die: A body with a crushed soul was no different from a ragdoll.

But the unholy priest mercilessly continued his attack against the heroes—who were practically living corpses at this point.

"Reload," ordered Shinichi.

"Yes, sir. *Apport.*" With that, Celes magically transferred the buckshot stored by the magic conductor into the large cannons. Once they were locked and reloaded, she aimed them at the men—they were as good as dead. "*Fire.*"

The horrendous sound ripped through the air again, and four thousand bullets whizzed toward the heroes, but—

"*Fortress,*" chanted the Demon King.

Just in the nick of time, a wall of light appeared in front of the heroes, protecting them from the pelts of iron.

"Why...?" started one of the heroes.

"Geez, you maggots. You're not even worth killing. You call yourselves *heroes*?!" he boomed, berating the dumbfounded bunch with the full extent of his wrath. "Why aren't you fighting? Why aren't you struggling to live? Gather your courage and face your enemies regardless of their strength... Isn't that what a hero is?!"

"—Ngh?!" As they were reprimanded by their enemy, they lifted their heads, as if their eyes had been opened for the first time.

But they still lacked the energy to get to their feet.

"But we're no match for—"

"Please don't give up!" An energetic voice suddenly rang across the battlefield, cutting through the despair.

The heroes turned around in surprise to see a figure with flowing hair as red as the rising sun, wearing a crimson scarf that was fluttering in the wind. The physical embodiment of justice. Her name was— "Arian the Red?!"

"I heard she'd disappeared after Hube sexually harassed her. What's *she* doing here?!" asked one of the heroes.

"Wait, she's not alone!"

Behind her peeked out a girl with flaxen hair in the robes of a priestess, who chanted a prayer of mercy for the heroes. "Please heal their wounds, *Area Healing*."

A warm magical light trickled down on them, washing over them and healing their wounds. It was as if it lifted their broken spirits.

"That's Saint Sanctina!"

"Why is she here?!"

There were some rumors that had been drifting around here and there that the Saint had become involved with a young singer, leading her astray and causing her to turn her back on the church. With this information, the heroes weren't sure what to make of this series of events.

But Arian shouted across the field, brushing away their last remaining doubts. "You may have heard tales that I'd disappeared or that Sanctina betrayed the church. They're all lies to mislead the enemy... That's right, it was all to defeat that pawn of the Evil God!"

"Wh-what?!"

With extra-dramatic flair, she put her all into her performance, and the crowd believed her instantly.

"You may reprimand us later for deceiving you. But right now, I'm asking you to gather your courage and stand up," Sanctina cooed.

"Lady Sanctina!"

Her eyes welled with tears—as expected from years and years of make-believe, playing her saintly part. She'd brushed up on her acting

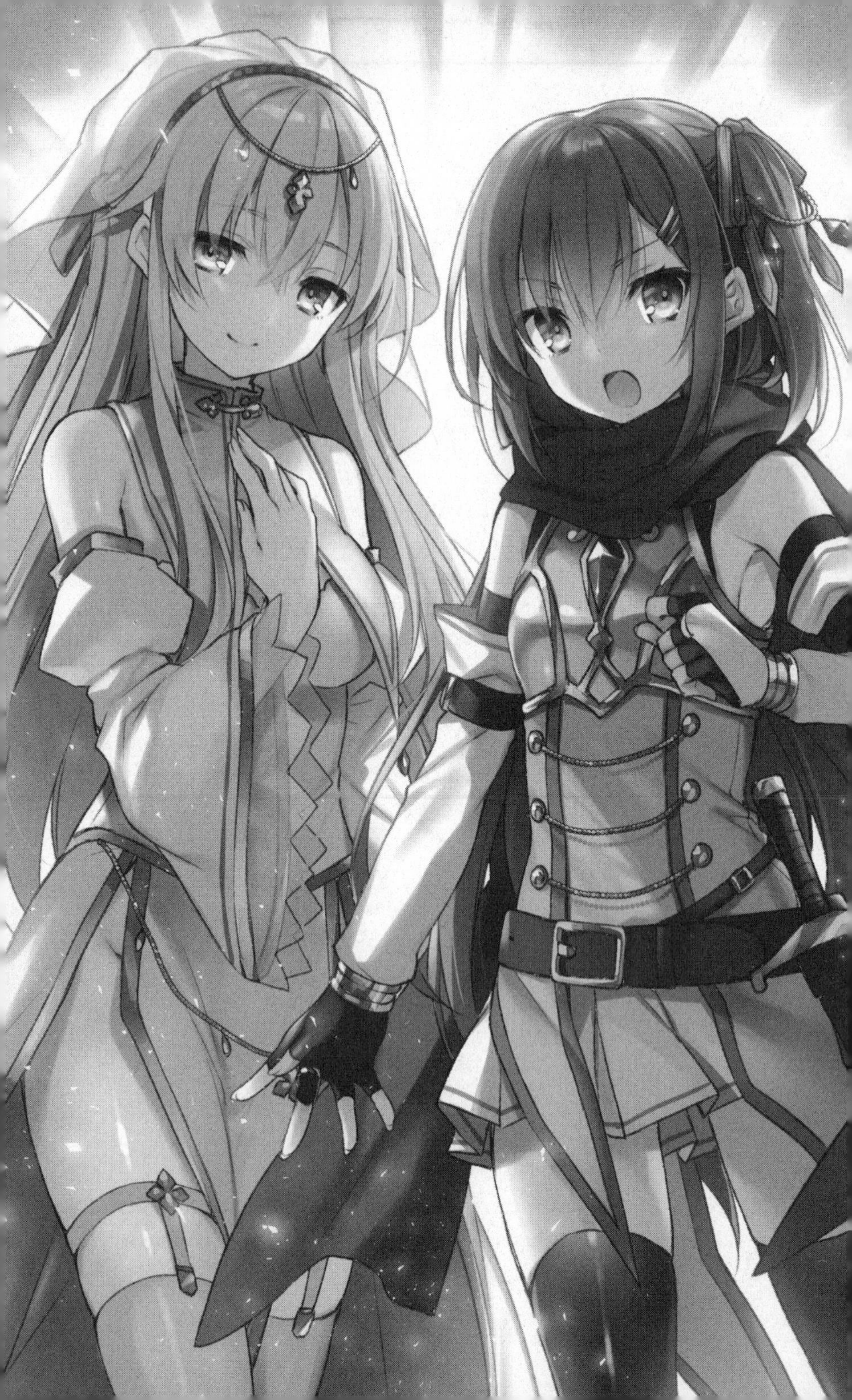

skills. The heroes were moved by this scene and rose on their shaking legs at her beckoning.

Arian smiled at them as she walked slowly up to the Demon King. "We're not allies. But right now, I think we have an even greater enemy facing us."

"I know." With a nod, the Demon King and Arian looked up at the massive dragon towering over them.

As the others witnessed the almighty Demon King stand side by side with a hero, they broke into a smile, faces beaming with optimism— the polar opposite of their shell-shocked expressions moments before.

"We can win! We can defeat it!" the men started to chant.

Inside the Black Boulder Dragon's head, Shinichi was holding his breath and desperately trying not to laugh at the scene that was unfolding like some cheesy manga for young boys.

"Heh-heh-heh. Oh wow, this is hilarious...!" He gasped between chuckles.

"I can't laugh at this. The heroes are too pitiful," snapped Celes, questioning whether Shinichi actually was an unholy priest. Despite taking part in his underhanded schemes, she was starting to feel a bit afraid of him.

This was all part of his plan: The Demon King stepping in to protect the heroes; Arian and Sanctina descending down on the scene.

He knew that they couldn't defeat an army of undying heroes. And if it wasn't possible to make them all allies, he needed to dispel their hostile attitude for a moment.

The only time two enemies came together was in the face of a common enemy. He called it, the "My Enemy's Enemy is My Friend for the Day! A Third Party Makes a Violent Intrusion!" strategy. It was an ingenious plan, if he could say so himself. It used the appearance of an incredibly powerful enemy—the Evil God, in this case—to allow the humans and demons to work together because they'd have *no other choice*. Plus, if they could make some false accusations toward that annoying stalker of an ex-bishop, thereby destroying all trust in him—well, that's killing two birds with one stone.

"It's all thanks to their discontent and distrust of Hube. Even if evil has taken root, justice will win in the end!" Shinichi cackled.

"Exactly what part of you is just?" asked Celes.

"Well, I might be evil, but Rino's the total opposite, so we're all good!" Under his mask, Shinichi's smirk was so diabolical, he'd never let Rino, the Super Justice Lover, see it.

As the director of this grand play, he added the finishing touches. "Mwa-ha-ha! You're no match for Elazok's power! The Demon King's scarred with injuries, and you've added a measly two heroes! Hellsaur, finish them!"

The hair-raising sound erupted for the third time, but the Demon King and Sanctina used *Fortress* to repel the rain of iron bullets. Arian drew her magic sword as she dashed toward the dragon.

"Here I come, Shin—er, I mean, unholy priest True One!"

Just like a scripted pro-wrestling match, the audience—the heroes, in this case—wouldn't buy it if they didn't fight with everything they had. She dashed across the ground faster than the wind, slashing at the dragon's thick leg.

"Hyah!"

Backed by Arian's half dragon strength, the razor-sharp magic sword made by the hands of the dvergrs could slice through diamonds with the ease of ripping through paper. It cut easily through the obsidian armor on the dragon, and clumps of dirt spilled from the wound.

Even Shinichi's smile widened at the marvelous attack. "Way to go, Arian. All right, time for our counterattack!"

"Impossible," Celes said.

"...Excuse me?"

"We have no way to attack the ground."

"Uh, we're giant. Can't we just stomp around or sweep our tail?"

"We can't move because this whole thing is too heavy. In fact, if we move too much, we'll destroy it."

"Are you kidding me?!" screeched Shinichi in shock, but it should have been obvious from the get-go.

The Black Boulder Dragon was just a golem, which have bodies made from dirt. Not even special dirt. Just your regular, old, run-of-the-mill dirt that you could find anywhere.

The best ones ranged from doll-size—like the ones they used for Rino's live performances—to twice the size of a human being, max. Any bigger than that, and they wouldn't be as operable.

Now this Black Boulder Dragon was over a hundred feet tall. It held together, strengthened with a *Protection* spell. Its outer shell was made of obsidian to support the inside, but that meant it couldn't move much more than its cannons and head.

"Gah! Okay then, you'll have to use magic to—" started Shinichi.

"That's also impossible," interrupted Celes.

"...WHAT?"

"I have almost no magic left." She pointed to the Tears of Matteral behind them. That had been acting as her primary source of magic. Her face showed visible signs of fatigue.

The massive magic conductor should have been sparkling, full of tens of thousands of people's magic. By now, it'd turned dark and cloudy—a small shard of light flickering inside like a candle in the wind.

"I expended more of my magic than I expected, holding the large body together and reducing recoil when we fired the cannons."

"I still feel like that was too fast..."

"Oh, maybe it's because I cast *False Dragon Breath*, which used 90 percent of my magic."

"That's obviously the only friggin' reason!"

"I've never used so much magic at once. It was fun." She flashed a grin.

"So...cute... I mean, stop messing with me!" They continued to banter.

Meanwhile, at their feet—

"Urgh, I suddenly feel sick for some reason!" With her woman's intuition alerting her that Shinichi was flirting with Celes, Arian let her anger out by hacking away at the feet of the Black Boulder Dragon.

The sight suddenly brought back the heroes' spirit.

"Look! The dragon isn't moving anymore!"

"I don't know why, but this is our chance! Let's get in there, too!"

"Yeah, let's not forget that we're also heroes!"

Surrounding the Black Boulder Dragon, they put the last of their remaining strength into their swords and magic. Individually, they were weak, but collectively, they started to tear though its titanic body.

"We won't be able to last much longer," Celes warned.

"You bastards... Those bastards—!" shouted Shinichi, letting out the cry of a small animal backed into a corner.

That was the signal to end the charade.

"Heroes fall back!" boomed the Demon King, as waves of powerful magic swept from his body.

"Everyone back off!" ordered Arian.

"Uh, yeah!" They hurriedly clambered away from the half-destroyed beast.

The corners of the Demon King's mouth twitched upward as he faced off against the golem. "*Dragon Breath*, hmm? ...Something I haven't seen in a long time."

It was the same spell that'd been cast by his wife and greatest rival—the Blue Princess of War, Regina.

That was why he needed to respond with an equally powerful spell.

"Blue flames that shine below ground, savior light that created our demon world, show one moment of your destructive power, turn my enemies to ash—"

He'd used this once before against Ruzal's party, but unlike that time, he wasn't shortening the incantation or holding back one bit. He poured all his remaining magic into the spell and created the sun of the demon world above the surface.

"—*Blue Raging Flare!*"

A brilliant orb of fire bathed the world in blue as it bolted toward the Black Boulder Dragon.

"You trying to kill us?!" cried Shinichi.

"*Fly.*"

At the last second, Celes grabbed him and launched them out of the dragon. Shinichi looked down as it was swallowed up in the flaming tempest, leaving behind no trace of its existence.

A violent gale of hot wind scraped the surface of the world.

"Agh!" Arian, Sanctina, and the army of heroes dashed away from the flames, but they were knocked off their feet, tumbling across the dirt.

The only one standing was the Demon King, stock-still and unfazed by the wind. He glanced up at the mushroom cloud blooming over the site as dissatisfaction crossed his face.

"Even if I was slightly worn down by the heroes, I seem to be losing my edge." He reflected that he needed to hunker down, get it together, and retrain if he ever wanted to show his face to his wife again.

Covered in debris and grime, the group—including Arian—only had it in them to sigh.

"He really is incredible…," she mused.

"There's no way we could have ever have won against him…," Sanctina commented.

Behind them, the rest of the heroes still rolled around in the dirt as shock passed over their faces. But they were beyond fear. They couldn't begin to understand just how powerful their enemy was.

"Mwa-ha-ha. An impressive display of power. Hats off to the Blue Demon King for standing against Elazok. Out of respect for your good fight, I will let you be—for now."

"No matter how you look at it, we were utterly defeated," murmured Celes, but Shinichi decided to ignore her matter-of-fact comment as he threw his last words down at the Demon King.

"But don't make the mistake of believing this is all there is to Elazok's power. Prepare yourself! There will be a second or third assassin to take your life. I'd sleep with one eye open if I were you. Mwa-ha-ha!"

"...I apologize for the inconvenience, but it's getting difficult to hold us up with *Fly*."

"Just a bit longer, Celes!" he whispered as her control over magic started to waver.

Shinichi, aka the unholy priest, the True One, disappeared into the sky.

Arian watched them go before inching up slowly to the Demon King. "Now I don't think we know each other enough to be on friendly terms. But a greater enemy has appeared. Don't you think we should put a hold on our fighting for the time being?"

She offered a small, pale hand, which the Demon King enveloped in his massive, blue one.

"We have never desired war with the humans. All is good as long as I can feed my darling little daughter some delectable delights."

The two species gave each other a firm handshake.

Following Sanctina's lead, the other heroes started to clap their hands. The sounds of applause rained down on the two. Arian and the Demon King gave each other wry smiles as they continued their handshake.

"I figured this would be embarrassing, but I'm starting to feel reeeeeally guilty," Arian admitted.

"Heh, I suppose we've joined the ranks of the sick and twisted," he replied.

In the future, this moment would be remembered as the "Day of Friendship between Humans and Demons."

But the masterminds behind it knew it was nothing more than an uncomfortable charade.

Regardless, that was how the pointless fight between the demons in Dog Valley and the undying heroes came to a temporary halt.

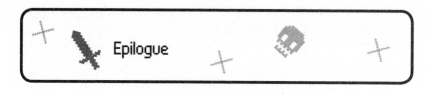

Potato Village was a few hours away from Dog Valley by walk. The faces of the villagers remained dark and cloudy, long after the deafening roars finally subsided. They started in the wee hours of the morning.

"I wonder if those heroes who passed by yesterday managed to defeat the demons?"

"Dunno. I think we might see them pass by again, beaten up and bloody as they scamper away like the troops from Boar Kingdom."

The villagers gossiped among themselves for a while, but they eventually headed off to work in the fields. They didn't have the luxury of standing around, trembling in fear.

Just as the sun started to rise, one young man noticed a strange figure approaching them.

"Ah, that's…"

He recognized the resplendent priest robes hanging on a man in his thirties. The man was unsteady on his feet, dripping sweat as if he'd been running until a moment before. His face was contorted, tormented.

"Are you all right?!" cried a young man.

"That…heretic…"

The young man ran up to him, offering him a shoulder to lean on, but the man remained unresponsive, his eyes empty. He didn't even seem to notice the young man there.

I bet he's an important priest. He must have run away from the demons upon his defeat. I gotta find him a place to rest somewhere.

After he led the priest into his own home and set him down in a chair for the time being, he dashed off to the village chief's house to ask him for guidance.

"Hey, I need to talk to you," he called out upon entering the house.

He didn't even bother to knock. That wasn't unusual in their village. Their population came out to a grand total of one hundred. Everyone knew everyone.

When he peeked in from the entryway, the young man could see into the bedroom—where the chief was lying, stark naked, with the pink-haired servant of the merchant Manju, Ribido, by his side.

"Chief, are you…?"

"Ah! I-it's not what you think!"

"Hmm, is it morning already?" Ribido rubbed her eyes and languidly lifted herself from the bed, next to the village chief, who was trying to stammer out some excuse—*any* excuse.

The young man bashfully looked away from her well-endowed figure and turned, speaking toward the wall. "I need you to come with me. There's some guy who came running all the way to the village. I think he might have been one of the priests who went to Dog Valley."

"Wh-what?!" sputtered the chief, scrambling to yank on his clothes. Together, they sprinted out of the house.

"Mr. Priest, we're coming in." The chief rapped his knuckled on the door politely before tugging the door open.

But the door didn't budge an inch.

"Why isn't it opening?"

"Hmm? That's weird." The young man gave it a good yank, but it didn't unlatch, or give even slightly.

This was particularly odd because it didn't have a lock or anything fancy on it. The only thing that the young man used to keep the crude door closed was a dead bolt on the inside. But it was like the door had been fused into the wall.

"Mr. Priest, please open the door!" The young man's voice went up a notch.

Nothing.

Just as the pair shot each other a look of confusion, a shout echoed through the house.

"...No...I did it...for..."

They couldn't hear it very clearly through the door, but it sounded like the priest was having a conversation with someone. He was desperate, as if backed into a corner. Then—

"Please forgive me... No! No... GAAAAaaaa—!" A bloodcurdling scream rang out inside.

"Mr. Priest, what's happening?!" The young man pounded on the door with his fists.

"Hmm? What's going on?" a drawling voice asked from behind them.

The young man whipped around to see Ribido, properly dressed in her maid uniform and sleepily rubbing her eyes.

"Well, there was this priest guy who came running from Dog Valley, and he shut himself in my house, and now we can't get the door open, and there was this horrible scream from the inside, and I have no idea what's going on..."

"Ahh, that's terrible." For a brief moment, her eyes glinted sharply, but in the next second, she flashed her stupid, goofy smile.

Pushing him aside, she placed her hand on the door's handle. No sooner had she concentrated and mumbled than the door unlatched in a breeze.

"It's open!" she announced.

"Huh? That's weird..." The young man scratched his head.

It didn't occur to him that the door had a *Hard Lock* spell on it and that the promiscuous maid in front of him had cast *Dispel*.

Either way, the door was now ajar. He walked into the house.

"Mr. Priest, are you okay?"

Slowly and fearfully, he took stock of the room before casting his eyes on a figure kneeling in the middle of the floor as if confessing his sins. His back was turned to them.

The young boy found it strange that the priest didn't move even a muscle as he entered, but he walked up to him, relieved. "Oh good. I was worried because we heard this terrible scream—"

As soon as he placed his hand on the priest's shoulder, the body crumpled brittlely to the floor.

"GACK—!" The young man screeched as he stumbled and fell on his butt.

The priest figure disintegrated into sand, leaving his ornate robes behind in a heap.

"Wh-wh—? What the—? What the hell happened?!"

"C-c-calm down, just calm down!" stammered the village chief.

"But someone just crumpled and…died?!"

The chief was losing his mind; the young man was in shambles.

Ribido stood there for a moment in quiet contemplation before beaming at the two men. "It must be a prank. I'm sure someone used magic to make a golem!"

"…Golem?" asked the young man.

"Yes. You know, a magic user can fashion dirt into a human-shaped doll, and they can move just like humans."

"Yeah, but…" The young man tried to say that the priest had definitely been an honest-to-goodness human, but clamped his mouth shut on second thought.

Though some other villagers had seen the priest approaching, he was the only one who had been close enough to peer into his face. Even if he insisted on the truth, there was no one who could back him up.

On top of it all, it was easier on his psyche to think this was a prank rather than fully process that a human had turned into sand—meaning they'd been destroyed beyond the point of resurrection.

"O-oh yeah, a prank…"

"Hee-hee-hee, I'd love to play a prank on you, too. ♡"

"Hey, Ribido?!" the chief gabbled as he watched her cuddle up to the relieved young man.

"By the way, what were you thinking, fooling around with Mr. Manju's servant?"

"Well, it was consensual! Plus, with my wife passing away, I was startin' to get lonely..."

"Okay, boys, I need to clean up so please take it outside."

She chased them both out of the room. The young man was getting visibly fed up with the chief, who was up in arms, trying desperately to defend himself.

Once they left, her expression hardened as she lifted the robes of the cardinal off the ground. "I need to report this to Shinichi."

He was really going to chew her out for forgetting to report on the movements of the heroes, forgoing her duties to spend the night fooling around with the chief. But that was the least of her worries.

"It'll be too suspicious for me to hold on to all of it. And a pain. There's no way to resurrect him, so this'll do." She took a handful of the sand and put it in a bag before sweeping up the rest and dumping it outside.

When she finished cleaning the house, she sent a telepathic message to Shinichi—just as he was caring for Celes, who'd collapsed from exhaustion.

Cardinal Hube was working for the God of Evil.

This shocking truth finally made its way to the Archbasilica. Through a chain of telepathic messages, the survivors of the savage battle and the resurrected heroes at the Cathedral of Boar Kingdom sent their updates to neighboring cathedrals, which then reported to others near them as the news traversed the continent.

There were some heroes that argued against that story—namely the ones who'd been killed by the Demon King before the appearance of the True One. But with Hube's disappearance, there was no one to provide an alternative explanation. Eventually, everyone gave up trying to defend him, instead adding their angry voices to the din.

The three cardinals cradled their heads in their hands as they sat in the prayer room of the Archbasilica, which had fallen into complete chaos.

"Why the hell did this have to happen...?"

"Indeed..." Effectus hung his head, betrayed by the so-called messiah, and looked as if he'd aged ten years, as Snobe rambled on, lost and confused by the news.

Vermeita had on a tense expression, scrunching her face as if plagued by a persistent headache. That's what it looked like on the outside anyway.

"Yes, but nothing will happen if we sit here grumbling in self-pity. Let us discuss the future."

"You say that, Cardinal Vermeita, but how can we possibly get this under control?"

They'd welcomed the young cardinal with pomp and circumstance in front of all those people in the Holy City. But it'd been discovered that he was an unholy priest serving the god Elazok, the exact antithesis of a priest in the service of the Goddess.

"Rumors are already flying around. Some of the people are screaming their heads off, blaming us for selecting him as cardinal. We're absolutely done for."

If they let the situation escalate, the masses would start to riot, claiming that the other three cardinals were also unholy priests. If that happened, they wouldn't just lose their status: The church itself would crumble.

"I'm aware. Which is why we must make it public that we were neither deceived by him nor working with him. We must tell the people that we were frightened. We must tell them that we had to go along with him because he threatened to kill the people of the Holy City," Vermeita suggested.

It was a lie that Hube had threatened to use the people of the city against them. But it wasn't completely false. After all, they *were* intimidated by him.

"We must show penance, of course. We lacked the strength necessary to stop him. We will step down as cardinals and... Yes, create a new rank of 'archbishop' below cardinal. Why not move to that rank instead?" she continued.

"Hmph, I'm sure we can negotiate with those terms."

They'd be punished with a change in title and reduction in their salaries, but they'd remain the three highest ranked people in the church. The result would be that things would remain more or less the same, but few members of the clergy would complain. After all, the majority of the church had been deceived by Hube's ways, meaning many of them were afraid their own faults would come to light, especially for accepting the brand of a fake hero.

"The people may not approve, but we can rebuild their trust in the future."

"Hmph, they have no power or money. The weakest dogs bark the loudest," Snobe spat, unusually frank with his insults.

Vermeita smiled at him. "That's what we'll do about this Hube situation. But what should we do about the demons?"

"Indeed. There was a report that heroes at the battle took it upon themselves to declare peace with the demons, but we cannot allow this as followers of the Goddess." Effectus had been silent until now but snapped his head up at the mention of demons.

Vermeita cringed inwardly, but she'd prepared an answer in advance. "You're talking about how the hero Arian and Saint Sanctina appeared on the battlefield and agreed on a cease-fire with the Demon King."

"Indeed. We cannot allow—"

"Yes, you're right. We cannot allow that. But it would be reckless to continue the war against the Demon King. We couldn't defeat him with ten thousand heroes. And there are more dangerous enemies in sight—the agents of the God of Evil."

"Hmmm…" Hit with cold, hard facts, Effectus shut his mouth with a sour expression.

But Vermeita knew these zealous believers wouldn't accept logic alone. She showed outward sympathy with the cardinal.

"Cardinal Effectus, this is a temporary cease-fire. This doesn't mean that we will be building a relationship with the demons. Once we have defeated the agents of the God of Evil, we will turn our swords back to our original enemy and finish them off."

"Indeed. That is the Goddess's will."

"…Heh." Snobe let out a quiet snort at the sight of Effectus brought under control with ease.

With these plans, they would by and large be able to take control of the chaos around them. Their only remaining issue—

"That leaves the unholy priest. That bastard Hube will likely make an appearance again someday."

"……"

Both Effectus and Snobe's expressions clouded over again, chilled to the bone from imagining Hube returning one day to exact his revenge. He'd made a run for it from the battlefield in Dog Valley. They wouldn't know when he'd get them back.

"Yes, terribly frightening…" Vermeita forced her face to copy their dismal expressions, though she had intel from a certain dirty person that Hube's days were over. Not that she was going to let the others in on that. "In either case, we can't sit here worrying. First, we must deal with the problems immediately in front of us. Like the former prisoners resurrected at the Cathedral of Boar Kingdom. We must discuss the best course of action to handle these doll-people…"

Vermeita continued to dominate the meeting. Night had fallen by the time they were adjourned.

But Snobe hung around after seeing Effectus leave. He abruptly stopped Vermeita from following suit.

"Cardinal Vermeita, I was hoping you could tell me something—no secrets, no tricks."

"What is it?"

"You don't believe Hube was an unholy priest."

It wasn't a question. It was a statement.

As I thought, he isn't so easy to deceive.

Vermeita wasn't surprised. Effectus might have a one-track mind, but this man was clever. After all, he needed to be to satisfy his greedy desires.

"I know the Goddess exists, of course, which means I don't find it strange that there actually is an Evil God—servants and all. But the power that Hube displayed…"

It was theoretically possible that the Evil God could act like the Goddess and mimic the ritual of granting people the status of an undying hero. Plus, the power to erase the prisoners' memories and turn them into dolls was a power that seemed appropriate for the Evil God.

But to take away Cronklum's status as an undying hero—it wasn't believable that the God of Evil would have the ability to remove the Goddess's protection.

"It's said her protection is like a *Geas* spell. It can only be removed by the original caster or someone who is much, much more powerful than them. If we are to believe anything in the holy book, I find it unlikely that the Goddess and the Evil God are that different in power. Which means…"

…that Hube had actually received his power from the Goddess Elazonia herself. It meant he actually was the messiah.

Snobe didn't say these final words aloud. Vermeita didn't push it.

She nodded quietly, agreeing with his points. "Yes. I doubt there is any such thing as an unholy priest in this world."

"…I see. Thank you." He was surprisingly candid with his gratitude. With a stern expression set on his face, he left the room.

Cardinal Cronklum has been turned into a simple old man. Both

Cardinal Snobe and Cardinal Effectus have lost a lot of support. Cardinal Snobe has also lost more than half of his funds. He can't prevent his own decline... Hee-hee-hee, it really does look like I might have a shot at becoming the next pope.

Vermeita smiled to herself as she realized her dreams were within reach—dreams of creating a wonderful place where boys could love each other. But a shadow remained over her heart.

"...Lady Elazonia."

She gazed up at the statue of the Goddess carved by the first pope. Vermeita might have her own dirty desires and not be as pure-hearted as Effectus, but she'd believed in and loved the Goddess.

Right now, she wasn't so sure.

"Do you really hate the demons that much?"

Why would she grant Hube that much power to destroy so many people's lives—just to destroy them? She knew she wouldn't be given the answer.

But there was another answer that she wanted to know.

"Are you really an ally to humankind?"

The cold, stone statue remained silent.

As an inexplicable heaviness pressed into her chest, Vermeita turned on her heel and left the prayer room behind.

The cease-fire released the demons from any imminent threats from the undying heroes. They were hosting a multiday banquet at the Demon King's castle to celebrate the occasion.

"Bwa-ha-ha! Eat your fill, everyone! Drink as much as you wish!" boomed the Demon King as he gulped down the contents of a casket of ale.

All around him, the demons ate merrily, even before receiving orders from their king.

The dishes filling the table were worlds apart from the meager spread of their first banquet to celebrate the defeat of the first heroes in Ruzal's battle party. Now they had potatoes and dark rye bread from farming villages in Boar Kingdom. They had goat steak, ale, and other delicacies from Tigris Kingdom. The table was overflowing with delicious dishes from all around the human world.

"Wowww. Just as yummy as the first time!" Rino grabbed her favorite food of all—french fries—and melted into euphoria.

"Yes, it's wonderful." Celes cast aside her deadpan mask, forgetting to maintain her stoic look in favor of a beaming smile. She was the real MVP this time.

Shinichi had made her goat-milk ice cream to express his thanks.

Even Sanctina grinned from ear to ear as she watched the scene. "My heart is about to burst from joy, just seeing Lady Rino look so blissful. And everyone else, too."

"Sanctina, do you have a thing for Celes now?" asked Arian.

"Lady Rino is my one true love. But I like all beautiful women. Including you, of course."

"Th-thanks..." Arian took a step back, suddenly a little uneasy.

She looked up at Shinichi next to her. He was busy chowing down on a sandwich with sliced goat meat, but he looked dissatisfied.

"Eh, forty points. An F. Aside from the ingredients, the only seasoning is some mineral salt. It tastes bland. I could try to make some mayonnaise from eggs, but it won't do much good if I can't find some black pepper..."

"Shinichi, you really don't go easy on food."

"Well, I can't help it if my standards are high," he replied.

His palate was used to modern Japanese cuisine, meaning these ingredients and cooking techniques seemed unrefined to him.

"Gah, I'm craving some rice just thinking about it."

"Rice?"

"It's a grain, kind of like wheat, eaten a lot where I'm from. It's Japanese soul food."

"...Oh, cool." Arian looked away with uncertainty, which Shinichi didn't notice since he was lost in thought.

We've got a temporary solution. With Vermeita's help, we can slowly reduce prejudices against the demons. If we succeed, we might not be attacked again by any heroes.

They now shared a common enemy: The God of Evil. More importantly, most of the clergy members in the church were terrified of one hell of a strongman, the Demon King. This fear had been pounded into their brains.

As long as the demons didn't try to expand their territory, they probably wouldn't have any more wars with the humans.

Plus, it's iffy whether Tigris is gonna actually drop ties with the church after this mess.

To begin with, Tigris Kingdom had been fed up with the church for their violent tendencies. All they wanted was a healthy relationship on equal terms.

The people of Tigris Kingdom had never wanted to display full-out hostility with the church. On top of that, the incubus's brainwashing efforts had been successful, filling the holy warriors who'd formerly worked under Sanctina with love. They became sexual deviants—er, *servants*, working at the cathedral to heal the ill.

Other than a few complaints from the male patients that the warriors stroke their chests from time to time, I think that's a pretty big improvement from manipulation.

Regardless, the kingdom's relationship with the holy warriors got better, and they'd successfully chipped away at the church's power, meaning the church wasn't going to attack Tigris Kingdom anytime soon, especially considering that they were allies of the demons.

There's not really anything left for me to do.

"Do something about the humans who keep coming back to life!"

"Give my beloved daughter, Rino, all the yummiest food in the human world!"

He'd completed both missions that the Demon King had given him. There wasn't any reason for him to stay here longer.

"Um, Celes. Your ice cream earlier? It looked really yummy. I'd like to try making it next time!" Rino exclaimed.

"Of course. Sir Shinichi showed me how to make it. Next time, we shall make it together."

"Whoa, whoa, whoa. Hold up. If you want *Ice*, Daddy can make plenty of that!"

"Your Highness, I don't think that's the same thing, *oink*."

Shinichi watched as the Demon King family, surrounded by a crowd of demons, merrily carried on. He smiled softly, quietly standing from his seat to leave the banquet. Once everyone had passed out cold from the drinks, he slipped out of the Demon King's castle, taking a small amount of gold with him.

"It's already been three months…," murmured Shinichi, suddenly feeling sentimental as he looked back at the Demon King's castle bathed in the silvery moonlight.

Ever since the day the Demon King had summoned him to this other world, he'd been so busy with fighting off the undying heroes or trying to improve meals at the castle that the seasons had seemed to change in the blink of an eye. This constant barrage of new experiences made him feel like his life back on Earth was just a dream. The weight of the smartphone in his pocket was the only thing that proved his life on Earth hadn't been a lie.

"All right, time to go!" He pushed aside his feelings of longing, turned his back to the castle, and—

"To hell?" Celes angrily blocked his path.

"Ah! Celes, why are you here?!"

"That's my line," she spat unhappily.

Beside her were Rino and Arian, tears brimming in their eyes.

"Shinichi, are you going to leave us…?" Rino sniffled.

"Are you abandoning me…?" asked Arian sadly.

"No, I'm… Wait, why are you three here?!" Shinichi repeated, instead of facing his throbbing heart.

The two looked up at him with dewy eyes, like puppies left out in the rain.

Celes pointed at Arian. "She was trying to sneak into your bed at night and saw you leaving."

"Was not! I was worried that Shinichi was going to go home— Hey! You also tried to go into his room!"

"I had a question about how to make ice cream."

"You liar! I noticed that you'd changed into a freshly washed maid uniform!"

"I have no idea what you're talking about."

Their bickering put Shinichi in an awkward position. He rubbed his temples timidly.

Rino's small hand latched on to his. "Shinichi, do you hate us…?"

"No, I don't. I left the castle because I love all of you."

She looked relieved as he softly stroked her hair. "Good. If you hated us, I would be so sad, I'd die."

"And I would die, too," he replied.

The triage of her father's *Blue Raging Flare*, the lesbian's *Holy Torrent*, and the dirty-minded maid's *False Dragon Breath* would burn every last wisp of his soul away. Rino pouted at Shinichi as he felt a cold sweat drip down his face.

"It's so mean of you to leave by yourself without telling anyone!"

"…I'm sorry. Half of it's because of my own selfishness. The other part is I don't really know where I'm going or how long it'll take, so I didn't want to make anyone come with me."

Celes and Arian finished up their argument. Arian came up to Shinichi and buried her face in his back as he made excuses.

"You still act like we're strangers… I told you that I gave you my life, my heart, my everything…"

"I know; I'm really sorry."

"*So will you trust me? Will you put your life in my hands?*" That's what he'd asked of her. If he abandoned her now, he'd only seem cool and unemotional on the surface—when he was actually just irresponsible.

Maybe the weight on my shoulders—the lives of all those people, the demons, the people of Tigris—maybe it's made me a pushover...

Shinichi was taking a good look at himself when Celes took another jab at him, a huge grin on her face. "Oh yes, you have yet to make an honest woman of me. You've seen me naked, after all."

"Huh? Does that mean you'll make me honest, too?" asked Rino.

"*...Shinichi?*" Arian's wet blue eyes sharpened, glinting with rage. Her pupils pointed vertically, long and thin, reminiscent of a dragon's eye.

Shinichi tried to change the topic in a fluster. "No, well, ahem... First, I was thinking that I would spread the Evil God's threat to humanity throughout various regions to make sure the cease-fire continues."

"Hmph, and you'll tell me everything afterward." Arian pinched Shinichi's back, but he just endured it and continued talking.

"I think the church will be on its very best behavior for a year, but if there's no threat from the Evil God during that time, people will forget him and come back to attack the demons again, right?"

The best-case scenario would be if Vermeita became pope. She'd be able to change the church. But there was no guarantee that things would go that well.

"So I was thinking that I'd start a bunch of rumors that the Evil God is here."

"I see. I understand what you're suggesting. However, I wonder if one weakling would be sufficient to deceive people," said Celes.

"Urgh..." Words escaped him. She was right.

Sure, Shinichi had created his own specialty spell, *Element Conversion*, thanks to the knowledge that he'd gotten on Earth. But his magic abilities weren't greater than an average human's. He couldn't use an *Illusion* or *Fly* spell by himself, so he wouldn't be able to convincingly act as a servant of the Evil God.

"I'm sorry. It would be impossible without you, Celes."

"As long as you understand."

"Hmph…"

"I can help, too!"

As Celes held her head high as the chosen one, Arian enviously puffed her cheeks out. Rino volunteered, waving her hand to appeal to him, too. Shinichi calmed the two down before Celes pushed the conversation further.

"You spoke as if that was only your initial plan. What else do you intend to do?"

"Spreading these rumors is a way to fill my time while I'm working on my main goal," replied Shinichi. He looked up at the stars glittering in the sky and spoke as if he was trying to send his words to someone up in the heavens. "I intend to uncover the true nature of the Goddess Elazonia and destroy the system that makes the undying heroes."

It was a declaration of war from a human against a god—a goddess who'd warped this world.

"So no more heroes?" asked Rino.

"Yep. If I don't do that much, I won't be able to forge a friendly relationship between the humans and demons, much less guarantee a future for the human world."

"No future?" asked Rino in confusion.

Shinichi smiled. "It's all fine and good that these resurrection spells exist. I think it's amazing that you can learn from your mistakes even after you fail, you know, even if you're punished with 'death.'" He had one particular person who'd failed in mind. "But there's something wrong with 'heroes' that won't die. I know this feeling of absolute security will chip away at their hearts, making them weak and foolish. And yet, they're the ones in positions of power, controlling people's lives in any way they see fit."

All the corruption in the church was rooted in these heroes. Their arrogance could be attributed to it. They just didn't value their lives.

"...You're right." Arian nodded as she reflected on her own status as a hero, far too serious for her own good.

In an attempt to console her, Celes patted her on the back before addressing Shinichi. "I still find it ironic that their physical strength as undying heroes is the driving force behind their demise, their weakened emotional states."

"There's a saying, 'A healthy mind lives in a healthy body,' but it's not always true. Now that I look back on it, the cardinals weren't half bad."

"In what way?" asked Celes, scrunching her face up at the memory of the Holy Mother's rotten smile and causing Shinichi to chuckle dryly.

"Their methods to spread the Goddess's word were honest, I think, and fair. Like, they were healing the wounded and defeating the monsters, and that was it. Tigris Kingdom had a few bones to pick with them, but they didn't resort to brute force to try to get them under their control."

The church could have had their heroes suppress the dissenters anytime a new one cropped up. And yet, they only used these fighters to keep the demons in check, not letting them turn on their fellow humans or lay a single finger on them.

"I'm sure that they verbally threatened that they'd dispatch the heroes on any unsavory characters. But I've never heard them follow through. Unlike Eument."

According to the stories, the first pope had unleashed his powers to destroy the heretical city of Mouse, casting the same *Solar Ruin* spell that Sanctina had once tried to use against the Demon King. It served as an example of the potential consequences of going against the church.

"There's always gonna be people who are totally convinced that they need to massacre those who go against her. Like the second or third coming of Eument—or Hube."

"Which is why you're suggesting we eliminate the heroes," finished Celes.

Shinichi nodded emphatically. "Letting her law rule the land... Where's the fun in that?" His eyes darted for just a moment to Arian's right hand.

That single glance was enough to enlighten the half dragon in love. *Oh, Shinichi. You're trying to destroy the heroes for me...*

The symbol of a hero was still on the back of her hand, even though it was hidden under her glove. And there was the mysterious death of Hube—another hero emblazoned with this symbol—after he'd fled from the battlefield.

I only saw the robes and the sand when you told me about his death. I guess it still hasn't hit me...

But Shinichi had understood. He was certain of their next steps.

If they didn't do anything about the Goddess, the other heroes— including Arian—could be murdered in the same way. That was the reason he needed to find the Goddess and destroy this system that churned out these heroes and twisted this world out of whack.

"Thank you, Shinichi." Arian hugged him from behind as she tried to hold back her tears of happiness.

He was a bit surprised by the sudden embrace, but he smiled and—

"If you're gonna try to press your boobs against my back, they gotta be bigger."

"Hey!"

"Wait! I'm just joking! Please stop with the whole red draconic aura thing! Please don't murder me!" As her eyes started to well up, Shinichi threw himself on the ground and groveled for forgiveness in front of Arian, who might have discovered a new power.

It was so like him to act this way. Celes and Rino shared a smile.

"Well, now that we know the goals of the mission, we should leave before His Ever-Annoying Highness wakes up," the maid suggested.

"Yessiree!"

"Hold up. I get that Celes needs to come with me, but are you sure it's okay for you, too, Rino? Won't your dad be worried?"

"It'll be okay because I'll be with you."

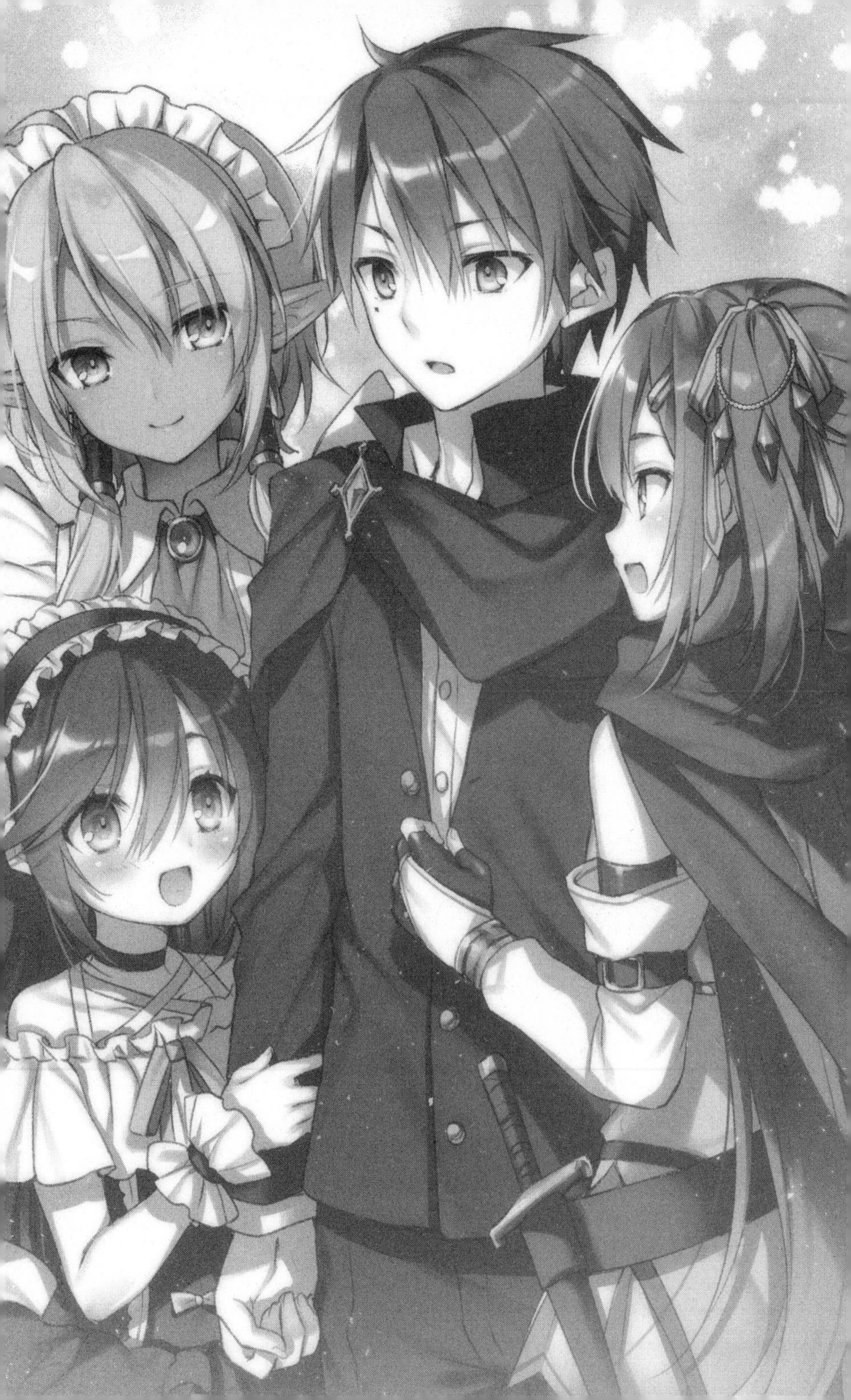

"Yeah, that's exactly why I'm worried…"

…*About MY life*, he wanted to say.

But the gifted maid (who sometimes took life at her own pace) had taken some extra precautions.

"I imitated Lady Rino's handwriting and left a note saying, 'If you follow us or get in the way, I'll never ever talk to you again.' We should be all right."

"You're demonic…"

"No, I'm a dirty-minded dark elf."

"Ha! So you admit it! I mean, that's not what I was trying to say!" He jokingly slapped her on the shoulder as she sighed.

"Well, if we *Teleport* back once every five days or so, we might be able to keep him from perishing from loneliness."

"Are we supposed to praise him for lasting that long?"

It was the unfortunate truth that Shinichi couldn't just play it off as a joke, especially for any matters that concerned the world's biggest helicopter parent.

"By the way, where's Sanctina?"

"… Recently, I noticed that Lady Rino's socks have been disappearing from her dresser. And I've found some familiar stockings in their place."

"Yeah, let's leave her out of this one. To put it bluntly, we can't take her with us."

For the time being, Sanctina wasn't so out of control as to steal Rino's underwear, but it would be too precarious to let a beast tag along. He didn't know when she might pounce and rob Rino's innocence from her.

"Oh, we're going to leave Sanctie behind…?" asked Rino sadly.

"Uh, well, you know, she has to work, heal those people in Tigris Kingdom." Arian scrambled to find an appropriate explanation to successfully convince her.

With that, the four finally started their new journey.

"Which way will we head first?" asked Celes.

"I'd like to do some research in the Holy City. Then I was thinking of heading east. Maybe we'll even find some rice there."

"Oh, you were talking about that earlier! I want to try it, too," said Arian.

"Wow, I'm so excited!"

They'd already forgotten the purpose of their real mission as their trip took on the air of a culinary tour across the continent.

The four set off underneath the starry sky, laughing and chatting among themselves, with a mission to defeat the Goddess's heroes and create a happier world.

Afterword

Greetings to all my Famitsu Bunko readers. It's me, Sakuma Sasaki, the one who hasn't stopped thinking about "prism glasses" ever since I read about them in a certain sleep-centered manga. I mean, they even let you read while lying down!

With your support, I was able to get this third volume out without a hitch. Thank you.

The last scene has some serious "the real battle has just begun!" vibes, which I know is usually reserved for final volumes. But not to worry: I'm busy plugging away, hard at work on the next installment of this series.

I imagine it'll involve the grand reveal of the Goddess Elazonia, who has been shrouded in mystery until this point. And I'll give you another tiny spoiler: The idol performances in the second volume are going to become a really important key to this complex puzzle.

Well, that's the goal anyway. But things don't always go according to plan, now do they? For my sake, it would be best not to get your hopes up too high.

I'm about to run out of space. For my final words, I'd like to thank Asagi Tosaka for the illustrations, my editor Kimiko Gibu, all the people involved, and my readers.

Sakuma Sasaki, July 2017

VOLUME 3

Afterword

Hi, it's Asagi Tosaka.
Thank you for picking up the third volume of *The Dirty Way to Destroy the Goddess's Heroes!*

If I'm being honest, my favorite character in this series is Celes. I was extremely excited to draw her in a bunch of scenes, especially since she was hard at work in this volume.

I desperately wanted to draw the scene where she kicks the wall, trapping Shinichi—from his perspective. I've taken the chance to do that here.

Mmm. Dark skin and white panties. A match made in heaven...!

All right. Thank you for sticking with me until the very end!

I pray we meet again soon.

Asagi Tosaka